THE PROVING GROUND

"I can keep the police off your back provided you close down some of your operations and at least try to go straight. There is also a good deal of money in it for you, although I'd guess it would not be a priority with you."

"If I'm to close down some of my profit-making schemes then money is a top priority. If I'm sticking my neck out I want paying enough to compensate losses and a high profit margin on top. But first I want to know the name of the guy I'm up against before I decide. And I'll need a photograph."

"No." Ewing finished his drink slowly. "I'll deal with that *after* you've decided." It was a shrewd move; Jacko now knew it would be someone of importance. "I cannot take the risk of giving you the name without first receiving your promise of help."

**Also by the same author,
and available from Coronet:**

Fall-Out
Exchange of Doves

About the author

Kenneth Royce, ex-army officer and business-
man, one of the best-known and consistent of
suspense novelists and adventure-story writers,
has published eighteen previous books, the
most recent of which are *The President is Dead*,
Fall-Out and *Exchange of Doves*. He has been
widely translated and several of his books have
been adapted for television. His character
Bulman, in a variety of series, ran for eleven con-
secutive years – making him the longest serving
detective on British television.

The Proving Ground

Kenneth Royce

CORONET BOOKS
Hodder and Stoughton

British Library C.I.P.

Royce, Kenneth *1920–*
the proving ground
I. Title
823.914[F]

ISBN 0-340-56240-4

Printed and bound in Great Britain for Hodder and Stoughton Paperbacks, a division of Hodder and Stoughton Limited, Mill Road, Dunton Green, Sevenoaks, Kent TN13 2YA (Editorial Office: 47 Bedford Square, London WC1B 3DP) by Clays Ltd, St Ives plc.

FOR STELLA

Prologue

Even with the windows down it was sweltering in the car. Before driving off Samson removed his jacket, but the moment he was clear of New Scotland Yard he loosened his tie. His white shirt was soaked and his eyes smarted as sweat trickled into them. He was a big man, much of the muscle turned to fat, but he was still powerful, strong hands gently moving the steering wheel.

He sat impatiently as the solid mass of cars moved forward a few feet at a time, petrol fumes adding to the stifling heat. But there was something else riding in the car with him like an unseen passenger: a touch of evil. He had overturned a stone, only a small one, but what was underneath was more than frightening.

He pulled the knot of his tie right down and undid the top shirt button, something he would not do in front of his subordinates. For Samson was a disciplinarian; a quiet man much respected in the Force. At forty-six he was young to be an Assistant Commissioner.

He moved forward slowly, then stopped again. As if the unusually prolonged heat-wave was not enough, a rail strike was adding to the misery and bad temper on the roads. Like everyone else, he wanted to get home to a cool drink and a sensible change of clothing. And he then had to do some very serious thinking.

He glanced at the thin document case on the seat beside him. He wished the contents were more adequate; there would be a great deal of work to do before the file filled out and he now knew that much of it would be dangerous. He was on a special, one-man enquiry commissioned by the Prime Minister through the Commissioner of the Metropolitan Police. It was an unusual step and once he learned the nature of it he wondered why Special Branch, or even MI5, had not been called in instead. Further enquiry might show why, but meanwhile he had been told that he had been selected because of his undoubted integrity, and because he was a damned good copper.

Joseph Samson was nobody's fool. He had few friends but those he did have were friends for life. As he gazed through the windscreen, the heat spiralling in waves from the body of the car, he saw the endless tailback of traffic as symbolic of the maze of his investigation; so far it had been impossible to cut through, and, like the jam he was in, could only move forward at a tortuously slow pace. There would be no big, or sudden, breakthrough.

When eventually he reached the London outskirts, conditions were little improved and he did not really pick up speed until he was well clear of the capital. He lived not far from the tiny airfield at Denham in Buckinghamshire. He had inherited the house from his father and he loved the large shrubbed gardens and the wide lawns. It was not isolated, but was well secluded.

When eventually he swung in to the semi-circular drive off the tree-lined avenue, he was soaked, but relieved to be home. He stopped the car, as he always did, in front of the double garage at one side of the house, switched off the engine and struggled out under the cool canopy of trees.

He had one foot on the gravel as the first bullet struck him behind the ear. As he crumpled in silence, reflex action making him cling to the door frame, someone he could not hear ran up behind him and the second bullet was fired at point blank range into his temple. Samson still clung to the door frame although quite dead, then slowly slid down to the gravel.

1

"Close the door." The grim-faced Commissioner returned to his desk after briefly shaking hands with his visitor. Newssheets were spread over the desk. The rail strike and the heat-wave had made way for the headlines carrying the story of the brutal murder of Joseph Samson.

Sir Walter McNally, arguably the most important police chief in Britain, gazed sombrely at the youngish man opposite him. They had not met before but the Prime Minister had personally telephoned the Commissioner telling him to expect a visit from Thomas Ewing. He would represent the PM and carry full authority in this tragic matter. McNally was not happy about dealing with strangers even if personally vetted by the PM.

Ewing carried a City image; dark-haired and well-dressed in a light barathea suit over a silk shirt and club tie. "What have your men come up with, Sir Walter?"

No preamble; no show of regret, or what a dreadful business it was and how was the widow taking it. McNally was angry; Samson had been one of his close friends and had been shot by some gun-happy shit who was still roaming loose in spite of a massive manhunt. And then he was partially relieved. Perhaps Ewing was right and, anyway, so far as he knew, he had not personally known Joe Samson. "We've been working through the night. As you would expect," he added bitingly.

Ewing sat crossed-legged, apparently relaxed, but gaze sharp. "I understand your feelings, Sir Walter . . . "

"No, you bloody well don't," McNally snapped. "You have no idea of my feelings. So cut the crap, Mr Ewing. You're here solely because Joe Samson was working on something for the PM. Perhaps that's why he is dead. It was a professional job."

"I'm sorry. I don't mean to insult you, but are you sure?"

McNally calmed down. He could not stand these Whitehall slickers, they so often appeared bloodless to him. But he must control himself. "Ballistics have come up with an early result. They believe Joe Samson was killed with a Ruger ·22 semi-automatic sporting rifle, possibly sawn down."

"Is that significant?"

"Yes it is. Look, I'm sorry I blew my top, but I had a hell of a lot of time for Joe Samson. There are few of his kind about."

Ewing held up his hands in surrender. "I asked for it. I should have shown respect. How significant is the weapon?"

"It's a professional killer's weapon. Many pros prefer a ·22 because the victim is less likely to jerk which makes it easier for a second shot."

"A contract job, would you say?"

"Unless he had an enemy who was also a professional killer, it looks that way. But it's all too early to say. We are working on every angle. We need some luck; no one seems to have seen anyone although it was still light. The gardens provide ample cover; it would be possible to hide in them for hours without discovery. The houses in the area are well separated. A pro would not panic, he would choose his moment to hide." McNally stared across the desk at the younger man and added, "What precisely was he working on?"

"I can't tell you. That is no slight, Sir Walter. You were involved only in so far as the PM wanted you to recommend a top-ranking policeman to do a special investigation. To involve you beyond that point would be politically foolish, and we must keep you above it. We cannot have our top policeman tied up in some clandestine action. There are too many groups waiting to crucify you."

McNally braced his stocky figure. "I'm trying to conduct a murder enquiry. If you stand in my way or withhold any kind of useful information I will hold you as an accessory."

"I am sure that you would, but you would not hold me for long."

"Nobody is above the law and that includes the PM."

"I shall have to refer back first."

"You had better hurry. Time is all-important. I want an answer today, this morning preferably."

"I'll do my best."

"You'll do better than that. Midday is your deadline. The press have a way of ferreting these things out."

"I hope that is not a threat of a leak to the press."

"It's a promise if I find anybody trying to foul up the search for Joe Samson's killer. He is not going to die in vain and if you can't trust me then just who do you think you can?"

"It's not a question of trust, Sir Walter. We cannot risk compromising you."

"I'm already compromised. I appointed Joe. Nobody told me it would be so dangerous." McNally flicked open a file, glanced at the first page, then at Ewing. "There's something else you can tell the PM. Earlier this year, in a suburb of Canberra called Deakin, an Assistant Commissioner in the Australian Federal Police was shot dead as he left his car on arriving home."

McNally derived satisfaction as he saw Ewing's smooth composure fray a little.

"He parked in his next-door neighbour's driveway, which he always did because she was elderly and it gave her comfort to have a car visible, a deterrent against burglars. His name was Colin Winchester. He was shot behind the right ear and then from close up through the temple. He too, was considered to be on an investigation of some kind."

Ewing was clearly startled. "Did they find out who did it?"

"No. Nor why. There are theories that it was done by Calabrians, some of whom live around the area. Some

11

Italians call them La Famiglia or the L'Onorata Society. That might have a familiar ring; the Family or the Honourable Society? In Italy they are often known as the Calabrian Mafia. The vast majority of Australian Italians are good, hard-working people, making a decent living and well liked out there. They are embarrassed by this sort of thing. And some are compromised."

"This is surely a coincidence. Policemen do get killed in the line of duty."

"How many of that rank? But your coincidence does not end there, Mr Ewing. The weapon used is believed to be a Ruger ·22 sawn-off sporting rifle."

Ewing sat upright and, for once, floundered.

"Once we had some idea of the weapon used I contacted Canberra. The answer was quick. At the time Colin Winchester was killed he had been head of the Canberra Police Force for six months. There seem to be a good many rumours but no hard evidence as to a possible motive." McNally gave Ewing an icy stare. "The sort of situation we have right here and now."

Ewing did not bite. "You mean they have absolutely no idea at all?"

"Oh, there are plenty of ideas. It sometimes seems as if nobody is anxious to take on organised crime over there. The drug barons could be behind it. It is also rumoured that Winchester had been tipped off about wide-ranging police corruption. Who knows? I find myself in exactly the same position here and I don't intend to stand for it."

Ewing leaned forward. "Is there some link between these two murders?"

"There is the obvious link of the same kind of weapon. If we are lucky enough to show that it was actually the same weapon then I would consider that a pretty conclusive link, wouldn't you? Most probably the same killer."

"That would indicate only that the same killer was hired; it would not link motive."

McNally inclined his head and pushed it forward pugnaciously. "Then provide the motive for me. You must know it."

Ewing rose and adjusted his tie. "I'll get an appointment with the PM just as soon as I can. I really am sorry about the Assistant Commissioner. But you do realise that his death may have absolutely nothing to do with the PM's private enquiry."

McNally was left with the frustrating feeling that Ewing's parting remark was to set the ground rules for what would follow.

Thomas Ewing was not a Member of Parliament, yet the Prime Minister had chosen to use him as an advisor, though precisely about what nobody seemed to know. Some thought him to be a link with the Security Forces. As the Prime Minister had several prominent advisors on various issues, much to the chagrin of some Cabinet Ministers, Ewing caused no stir and little press interest. His contacts were wide and varied but he was, at the moment, concerned over which one he should turn to.

He was much more upset about the murder of Joseph Samson than he had shown to Sir Walter McNally whom he trusted and respected. Just the same, someone, somehow, had got to know just what Joe Samson was involved in. The Police Commissioner himself did not know and Samson was hardly likely to advertise his brief; he had been warned of the dangers from the outset.

Ewing suddenly felt himself very much alone. At forty-five he was still a bachelor although there was an attractive divorcee in whom he had more than casual interest, but she had much too much money and he was too independent. He was by nature a loner but was immensely loyal to the Prime Minister or, for that matter, to anyone for whom he worked. He was not wealthy but he lived comfortably and was compensated for lack of wealth by an interesting and varied life covering issues he largely handled alone. He saw himself as a superior odd-job-man, handling work which came under no identifiable umbrella. When he needed help he had always known where to find it. Until now.

He turned into a pub in Victoria Street whose doors were wide open; there was an overspill of customers on the pavement, men without jackets, women in flimsy dresses. The heat inside was almost unbearable, the place crowded and full of smoke and sweat.

Yet Ewing, correctly dressed, did not so much as adjust his tie or undo the middle button of his jacket. His dark, good looks were untouched by sweat as he eased his way to the bar to order a Campari and soda with ice, suggesting that he felt the heat without showing it.

As he sipped his drink he decided he would have to see the PM very quickly and suggest a completely new turn of operation. Should he also see the Home Secretary? He would have to be careful; there could be no suggestion of a leak on this one. Yet somebody clearly already knew.

They met on the terrace of the House of Commons later that day. The Thames had lost its usual turgidity and was reflecting the sun like a cracked mirror. It was cooler on the terrace, which was, at the moment, crowded. The two men headed towards the far end to obtain what privacy they could. They stood against the balustrade, facing the river and St Thomas's Hospital on the opposite bank.

The Right Honourable James Dawson knew Ewing and was not keen on obscure advisors to the PM. But the PM had made the suggestion, which meant an instruction, that the two men meet.

Ewing came straight to the point; "I'm looking for someone who is competent and discreet enough to make some enquiries for me."

Dawson watched the rivulets from the glass of lager he was holding trickle over his fingers. "Why don't you get a good detective agency?"

"This is far too confidential."

"Really?" Dawson was not particularly interested; he was wondering why he had been involved at all. "I can see no way I can help."

"The PM thought you might."

Dawson was irritated by the innuendo that an outsider might have more influence with the Premier than he. "I can't see how. If it's so terribly confidential why don't you approach one of your friends in 'Five'. If they are unhappy about it they can refer it back to me."

"I don't think the PM wants to involve them, for whatever reason."

"The police then. I can introduce one or two top coppers to you. If it's that important." Dawson was becoming bored.

"I've tried that already. With tragic result."

At first Dawson was furious at the notion that Ewing had approached the police without first referring to him; the police were under the Home Office. The penny was slow to drop. "Not Assistant Commissioner Samson? Good God. Why wasn't I informed?"

"The PM wanted it done on the quiet. It is a non-political matter but important just the same. Nobody could foresee this happening."

"You mean nobody had the foresight. You realise that I am in direct touch with the Commissioner on the murder enquiry. Anything that comes out of it will come to me so why all the secrecy?"

"The insistence on secrecy is not from me although I agree with it. My feeling is that even if a murderer is found the motive will still be missing."

Dawson drank some of the cooling lager and gazed across the Thames. He was silent for some time. He drained his glass and balanced it on the balustrade. He looked at Ewing and found no envy or resentment and was suddenly pleased he was not directly involved. "You are either talking of a mindless assassination or a cover-up of immense influence. That's hairy, Ewing."

"Yes. Can you help me?"

"Outside official channels?"

"Yes. I think it is the only chance we have."

Dawson was uneasy. "Are you saying the risk is too high to be tackled officially? Are you implying corruption in high places?"

"Not corruption. Samson was trusted beyond reproach. Look what has happened to him."

"But I'm the last person to have personal knowledge of a capable person outside our own police forces and our

Security Services. I'm not in direct touch with those sort of people."

"Then the PM has misled me."

Dawson stiffened. He was suddenly worried. He began to wonder if some of the secrets he had kept to himself were already known in certain quarters.*He hoped not, for it could mean that he had yet to pay the price. His memory did not have to go back too far. "I might know of someone. If he's still in the country. He's known to 'Five' but I imagine you would not want them to know if he is to help you?"

"Better not. Otherwise we might just as well go to them direct. May we keep this strictly between the two of us, Minister?"

"It's certainly not something I would want to advertise. The press would make good copy of it. Have you a pen and paper?"

Ewing smiled for the first time that day. "No, but I have an excellent memory."

Willie Jackson, variably known as 'Glasshouse' Willie due to his short term in a military prison, or simply 'Jacko', arrived home late. He had been to his second-hand clothes warehouse in London's East End where he kept a good selection of stage clothes for hire.

As he parked his red Ferrari he noticed the white Daimler Sovereign across the street. There was a stranger in the camp. He parked in his usual slot which was strangely kept free for him, climbed out, locked the car, and mounted the steps of his terraced house.

A good many people of all colours and creeds were camped out on the steps of the rows of houses, trying to get a little relief from the oppressive heat-wave. Jacko returned a few waves from friends but his gaze rarely left the Daimler. Trouble; it pointed at him like a bloody sword. Coppers would not be so obvious but the sleek car represented authority of some sort and whoever sat in it was waiting for someone.

*See *Exchange of Doves*

As Jacko turned the key and opened his front door, he heard the footsteps crossing the street towards him. He turned round and saw Thomas Ewing, still clad in his lightweight barathea, heading straight for him; Ewing was so smart and looked so cool that he drew wolf whistles from some of the watching women. Ewing mounted the steps as Jacko waited for him with the door wide open.

"You want me?"

"If your name is William Jackson, yes."

"Are you carrying a warrant?"

"No. Nothing like that." Ewing had reached the top step.

"Are you in security of any kind?"

"No. I just want to talk to you for a while. Privately, without half the street listening in. And I do carry a good deal of money."

"I wouldn't say that too loud if I were you. You've got to get away from here." Jacko shouted across the street to a black man who was sitting on the opposite steps. "Charlie, make sure nothing happens to his car while he's with me."

Charlie grinned as Jacko waved Ewing inside the house.

It was surprisingly cool and as they climbed the stairs Ewing realised that the house was air-conditioned. Jacko led the way into a large room which overlooked the street and Ewing at once noticed that the furnishings were expensive, if not to his more conservative taste. He had been warned that Jacko had money and was now seeing this for himself. But it worried him; a money incentive would be useless unless everything he saw was on credit.

"Take a pew, mate. And what's your name?"

"Thomas Ewing." Ewing selected an armchair and sank into it; he preferred a harder seat, one he could rise from quickly.

"Drink?" Jacko was missing nothing about Ewing but found him difficult to pigeon-hole.

"Campari soda would be nice." Ewing could see that Jacko's mohair suit was expensive but the cut was a shade too exaggerated, the shoulders just too wide, the waist a

17

little too tight. The knot of the plain silk tie was halfway down the chest and the top two buttons of the silk shirt were undone. The lightweight shoes were turtle skin.

It struck Ewing that the somewhat unnatural emphasis of the clothing was not necessary. Jacko was a powerful man, not over-tall but solid. His face, when not smiling which he seemed to do often, was granite in repose. A hard man. His fair hair, almost down to the shoulders, spoiled that image but the cool grey eyes restored it. His image seemed mixed and perhaps that was a deliberate ploy. He fell just short of being flash. Reliable? His record was also mixed.

Jacko handed Ewing his drink and sat opposite with a can of beer. "What do you think? You've taken long enough sizing me up." His accent was London, verging on cockney.

"Cheers," Ewing raised his glass. "I don't know whether you're trying to fool the world or yourself. Perhaps you are just poking fun at everybody."

Jacko took a swig at his beer. "Okay, matey, I've some work to do; what do you want?"

"Your expert help."

"You can't afford it."

"I think I agree. Queen and Country?"

"Balls. They've already had the best years of my life and then threw me in stir."

"You were rather a naughty boy at the time." Ewing carefully placed his glass down on a drinks mat on a side table. He reached inside his breast pocket and produced a sheaf of papers stapled at the top. "I don't really need these but I wanted you to know that I have access to them which suggests I am in a position of some authority. These contain your army record and your activities since. And your police record."

Jacko laughed. "You know how to keep things going, cocker. But I have no police record apart from the military."

"Oh, but you have. You have no arrests, of course, but you are preciously close to them."

18

"That sounds like a threat, matey. Don't spoil a cosy chat."

"It's not a threat, not yet. But I could easily close down your more profitable enterprises which are largely based outside the law." Ewing smiled quite warmly. He much preferred to deal with this man with his varied record than with the Home Secretary.

"If you're trying to get me on your side you're going a bloody funny way about it. Now cut the crap and just tell me what you want and we can take it from there. I need another beer; you want a top-up?"

Ewing shook his head as Jacko went to a small bar in one corner of the large, airy room. When Jacko returned with another can Ewing said, "I want you to look into the background of a certain person. It could take time and you could encounter a good deal of opposition. I can give you very few leads."

"Are you some sort of copper? That's a police job. Why don't you give it to them? Unless you are not as well connected as you imply."

"We've tried the police. With a disastrous result." Ewing reached for his drink to give time for the remark to sink in.

Jacko stared across the room, dangling the can between his straddled legs. He missed the point because he was not thinking in such wide terms. "You've lost me."

"Have you seen today's front pages?"

Jacko slowly understood. "The Assistant Commissioner? You can't be serious."

"I'm totally serious."

"But you're off your rocker, mate. If he couldn't do it what chance have I, for chrissake?"

"I'm told you are very good."

"Who told you that . . . " Jacko held up a hand. "Don't tell me. Neither of us would want to mention his name, right? That wasn't me. That was a mate of mine, Sam Towler. You won't get him, he's abroad somewhere with his wife, Kate. I merely helped out."

"I know nothing of this nor do I want to. My source has great confidence in you."

"Your source is unreliable, and you can take it from me that I know what I'm talking about. For God's sake there must be plenty of agencies you can contact."

"Let me try to explain. I do not want to use any official source. Assistant Commissioner Samson was as honest as they come and a careful man. Yet someone knew what he was doing. I do not know the extent of penetration our culprit has. Undoubtedly he has a lot of friends in all sorts of official places. He is clearly on the old-boy network. I don't want a repetition of what happened to Samson. And few, if any, of the official sources have your particular expertise. You are a survivor, Mr Jackson, and not by accident."

Jacko twiddled with the can of beer. "I'm left wondering what sort of expertise you're talking about. You're blackmailing me; 'help or I'll jail you'. How am I supposed to trust you?"

"During demonstrations at Hereford to impress visiting politicians, a soldier would sit in a chair with a wide board behind him, while one of his colleagues fired a Heckler and Koch to outline him with bullet holes. You were the man with the gun. You are not only a crack shot but had the complete trust of your colleagues. You clearly have a steady nerve and a clear head and you know what danger is all about."

"I've also sat in the chair."

"I know you have. Look, Jacko isn't it? Your particular circles will be free of infiltration. Don't you see?"

"If this guy is as deadly as you say I wouldn't be too sure of that. He must have contacts with contract men unless he's doing it himself."

"But he won't be looking in that direction. If you beaver away quietly you will probably not run into that sort of situation."

"What's my incentive?"

"Having met you, satisfaction I would say. But I can keep the police off your back provided you close down some of your operations and at least try to go straight. There is also a good deal of money in it for you, although I'd guess it would not be a priority with you."

"If I'm to close down some of my profit-making schemes then money is a top priority. If I'm sticking my neck out I want paying enough to compensate losses and a high profit margin on top. But first I want to know the name of the guy I'm up against before I decide. And I'll need a photograph."

"No." Ewing finished his drink slowly. "I'll deal with that *after* you've decided." It was a shrewd move; Jacko now knew it would be someone of importance. "I cannot take the risk of giving you the name without first receiving your promise of help."

2

Two days after the murder of Joe Samson, Dickie Ashton was taken to Heathrow Airport in a Rolls-Royce driven by his chauffeur. Seated in the rear beside Ashton was a very attractive woman in her mid-thirties. Auburn hair flowed from under a wide-brimmed straw hat, and she wore a cool designer creation. The heat-wave continued but any car belonging to Ashton, entrepreneur, commercial banker, millionaire, was bound to have air-conditioning.

Ashton was forty-six, wide-eyed and never far from smiling unless conducting business. Fair-skinned and already thinning on top, he nevertheless conveyed a great deal of charm and possessed a quick wit. He appeared to get on equally well with men and women.

"Liz, it was good of you to come for the ride. I hate travelling alone." Ashton turned to the girl with an affectionate smile. "Sorry to tear you away from your boyfriend, though. I hope he understands. Stan will drive you back to wherever you want to go." He briefly patted her hand.

"He's not my boyfriend, you know. But I must admit I'm fond of him."

"And I must admit I don't recall him too clearly. Perhaps I haven't actually met him. I'm dreadful on names."

She knew that he was not. "How long will you be in Spain?"

"Oh, just long enough to wrap up a deal. A couple of days should do it."

When Ashton was dropped off at London Airport, carrying only one small case, Stan Bates drove Liz Mitchell back to London and dropped her off, at her request, at the Ritz hotel where she ordered tea.

She was quite happy sitting alone watching the usual

crowd lightly sprinkled with a new intake. It was cool in the hotel and she was in no hurry. Since her divorce a year ago she had spent a fair amount of time alone; her husband's infidelity had shattered her at a time when she had believed her marriage was working so well. Only recently had she begun to take men into her circle again, but she was very cautious.

She had met Thomas Ewing at a political meeting. They had got on well from the start and had begun to date. She found she was still incapable of making too easy an association with men, and her meetings with Ewing had yet to blossom into an affair. Yet she enjoyed his company without commitment.

Dickie Ashton was quite another matter; he knew so many women that few took him seriously. He was good company and had pots of money and no particular reputation for womanising. On the subject of marriage he would either skate round the question or deny that he had ever been married. It was difficult to be sure with Ashton. He was far from being a playboy but was not a hermit either. He did not project himself as he might. If he made conquests then he was certainly discreet. Liz had met him at a party while she was still married and during that time Ashton had made no suggestion of a pass at her.

Her trip to the airport was simply due to a chance meeting; it had been a fun thing to do while she was at a loose end. She sat quietly, thinking over recent events, finding she was not too dissatisfied with them, but not completely happy either. She was afraid to cast her mind back more than a year; memory could be strong and recollection still bitter.

Thomas Ewing had been forced to call off their date for that evening, he had got caught up in something important and was genuinely upset by it. She closed her mind to his reasons; it was the only way she could handle it. She would go home and watch television. Before leaving the Ritz she briefly wondered how Dickie Ashton was getting on with his Spanish.

* * *

Ashton landed at Malaga Airport. It was a sultry day but, surprisingly, not as hot as London had been, The thin ceiling of cloud was low and created an uncomfortable humidity. He was quickly through controls and entered the Mercedes which was waiting for him. He climbed in beside the driver without a word and the car pulled out to head towards Mijas in the hills.

When they had been climbing for a while Ashton looked back to see the unending stretch of placid sea, leaden and dull and reflecting the overcast.

"No problems?"

"None. Your plane was waiting like you said and so was the rest of the money. I was flown to Scotland. From there I caught a flight to Amsterdam and from there to here." The driver had a peculiar accent. His English was hesitant and an Italian background was obvious, but the Australian twang mixed up in it was confusing. His name was Piero Cirillo.

Ashton was never fully comfortable in the company of this man, and indeed had met him rarely, but they understood each other very well.

Cirillo was wearing sandals on bare feet, cotton shorts and a cotton shirt open to the waist. He was not a big man, nor was he tall, but his body was very compact, brown and hardened and free of fat. Veins stood out on his forearms like blue sinews and the long-fingered hands on the wheel were strong. His dark hair was tousled but clean, his pinched features bland; a face almost without expression or emotion. When he talked it was like switching on a machine but the controls were his. The two men were complete opposites in appearance yet they had much in common.

"Did he have anything with him?"

"A thin case with a file inside."

"What did you do with it?"

"It's at the villa."

"Did you read it?"

"If I say no, you won't believe me. If I say yes, you

will be furious. I'm a professional. I am not interested in the file."

"Not even for possible blackmail?"

Cirillo's gaze did not leave the road. "You insult me and that could be dangerous. I work hard at what I do and there is none better at it."

"That's true. What did you do with the gun?"

"I still have it. An unsuspecting friend brought it over by rail. I picked it up in Madrid and motored back. I returned only this morning."

"That alarms me. It sounds very unprofessional."

"That's because you don't do your own killing and hire people like me. If I had discarded it the police might have found it."

Ashton did not want to interfere but was still concerned. "Do you always use the same weapon?"

"Do you always use the same business tactic? It depends on the job. I use whatever is right at the time."

The feeling of unease persisted. "Is it the gun you used in Australia? Suppose the police make a connection?"

"Then they will be confused and start to chase their tail. I don't like being questioned as to how I do my work. The job is done; that's an end of it."

"No," Ashton contradicted quietly. "It is only the beginning. I would be happier if you changed your tactics, and your weapon."

Cirillo branched off before reaching the white spread of the lovely hill town of Mijas, and they were now on little more than a dried-out track. The car began to rock and Ashton clung to the open window. And then suddenly, after topping a rise, the view of a large villa, white walls partially covered by a splendid mass of bougainvillaea, unfolded. The paved swimming pool was set to one side like a blue jewel. Even to Ashton, used to luxury, it was a splendid sight.

"If I had one like this in Australia I'd have coppers all round me," Cirillo said without a smile.

Ashton did smile. So this was one way Cirillo used his money. He did not come cheap.

The soft hum of the air-conditioning could be heard from somewhere at the back as Cirillo led the way in to the cool interior. "You want a drink?"

"No thanks. I want to get down to business and then get back home. No offence."

"That's the way I prefer it, too. What's on your mind?"

Ashton sank into a cane chair to face the superb distant view. It was difficult to reconcile the peaceful atmosphere of the place with the man now sprawled opposite him on a long settee.

Cirillo said, "Why are you wondering about me? It is too late."

Ashton shrugged. "I was merely wondering what you do in your spare time. You must have a good deal of it."

"I swim a lot. I make love to women. And I play golf; I belong to a club near here. What else do you need to know?"

"I already know what I need to know. It's such a pleasant place. I hadn't thought about it; it took me by surprise. This really is a lovely setting. So you don't get bored?"

"I'm getting bored now. Will you get to the point."

"Of course. I'm sorry. But first I would like the file."

Cirillo crossed to a magazine rack and unerringly pulled a buff folder from the mixture of papers and magazines. He gave it to Ashton and sat down again, brown legs raised on the settee, one arm along its back. He watched Ashton thoughtfully.

Ashton was not happy, disturbed at where the file had so casually been placed. Anyone could have taken it.

Reading his mind, Cirillo said, "Better than a safe. You worry too much. People always look behind pictures, under mattresses, in safes."

Ashton opened the file. There was very little in it but there was enough to inform him that Assistant Commissioner Joseph Samson had found the right track. He closed the folder and asked, "Have you an incinerator?"

"I'll burn it for you."

"I'd be happier doing it myself; it is not a question of trust but of putting my mind at rest."

Cirillo understood. He led the way out to a huge yard surrounded by earthen pots overflowing with blooms. Ashton had difficulty in associating Cirillo with flowers, but as they went past, Cirillo plucked off some of the dead heads.

There was an incinerator in the far corner and Ashton held the file while Cirillo put a match to it. When it was well alight Ashton dropped the burning file in the drum and Cirillo poured barbecue fluid on top of it. Ashton waited until there was nothing but ashes.

As they walked back into the cool of the villa Cirillo said, "There could be other files."

"That's possible but unlikely. Samson was working alone. I think we got to him soon enough. Well done." Ashton leaned back in the cane chair feeling it adjust to his position. "It is time to tidy up some loose ends. Somewhere, somehow, someone has got suspicious. Enough to appoint a very senior policeman to investigate. I want to remove any leads they might be able to follow. Make a clean sweep, however regrettable."

"How many loose ends?"

"There shouldn't be more than half a dozen. I've got to do a lot of thinking."

"So have I. That is a lot of risks to take."

"I won't quibble over money."

"You bet you won't. If I agree."

"It will make you very rich."

"I'm already very rich."

"I somehow think you are too young to retire. And I think you would find any other work difficult to do. You are what you are; we all are, Piero. It's too late for any of us to change, and would we really want to?"

"I suppose there is a time limit?"

"You would have to set your own limit, you know what to do. But obviously, the sooner the better if you are to claim the second payment."

Cirillo came close to a smile. "I would not take it as a job lot. Payment per hit. No other way."

"I can arrange for a Bahamian bank to pay as you go.

Payment is the least of our problems. It would be foolish if each one appears to be an assassination. That could lead back to both of us once some sort of link is made. They will have to be accidents."

"Are you sure there are no more than six?"

"Not absolutely. About that. It's no use me going off half-cock. I have to think it through. If I miss one and that person gets a whiff of what is happening to the others it could be very dangerous for both of us."

Cirillo did not appear too keen. "Do your homework first and then come back to me, once you know what you are doing."

Ashton realised that he had handled it badly. "It's okay. I know what I'm doing. I'll feed you with all you need to know and payments will arrive on time."

"How will the information arrive? The postal service around here isn't so hot."

"I would not trust the post anyway. I have some detail with me, and a telephone number for you to use as each job is done. We'll formulate a simple code. The remainder I will bring over personally by air when you have returned to base."

Cirillo gave the matter some thought. It was too early to criticise. He would have to take it one step at a time. He already knew that he could not refuse; this would be his biggest job. His main question lay with Ashton himself. He seemed to be such an unlikely person to issue contracts. But the matter-of-fact way he did so suggested that it was not the first time.

Cirillo preferred an indirect contact with his clients; Ashton worked the other way. He watched Ashton cross to the lobby to retrieve the small case he had brought with him. Cirillo had to admit that Ashton had the same outlook as himself; the job had to be done, no matter the reason, so get on with it without crocodile tears.

Willie Jackson was due to meet Ewing for the third time in two days. As far as he could see he was flying blind. There was virtually no information to go on. If Joe Samson had kept records then they had disappeared, probably taken the night he was murdered. Samson's wife was too distraught to see anybody and anyway, it was doubtful if she knew anything.

Ewing had tried to be helpful and had given Jacko names and addresses of Richard Ashton's family. It was them he would have to follow first. Jacko had vaguely heard of Ashton, a whizz-kid by all accounts. Good background so he had started off with the advantage of money. He was a toiler, a workaholic.

Jacko was not at all sure what he was expected to find but he took the point that a top policeman investigating Ashton had been killed by a pro. That meant Ashton had some deadly contacts, and was a man who covered his tracks thoroughly. Which was why Ewing, representing some top authority, perhaps the top authority in the government, was loath to use either the police or the Security Service.

It was difficult to believe, yet every time he cast doubt Jacko had to return to the outrageous killing of Samson; there was no escaping that single, horrific fact. There had been a leak, perhaps an innocent one, but it had cost a man his life.

Ewing arrived at Jacko's Notting Hill home – they had both considered it the safest place to meet – in mid-afternoon when it was steaming hot. The air-conditioning was a saviour.

"You've had a haircut," Ewing observed in surprise. Jacko's hair was not too far from a crop.

"I'm going back to the old job for a while. I have to feel right." Jacko handed Ewing his usual Campari soda and sat down to sip his beer. The two men were by now surprisingly at ease with each other. "Do you know a geezer called Nigel Prescott?"

"I've met him," Ewing said cautiously. "Why?"

"Don't trust the bugger. If you know him you'll also know he's the new head of MI5. Crafty sod."

"Are you speaking from experience?"

"Oh, yes. His side-kick Soames was just as slimy, but he had to retire on medical grounds."

29

"You seem to know a lot about them."

"I do. I wondered if you knew that I do."

"Nobody told me. I really know little about your recent past. You were recommended from a very high source. That's about it."

"Well I'm relieved to know that your very high source knows how to keep his mouth shut. Had he mentioned how we all met I wouldn't touch this job with a barge-pole. The man who knows more than anyone about all of them is a mate of mine who married Kate Parker."

"Am I supposed to know who Kate Parker is?"

"A lot of people do. But you can find out from someone else. You know, there's a lot about this job I don't like. You seem not to be able to trust any of your own crowd."

"We've made one tragic mistake and we don't want to make another. It's not so much a matter of trust, of course there are people we trust; we trusted Samson and rightly. It's a question of misjudgement. This thing is much deeper than we first supposed. There is now a big element of danger attached to it and you are used to danger, real deep danger. We have no policemen, or security officers, with your particular kind of experience. The training you've been through would kill most of them."

"I'll need a gun and ammunition."

Ewing smiled. "Come now. We know each other better than that, don't we?"

"I don't see why I should use my own gun."

"Because you'll be happier with it. God forbid that you have to use it. I certainly hope not. Okay, Jacko, we'll pay the cost of gun and ammunition. Let me know how much. Has the other money come through?"

"Yes. It was the one point that reassured me. I've checked direct with the Austrian bank; dollars as you promised."

"Then you are ready to start?"

"I suppose so. I don't promise results. If I reach a dead end then that's it."

"Delve into his whole background; family history, that sort of stuff. See if he is who he says he is."

Jacko looked across sharply. "It could turn out to be a big box of apples."

"If this goes the way I think, then you may find that most of the box is rotten." Ewing rose and seemed reluctant to go. "Be careful, Jacko. I think, at the moment, you have the advantage of surprise, but watch your back. Watch it all the time. The moment the first whisper that someone has replaced Samson gets around you could be on the hit list. I have to tell you this so that you can back out even now."

"That much I know," said Jacko with a wry grin. "It's the rest that worries me."

"It's been a pleasure dealing with you, Jacko. Good luck. You have my special number."

The two men shook hands.

3

Dickie Ashton flew back to London on a late flight and went straight to his apartment in St John's Wood. There was an underfloor safe in the huge, modern kitchen which he could open by inserting an ordinary knife under a block of four Amtico floor tiles.

He sat at the kitchen table and carefully went through some papers, making brief notes and setting them apart with some photographs, some of them very old. From time to time the telephone rang, he had an extension in the kitchen, but he ignored it and let the answering machine do its job in the study. He was totally engrossed for some two hours and it was after midnight when he locked the safe again.

It was a measure of the man that he had come straight in, not even pausing to wash after a tiring and vital day, to get down to those issues which really mattered. Only when he had finished did he begin to show his tiredness and remove his jacket and tie.

He went to the answering machine and picked up the messages, answering some straightaway in spite of the late hour; those who did business with him were quite used to this no matter how inconvenient. He did not have to account for his whereabouts all the time but he knew that constant absence would raise queries in some people's minds. So he avoided bringing that sort of attention to himself.

He went into the spacious lounge and poured himself a drink at the long, impressive bar running the length of one wall. He sat on a stool in front of the bar, soft lights springing from cornices around the room and shadowing the folds in the heavy drapes.

It was lonely yet he did not feel alone. Ashton trusted very few people and his real friends were difficult to nominate. He could enjoy company as a superficial pastime but was quite happy alone with his thoughts; he was a man who could not tolerate interruption when working, as many had found out.

Ashton had always applied cold logic to any situation and would act on it. He had never dithered, right or wrong, and his mistakes were few. But now he was beginning to wonder. Something had gone wrong. Someone had got a whiff of what he was doing and he wondered in which direction the danger lay.

The person who had tipped him off about Samson was himself a senior police officer, who had clearly not known, or come near to guessing, that the subject of enquiry was Ashton himself. Ashton always reacted very quickly to such situations.

Having a senior police officer killed did not worry him in the least, nor really did the repercussions. It had to be done, and that was that. But what would happen now? What course would they take?

This concerned Ashton very much. He knew where the blame would be laid and was equally sure that the crime would never be solved. It paid to use the best. But it would not stop there. Which was why he had flown to Spain. Destroy the chain of evidence, no matter how solid its support to him, and there would be nothing left to find. He was certain that Piero Cirillo was working on the problem right now. It would help, too, if he could find out who had requested the investigation in the first place; he thought he knew, and how to deal with it.

Jacko was anything but orthodox. He had long since learned that it was far safer to be unpredictable. He read through the little pieces of information Ewing had given him. None were in any way incriminating; they merely gave family and school backgrounds. He decided to call on the nearest to hand.

33

Stan Finian was a stockbroker who had been at Oxford with Ashton. Jacko decided to drive down to Haslemere in the Ferrari; it would be little use trying to tackle him while he was still in the City.

The house was no less than he expected on the stockbroker belt. It was big and rambling in a few acres of woodland and lawns. The drive was gravel giving a pleasantly expensive sound as Jacko drove round it.

Finian was not yet back but his wife was in with two teenage boys. Jacko was dressed conservatively for him but he could do little about his accent. "Evening, love. Is the boss home?" Jacko was warm and disarming when he wanted to be.

The blonde Mrs Finian had not opened the door fully but gazed at Jacko in tolerant amusement. "You mean my husband?"

"If he's Stan Finian, bang on."

"Does he know you?"

Jacko grinned. "Now I ask you, is that likely?"

"Then who are you and what do you want him for?"

Jacko pulled out a warrant card and held it up so that Mary Finian could see it. It had been one of Ewing's little refinements, a forgery nevertheless. "Sergeant Willis, Special Branch."

"What on earth could Special Branch want with my husband?" Suddenly she was not so sure of herself.

"Oh, it doesn't concern him directly, ma'am. Well at least I hope not. I'm not sure that I should tell you."

"You're not going to get anywhere if you don't, Sergeant. And you are not coming in either."

"Very wise, ma'am. You can't be too careful these days. And you shouldn't have taken the chain off the door until you were sure of who I am. It's about one of his friends; someone has threatened him and we wondered if your husband knows of any enemies he might have."

"Threatened? How? Who?"

"Well, your husband is certain to tell you if I get to see him so I might as well come straight out with it. It's a Mr Richard Ashton. Someone threatened to kill him. It's

34

probably a hoax or a crank but we have to follow these things up."

"Dickie Ashton? Who on earth would want to kill him? What a dreadful thing. I don't see how my husband can possibly help."

"Well, ma'am, friends often see more than the intended victim. You'd be surprised how many threatened people say they haven't an enemy in the world. But their real friends sometimes know better. They hear some of the whispering that goes on. We have to contact all his friends."

"I do understand, Sergeant. You had better call back. After seven; he's rarely in before then. I still don't think he will be able to help you, though."

"I'm sure you are right. We just have to slog away. Perhaps he doesn't see much of Mr Ashton these days."

"A fair amount. They've been good friends for years; they were at Oxford together."

"It's nice when friendships last like that. Friendships should last forever."

"Well, I can't see this one ending; they get on far too well. Tell me, why is Special Branch involved?"

"There is a political side to it. Maybe this crank doesn't like Mr Ashton's politics or something stupid like that. I just do what I'm told and make enquiries."

Jacko offered a disarming smile. "You've been very understanding, ma'am. And very helpful. I don't think there is any need for me to call back. Just one thing, though. It could be dangerous to Mr Ashton if news got back that we're contacting his friends. He virtually forbade us to do it, but it has to be done. And if the threat is real and the culprit finds out that Mr Ashton's friends are being contacted, it might hasten an attempt; it might even drag some of the friends into the danger line. By all means discuss it with your husband, but let it go no further than that, ma'am. Don't let Mr Ashton know that you know."

With her reassurances ringing in his ears, Jacko climbed back into the Ferrari leaving an excited and very puzzled woman behind. So Ashton had at least one friend.

*   *   *

Frank Stewart was an East End mobster who had taken pains, over the years, to improve his image and to look the City gent. He had achieved this in large measure. He dressed quietly, was clean in his personal habits, and spoke quite well. Tall, stockily built, only a broken nose suggested something of a rough past. He could have got the nose straightened but as it had been broken by a contemporary who went on to become a British boxing champion it remained as it was for a story to tell.

Frank's City image had not quite made the City and he was not foolish enough to think he could get away with it in the better clubs. But in general business it had seen him through and he had sometimes met quite important executives, although never the top echelon. He remained a useful link between crime and legitimate business and had a hand in both, the one having arisen from the other.

He had only been in prison once and that was in his early youth. So he was shrewd and careful and successful. He, like others in the underworld, was shaken by the slaying of Assistant Commissioner Samson. It was not that he was against knocking off coppers, but one this size caused a lot of ripples and filled the streets with snouts. It was bad for business.

Everyone in the underworld could see that it was a contract job and this worried them for the whisper was an outsider had been brought in; which meant he had gone back again. The big villains would all be suspect, and many in the second division of crime also, which included Stewart.

Jacko met Stewart in the Hot Pot, a basement club under a film agency, and between a wine bar and a strip club, off the south end of Dean Street in Soho. Jacko had telephoned him on the road back from Haslemere.

Both men were well known at the club and went to a small airless room beyond the so-called dance floor. It was unbearably hot in the room and Jacko fetched a fan from the bar and mounted it on a small table. Even so they had to remove their jackets and open their shirts. They sat at the small table, sweating profusely and adding to it by drinking ice-cold lager.

"Right, old boy. What can I do for you?" Stewart had practised for so many years that the words came out quite naturally even if Jacko found them amusing; Jacko had made no concession to his own background; people could take him or leave him.

"Who do you think topped Samson?"

Stewart almost shot from his chair. "How the bloody hell should I know? What a stupid bloody question." In one short sharp query Jacko had cut through years of effort and brought Stewart back to his roots.

"I don't think it's you, you berk. But there must be a whisper."

Frank Stewart ran a big hand over his flattened nose. Fifty, he was still muscular. "That was under the belt, Jacko." In spite of his prowess with his fists he knew that he could not take the less heavily built man beside him. Jacko would not fight in the same way but could be lethal. Stewart had a good deal of respect for Jacko for all sorts of reasons. "It was an outside contract. That's all I know."

"No," said Jacko. "It was an inside contract for an outside hit-man."

"Then you know more than me. What's your interest? You want to keep out of this."

"This sort of thing is not good for business. You know that. It's not our style of work. We don't hit coppers. But whoever has should be put out of business before the rest of us are shut down. Think about it."

"I have. None of us like it."

"You don't think it was routed through any of the really big boys?" When Jacko saw Stewart's painful look, he added, "I don't mean you, Frank; I know you're big enough, but I wouldn't be discussing it with you if I thought you were involved."

Thus elevated to the top division, Stewart gave the matter some serious thought. He moved his drink away so that perspiration did not drip into it. He was panting heavily, the humidity and heat in the room dangerously high. "I don't think any of our boys are involved in any way. That's the word on the street."

"Who then?"

"That's what everyone wants to know."

"But who hired him?"

Stewart sat back on his chair gazing at the half-empty glass of lager; he picked it up and drained it. "You won't get near him. Nobody will. He can pull too many strings."

"So who the hell is he? You seem to know."

"Of course I don't bloody well know. I'm guessing. He's someone in the City. Probably been laundering, amongst other things. Those bastards always get away with it."

"Did Sonny Rollins tell you this?" Rollins was one of the very big villains who had been operating by remote control for many years which was why he had never been caught. Rollins used Stewart quite a lot but was hardly likely to confide in him even if he knew something. But Stewart was light-footed and had excellent hearing.

It was a long shot. Jacko simply believed that information about Ashton was more likely to filter through the London underworld than through Ashton's friends, many of whom might be indebted to him. That was if Ashton was even half as bent as Ewing seemed to think.

"Well, not exactly. He does confide in me, of course. But I think they've done business together although I don't know if they've ever met. You know how it is."

"Has this guy got a name?"

"I can't tell you that. It wouldn't be fair to Sonny; he relies on me. And I think your interest is not exactly healthy."

"Which means you don't really know; you are not in Sonny's confidence. Too bad."

Stewart bridled. "Drop it. Sonny might get to hear of your interest, Jacko."

"He could only do that through you, Frank. And you know better. Is this guy trying to get into politics? If it's the same bloke I hear he's already been elected as candidate by his constituency selection committee. Is that the one?"

Stewart appeared very uncomfortable. He was caught between prudence and ego. Bragging about his knowledge could lead to trouble. Rollins was called Sonny because he had the features of a young lad and never seemed to age. Face lifts and silicone treatment had something to do with it but it would be a foolish man to tell him so. He could be very vicious by proxy; a trait he probably shared with Ashton.

Jacko had not intended to reduce Stewart down to size. He might need his help later. He said, "I understand, Frank. You are loyal and that's fine. But let me tell you my interests in this are for all our benefits, believe me. Let's get out of this hell and we'll meet again. Thanks for coming."

They left together, and after the basement back-room even the humidity on the streets was almost like a cold shower; their clothes were soaked in sweat and each carried his jacket over his shoulder.

They stood talking while they cooled down a little. Soho was quite busy, it was now almost ten although it was still fairly light. Eventually they broke up to go their separate ways and as Jacko turned round to head in the opposite direction to Stewart, he bumped into a man who was just about to pass him.

"Sorry, mate," Jacko apologised as the two men gripped each other to steady themselves.

"That's okay," replied Cirillo, his gaze beyond Jacko to focus on the disappearing Stewart.

It was over in a couple of seconds and Jacko had no idea that he had briefly held Samson's killer. He had picked up the mixed Australian accent, and realised that the other man wanted to hurry on, but that was all. As he walked on he did not give it another thought.

Cirillo caught sight of Stewart again and held back to follow him comfortably. Stewart was heading for the Piccadilly Underground station. Once satisfied of Stewart's intentions, Cirillo looked for a cab.

The underground would have been quicker but Cirillo was not too familiar with the system and it would be easy to lose Stewart in the late-night crowds. He was rushing the job and he did not like it; in this particular case refinements might not matter so much but he was being unprofessional and that worried him. Ashton wanted too much too soon.

He reached Islington and had the cabbie drop him off a block or so from where he wanted to go. He entered a gateway to a terraced house but, as soon as the cab had gone, came out and strode up the darkened street. By this time there were fewer people about and when he reached the back streets, fewer still.

He arrived at Stewart's address and gazed up at the tall terraced houses; there were lights on in most of them but many had curtains drawn across. There were lights on in Stewart's house too, and he wondered if he had arrived too late; he wanted to avoid breaking in but he did not want delays either. He drifted into a doorway and waited, moving from time to time when the street had emptied.

Midnight passed and still Cirillo waited. Most of the house lights had now gone out including some in Stewart's house, but two still remained on. If he had to break in he would leave it until after one.

He heard voices at the end of the street and rolled round the doorway just enough to see the outlines of a man and a woman at the corner of the street. The man could be Stewart, he was the right size; the woman might be a complication.

The couple seemed to be talking in quite a friendly way; it could have been no more than a chance meeting but it was obvious that Stewart had not come straight home. Cirillo was now convinced that it was his target standing some thirty yards away.

At last they said goodnight, they did not even kiss, and Stewart began to amble towards Cirillo, humming quietly to himself and still carrying his jacket over his shoulder, occasionally shadow-boxing with his free hand and moving his feet lightly.

Cirillo could now positively identify Stewart. He carefully checked the street to make sure it was empty, stepped out of the shadows opposite Stewart's house to cross the

40

road slowly, glancing at his watch, holding it up to catch what little light was left.

Stewart approached, watching Cirillo trying to read his watch in the dark. "It's twenty past twelve, old boy."

"Thanks, mate. I can't read the bloody thing in this light."

As they almost drew level Stewart said, "You don't live round here, do you?"

"No, mate. And neither do you any more." Cirillo shot Stewart through the heart at close range and the big man collapsed with a groan, making no more sound than the silenced gun. Cirillo pulled the body into the nearest doorway and continued on.

4

The murder of Frank Stewart caused little stir except to Jacko, and Sonny Rollins who had largely employed him. The police showed no surprise and some were quite pleased. Stewart was one more public enemy off the streets and he had evaded prison for too long. There was no escape from where he had gone.

The police soon discovered that the weapon had been an old war-time Beretta 9 mm which had obviously been adapted to take a silencer for nobody had heard a shot. After all, Frank Stewart had been shot almost outside his own house and his wife had been waiting up for him.

Ashton realised what had happened as soon as he heard the news. He was furious and relieved at the same time. He had given Cirillo carte-blanche on the order of executions but it had so happened he removed one of the least important first.

Later, Ashton was to appreciate the refined strategy of Cirillo in so crude an act. And perhaps the Australian was right to deal with Stewart first. Stewart would have had little knowledge but it could have been enough to point a finger and he was likely to talk under pressure. Whereas the really big fry were in the same position as Ashton himself in the sense that they all had too much to lose not to keep the common bond.

Jacko's thinking was quite different. He considered it a complete coincidence that Stewart had been killed the night they had met at the Hot Pot. Although the reason for the meeting could be connected to the killing, it meant that Stewart had known more than he had told Jacko. There would be no more to come from that source.

Ashton chaired a board meeting at Moor, Ashton and Roache, merchant bankers, or what the Americans called investment banks. He was perfectly normal in every aspect, dealing efficiently and unrelentingly with the business and afterwards full of jokes and anecdotes, while he had a separate word with each board member.

There was little friction during these meetings. Dickie Ashton was shrewd and knew his job. His judgement had made his colleagues plenty of money.

Sonny Rollins regretted losing someone as useful as Frank Stewart. He knew Stewart ran many rackets of his own and had made enemies; but if he had learned that it was Dickie Ashton who had removed one of his chief lieutenants, it would have caused serious problems between them.

"They do have a Detective Sergeant Willis at Scotland Yard. They won't confirm that he's in Special Branch but they don't deny it either."

Stan Finian turned to his wife who was applying the last touches to her not unattractive face before they went up to London to a select party Dickie Ashton was throwing at short notice.

She watched his reflection in the mirror. "Strange little man."

"Strange?"

"Well, he didn't seem like a detective really. He had almost a cockney accent."

"Some policemen do. Are you ready?"

"I know. But Special Branch, I ask you. They should do better than that."

"He seemed to get what he wanted from you without troubling me. He must know his job if he can do that."

She did not know which way to take him but suspected a jibe. "Well, do we tell him or not?"

"Dickie? About the threat? Certainly not. Your strange little man seems to have talked a good deal of sense."

* * *

Few declined the invitation to Ashton's party that evening in spite of the short notice, and among the guests was Liz Mitchell and any friend she cared to bring.

Her companion, as Ashton would have been willing to gamble, was Thomas Ewing who most people knew had the ear of the Prime Minister but few knew in what capacity. Ewing was not comfortable about the invitation but recognised the sense of going.

He and Liz made a striking pair. There were less than twenty people and most of them knew each other. They represented the City and politics and were generally dull so far as Liz was concerned.

Ashton presented each lady with a splendid posy and Liz pinned hers on. Ewing, who had met Ashton only twice before, found him disarming; to an extent that made him wonder if, for once, the PM had got it wrong. Ashton appeared far from being a copper killer. And without doubt his interest in politics was not only real but realistic. He had clearly studied a good deal and seemed to have more insight into human nature than most politicians.

Afterwards Ewing and Liz went out to a late dinner and Ashton quickly became the subject of their conversation.

"Did you know he owns a donkey sanctuary and two dog homes? He loves animals but simply has not the time to keep any himself; his movements are too erratic. He's an interesting man."

"How, interesting?" Ewing eyed the posy Liz was still wearing.

Liz smiled and placed her hand on his across the table. It was a spontaneous act which took them both by surprise, for Liz had tried hard to keep her feelings in check. It did not seem to matter any more. "That sounded like jealousy."

"It was. Let's face it. He has charm, wit and a lot of money."

"And no wife?"

The question drove him much nearer to base. Had he a wife? One would expect to hear of her if he had. Or had he ever had a wife? "Didn't you ask him?"

"Yes. He merely says he is not married; except to his work, his charities and his interests which did not seem to include women . . . or men for that matter. Perhaps he's too afraid to get involved."

"And perhaps he would be just bloody impossible to live with."

"Now that definitely is jealousy. It reassures me, Tom. Don't worry, there's no competition. Just give me time."

Later, when he was on his way back to his own apartment, Ewing considered Jacko's brief telephone report earlier in the day. Ewing had noticed Finian's appearance at the party with his wife and considered Jacko had been right not to pursue matters with Finian himself; it was clear that he was too close to Ashton and word might get back. This was going to be a constant problem.

Could Ashton really have had a hand in the killing of a gangster the previous night? He began to doubt his own judgement. But Jacko was not the type to delve into fantasy. Jacko had his feet on the ground. Ewing clung to that belief but could see why Ashton had so many friends, excluding the sycophants. He wondered if he had set Jacko an impossible task. An enquiry like this needed the weight of the whole police force and Interpol, but if that happened Ashton would certainly start covering his tracks again. It might do no harm to give Jacko a little longer.

"Then I hope they get the bastard."

It was not the answer Jacko had expected. He said to John Wheeler, "Can I come in to discuss it, sir?" Jacko had called on another of Ashton's Oxford contemporaries. Wheeler was an actor, not often seen on large or small screen, but he made a good living doing voice-overs for TV commercials. He stood in the doorway in shirt and tatty shorts appearing massive against the small door frame.

"Not if it means I help him."

"Just to gather information, sir. There's really very little we can do about these sort of threats, if someone is out to get him, then they probably will."

"Bloody good show. If you promise to let me be the first to know, you can come in."

Jacko grinned. He liked this larger than life character who made no pretences about likes and dislikes. With his beard, Wheeler appeared a bit piratical and Jacko thought he should be on the screen more. He followed the big man into the cosy comfort of a Hampshire thatched cottage; the actor seemed to have beam-dodging down to a fine art.

"Who is it, darling?"

A woman entered the room from the kitchen and Jacko immediately recognised her. She was just as stunning off the screen as on, and Jacko saw part of the reason why Wheeler was not as publicly exposed as his wife. They looked good together and had probably worked out their individual commitments to give their marriage a chance. He hoped it would continue to work for them.

Jill Wheeler made tea while her husband explained what Jacko was doing there.

"Oh, it's about that little shit, is it?" she remarked blandly.

Jacko warmed to them. "You don't seem to like him. You should be more careful in front of me or you'll finish up on the list of suspects."

"You mean we're not? You people can't be doing your job properly. Sit there, Sergeant, it's less spongy." Wheeler spread himself on a battered sofa and his wife passed round cups of tea and some biscuits on a plate.

It was surprisingly cooler in the cottage. Jacko could see a stream flowing through wide lawns. A duck landed on the water as he watched. It was very peaceful but Wheeler had seemed ready to shatter it at the mention of Ashton. "So why do you dislike him so much?"

"Hate is the word. I hate him; we both do."

"There must be a reason." Jacko reached for his cup.

"Are you sure you're Special Branch? You don't look like a bloody copper to me."

"Thank God for that."

"Are you a cockney?"

"Very nearly. Have you something against them?"

"Love them, dear chap. Salt of the earth. None better." Wheeler glanced at his wife proudly. "Jill's a much better actor than me, you know."

"I've seen her many times, sir. Terrific stuff. Tell me about Ashton."

"Nasty bit of work. Let me down badly more than once. Not to be trusted."

"Was this at Oxford?"

"Of course. The only way I could tolerate him was by compulsion. We were unfortunately there at the same time."

"Would you care to say how he upset you?"

"What's this got to do with someone wanting to put his lights out?"

Jacko tried to keep his face straight. "I'd like to see just how strong your motives might be."

As Wheeler hesitated his wife stepped in. "He did some dirty tricks on Johnny. Broke promises that meant a lot. Spread malicious gossip which it was impossible to disprove. Got him suspended from the OUDS for six months and one of his cronies to fill the gap."

"Why?"

"Because Johnny is the type to speak his mind. He caught Ashton performing a shabby little fraud on one of the undergrads and thumped him round the ear for it. Johnny should have reported it but it's not his style. From then on Ashton fixed Johnny whenever he could and sometimes it hurt."

Jacko watched Wheeler who seemed quite content to let his wife do the explaining. He asked her, "You witnessed all this? You were there?" She was clearly too young to have been there at that time.

She smiled. "No, of course not. Johnny told me later on. We hadn't even met then."

"So you can't be absolutely certain." He turned to Wheeler. "I say that with respect, sir. It's hearsay and does not constitute evidence."

"What happened later did," Jill interrupted. "When he found out that Johnny and I were going together

47

he tried to bed me several times and told me some horrible lies about Johnny. He did not really want me, he wanted to break us up. That is Dickie Ashton. After that our lives simply went different ways. We haven't seen him in years."

"Would it surprise you to know that he has a lot of friends, apart from buying them, I mean?"

"No. We've both seen him operate. Have you checked on the number of enemies?"

Jacko smiled wryly. "That's what I'm trying to do now, ma'am."

"If this threat is real why aren't the Met investigating? I mean it's a bit out of line for SB, isn't it?" asked Wheeler.

"Everyone asks that." Jacko was beginning to think that Ewing had made a mistake in issuing him with an SB warrant card, but Ewing insisted he had his reasons. "If there are political implications we can be drawn in. Depends where the motive springs from."

"You can't be short of motives for that bastard; he'll have climbed over so many backs to get where he is that there must be a whole trail of motives."

"That's not the way it comes out, Mr Wheeler. I don't think he would have been so crude."

"Call me Johnny, for God's sake. Life's too short to piss about. Maybe he's been cruder than crude."

"You mean intimidation?"

"Worse. I'd believe anything about that man. It would never surprise me if he closed a few mouths."

"You've put yourself top of the list. Can it be that he scored a few times over you and you have never forgiven him?"

Wheeler stretched himself on the sofa. "I'm not a bad loser, if that's the suggestion. It was the manner in which he beat me that I didn't like."

"Do you know anything about his background?"

Wheeler gazed at Jacko shrewdly. "This sounds as if you are now investigating him, not a threat against him."

"Do you?" Jacko pressed.

"He never talked about his background that I can recall." Wheeler looked over to his wife. "Do you know anything, darling?"

Jacko was quite happy to look at Jill Wheeler while she answered.

"While he was making his passes at me I asked him about his family. He didn't attempt to hide anything, always assuming he wasn't lying. He said his father was a Canadian who came to Britain some time after the war and has lived here ever since. I think he had a brother, and a sister who lives in Italy."

"What about his mother?"

"I don't recall him ever mentioning her. When he said the family came over from Canada I assumed he meant all of them."

"So he was born in Canada?"

"I suppose so. That should be easy enough to find out."

"If he was. How old do you reckon he is?"

"Forty-six, -seven." Jill queried it with Wheeler who nodded confirmation.

"Anything else you can tell me about him?"

Wheeler gazed across suspiciously. "You're not levelling with us are you? You've spun us a lot of bullshit about a death threat."

Jacko could have wriggled out of it quite easily but he thought he might have a couple of useful allies here. So he said, "It is certainly part of my enquiry to get as much background to Mr Ashton as possible, which I would have thought logical, wouldn't you?"

Wheeler was grinning slightly. He said to his wife, "What do you make of this crafty bugger, Jill?"

Jill used the kind of captivating smile Jacko had seen so often on screen. "Are you married, Sergeant?"

"No, ma'am. It would need a foolish woman to take me on. I don't lead a settled life."

Jill laughed. "You think we do? In our profession? But we make it work. What are you, mid-thirties? The best age of all. Experienced yet still young."

For once Jacko felt at a disadvantage. "With respect, ma'am, this has nothing to do with Mr Ashton."

"Oh, but it has. It helps us make up our minds about you. Whether we help you or not. I think we want to, don't you, darling?"

"If he's here really to dig out Dickie Ashton's past, I'm willing to spend time on it."

As they smiled at each other with obvious satisfaction, Jacko could not resist asking, "Have you ever been called Jack and Jill?"

Jacko, not wanting the distraction of driving, pulled into a lay-by off the A303 to London to make a call on his car phone. He rang Ewing on the special number.

"It seems Ashton was born in Canada."

"We know that much."

"Thanks a lot. Has anyone bothered to check on it?"

"Perhaps Samson did."

"Well let's do it again. I smell something fishy."

"I'll check with Public Archives in Ottawa."

"Check army records as well. His old man might have been in the Canadian forces."

"Anything else?"

"See if you can locate a brother, presumably in this country, and a sister who went to Italy. Nobody seems to know what happened to his mother or if she's alive or dead."

"All right. I've got to be careful how I lift this information."

"I thought it would all be on computer."

"Yes, of course. But computers need operators. Keep going."

As Jacko headed back to London, for the first time he felt he was on the fringe of something. It was a gut feeling that he was on his way. He hoped Ewing would come through with some quick answers.

Cirillo hired a car in a false name. He had a collection of passports but never carried more than two at a time. He

50

drove towards the Cotswolds, taking it slowly. Although he had lived some years in Australia he had never felt comfortable driving on the left hand side of the road.

If he had a weakness in his job it was one of navigation. He always got there in the end but often with difficulty. Scenery was lost on him, even at his beautiful villa in Spain the outlook barely touched him. The sea was to swim in, the sun was to get him a tan, and golf courses were for limited exercise and for keeping an ear to the ground and mixing with the crowd. It did not matter to him what people thought of him, but he recognised that he must put on some sort of show to convince them he belonged. It was a bore.

At least in the car he was alone which he much preferred to be unless he had the temporary company of a woman in bed. Once he had used them he forgot them. No woman ever knew him long enough to find out anything about him.

His hired drophead allowed the full blast of air to freshen him as he motored along; he did not find the heat-wave uncomfortable, he had endured far worse, but he disliked the high humidity.

He drove deep into the Cotswolds and pulled up on the forecourt of a pub so he could study his map. There were tables and sun-umbrellas outside the pub, every seat around them taken, and drink was flowing freely. He could have asked any one of the pub customers the way and would have received accurate directions but he would never do that. Cirillo would rather get lost than approach someone who might later identify him.

It took him some time to find the little village of Chelton. He turned down several wrong lanes but never lost patience as if it was all part of the deadly game and that he knew he would finally get there.

The stone church tower poked out above the cluster of Cotswold stone dwellings and the surrounding grass had withered to a yellow mass due to lack of rain. Some sheep were finding it difficult to graze and chewed away at roots.

Hannah Cottage; it was difficult to find in the country where street names were few and houses seldom numbered. And it was difficult to park without standing out as a stranger. Certainly there were tourists but they were closer to the pub, many of them in it.

It was impossible to park in the narrow lanes and leave passing space, so eventually, now more certain of his ground, Cirillo drove back to the pub and managed to find a space in the car park round the back. He walked out of the car park and away from the pub, keeping it between himself and its clientele.

He did not like the conditions he was working under. The English were naturally curious and someone would notice him. He kept walking, found the correct turn-off and was glad to be alone again. As he neared the cottage he approached warily. The cottage was quite isolated as Ashton had informed him it would be, the surrounding flower beds neglected. As he neared the perimeter Cirillo slowed down and looked around him. There was nothing so deserted as a quiet English country lane; nor were there so many eyes; country people knew how to observe unobtrusively. It was too quiet.

He reached the short, slatted white fence. It would be easy to step over the tiny gate but he unlatched it and went up the uneven, pitted path to the low, green painted door. There was no bell; he raised the horseshoe knocker.

The knock sounded hollow as if the cottage was empty and the sound echoed into the lane. Cirillo stood quite still under the overhang of thick straggling roof which needed re-thatching. The heavy door opened and a slight, pale-faced man of medium height looked inquiringly at Cirillo. The eyes were weak but the features finely drawn and intelligent; the clothes were rather shabby.

"Can I help you?"

Cirillo smiled disarmingly. "I hope so. I've called with a message from your brother. D'you mind if I come in?"

"My brother? I haven't seen him for many years. The last time we met we had a thundering row. However, you had better come in." As he turned to lead the way into

52

the dark interior, he observed, "You're an Australian of Italian descent."

"That's sharp of you." Cirillo wished there was more light; it was so gloomy inside, dark walls and heavy furniture.

"I've made a study of accents. Do sit down." He started to turn round when Cirillo hit him on the back of the head with a gun. Cirillo half caught the body then laid it face downwards on a rug so that the blood would not drip down.

Cirillo moved quickly. He found a bathroom on the ground floor and filled the bath, using a hand towel to turn on the taps. He returned to the living-room, carried the unconscious body into the bathroom, undressed it; lifted the frail form into the water, judged the position of the seeping wound in relation to the edge of the bath, lifted the head then cracked it down on the end of the bath hard enough to enlarge the wound and to blood-spatter the bath, but not enough to kill. He then held the head under water until the poor wretch was drowned.

Cirillo gazed round, found a bar of soap and threw it into the bath. He collected the clothes, folded them roughly and took them to the living-room to lay them on a chair.

He opened the front door a fraction, peered out, was about to step outside when he heard someone approaching from the back; there must be a path leading to the back garden, a short cut of some sort. He thought he heard someone trundling a bicycle.

Cirillo stepped outside, quietly closed the door, and hurried away. Once he had turned into another lane he broke into a jog. He had run away from jobs before but never in such an exposed situation; he was glad then that everyone seemed to be out drinking.

By the time he was in sight of the pub he was wet through with sweat. He slowed to a walk, keeping out of sight of the pub's forecourt. The sound of laughter and small talk grew louder as he approached. He went round the back to the car park; the place was now full, and he was not alone there but the two groups who had just arrived showed no interest in him.

He drove off, skirting away from the pub and out into the country before attempting to get his bearings. His clothes were clinging to him and he did not like the reason. Ashton's brother was supposed to live alone. Perhaps he did and was just being visited by a friend. But Cirillo, for once, was badly shaken. He did not like the feel of it at all and was quietly seething. Something was wrong.

5

Thomas Ewing met Jacko at his Notting Hill home. The two men, perfectly at ease together already, had even begun to like each other.

Jacko said, "They are getting to know your car here. If the fuzz put out a trace on your number they are going to think that one of the PM's aides is mixing with villains. We'll have to change our meeting place."

Ewing did not seem too put out. He was drinking his usual Campari soda, and gently rattling the ice in the glass. "You could be right. There is no trace of Ashton's father having served in the Canadian forces during the war. Nor, for that matter, is there any trace of the family as we know it. Ashton senior did come over here with a young son in 1953. There is no mention of any other child, nor a wife and sisters yet we believe he had both. Indeed, I have one address for you."

"If it's in this country I'll tackle it tomorrow. I'm running round like a blue-arsed fly at the moment so I'll sleep here tonight."

"The problem, Jacko, is that the Canadians, and they have really pulled the stops out for us on this, can find no trace of Ashton and father before they came over here. They came from Canada but archives have thrown up nothing of their births, marriages or whatever; not that could relate to these particular Ashtons."

"Maybe they changed their name?"

"If they did it by deed poll there would be a re-cord and there is none. They could have changed their name in some other country; it's easy enough to do. But we don't know whether they changed their name at all."

"Maybe just after the war records weren't so meticulously kept."

"Don't you believe it. Most Western countries were very alive to escaping Nazis forging their way in. Many succeeded."

Jacko had one leg draped over the arm of a sofa. "You don't think . . . ?"

"No. Nothing like that. I don't think that is the particular problem. But there is certainly some confusion over their background."

"Maybe Ashton isn't Canadian at all."

"Perhaps. He certainly lived there as a small boy and came to this country from there. Of that much we're pretty certain."

"Maybe he's an American? That would be easy enough."

Ewing smiled. "And maybe he's a South African or New Zealander, or a European. He will have had plenty of time to perfect his English. If he set out to confuse his background we won't find ready answers."

Jacko's red Ferrari caught the eye of the pub customers and those who did not at first see him could not miss the thunder of the engine. He pulled up outside the rows of tables and chairs, switched off and called out for directions to Hannah Cottage. He was met by some silent stares but an elderly man came over to his car.

"Hannah Cottage, you say?"

"Have I said something wrong?"

"Someone died there yesterday. You could be wasting your time."

Jacko froze slowly. Frank Stewart had died just after they had met; had this one died before? "Thanks," he said. "I'd better go and find out."

It did not matter to Jacko whether he was in town or country, he still drove with the insight of a London taxi driver. A brief glance at a map was enough to get him going, and the skill of map reading, like many of his skills, came from his time as a sergeant in the army.

56

He had served in the Paras and later, and for longer, in the Special Air Service; but his dismissal from that, culminating in a military prison sentence, was something he never talked about. The few who knew him well understood that he went berserk when his younger brother was killed in an accident. Up to that time nobody knew he had a brother. Nobody knew why it had hit him so hard, and Jacko was never to explain. It was done.

When he arrived at Hannah Cottage he parked outside the small gate leaving little room for any vehicle to pass. He climbed out to wonder why it was all so silent; the least he expected was a copper on the door. No curtains were drawn, no outward sign of tragedy. And yet he felt somehow the place was not empty. He hammered the heavy knocker and the door was opened almost immediately.

"Do come in."

There was no resemblance to Ashton in those features. The man was in his late forties, slightly on the stout side, thick grey hair and sad haunted eyes. "You don't even know me," said Jacko.

"It doesn't matter. I cannot stand the loneliness. Just talk to me for a while; I've just lost a dear one."

Jacko followed him into the gloomy interior much as Cirillo had done. It was not difficult to understand why it was blazing sunshine outside yet so dull in the cottage; the low ceiling and the old oak beams were one reason, the heavy, lack-lustre furniture another.

Jacko was made to sit down while his host went into the kitchen to make tea Jacko did not really want. A mass of creeper covered much of the latticed windows preventing the light getting through. It was as if the whole idea was to keep the cottage cocooned against the outside world.

The tea was brought in on a silver tray and made an oasis of light as an oak table was cleared of papers and magazines to make room for it. Jacko endured the ritual of tea pouring and sampling and finally faced his host across the small table. He used his usual introduction and produced his warrant card after which he asked, "You are Richard Ashton's brother?"

"Oh, yes. I am Michael Ashton." The answer was so subdued, so strangely uttered that there could be a trace of fear in it.

"Can you think of anyone who would want to kill your brother?"

"Oh, yes. I would happily do it myself."

"Are you serious, Mr Ashton? Or is that just a figure of speech?"

"I'm quite serious." The sad eyes gazed at Jacko, before he added. "You must forgive me. This is not a good time."

"Would you rather I called back later?"

"No. Please don't go. The place is so empty now. I hate being alone here."

"At the door you mentioned you had lost a dear one."

"Yes. He died here yesterday."

"I'm sorry. A good friend?"

"More than that. My companion. I loved him so much, Sergeant. Freddie was so kind, he would hurt nobody. I don't quite know how I will carry on."

"People do." Jacko showed no surprise. "You must possess strength or you would not have told me that. What happened?"

Ashton reached for his tea but his hand was too unsteady to hold the cup. He spilled some in putting it down. He looked at Jacko with his sad eyes and suddenly realised that he must appear something of a wreck. "You must forgive me, Sergeant. I simply haven't had the heart to tidy myself. It happened yesterday; the police say he took a bath, fell and hit his head against the side of the bath and drowned in a few inches of water."

"You sound as if you are casting some doubt on that finding."

"It's absolute nonsense. In all the years we have been together Freddie never used the bath down here. In fact he never used a bath at all. He always showered; every morning, the year round."

"You told the police that?"

58

"Naturally. They took the general view that there is a first time for everything. Freddie decided to have a bath and that's an end of it."

"Couldn't they be right?"

Ashton shot Jacko a barely concealed look of contempt. "Apart from anything else, Freddie would never use the bath because it is mine. He would never use it without first asking me."

Jacko felt the old warnings creeping back. "What do you think happened then?"

"He was forced to get into the bath and was killed."

The tea was almost cold but Jacko drank it for Ashton's sake. When he had finished he asked quietly, "But who would want to do such a thing?"

"Someone who thought it was me."

Christ! Someone was still going round clearing up. "Are you absolutely sure that Freddie had no enemies? Wasn't it possible that he had . . . " Jacko tailed off, unable to finish.

"Another lover?" Ashton smiled whimsically. "No, Sergeant. It was not that. The only enemy Freddie had was society itself. That's one reason the police were so unhelpful; they do not approve of my life-style. I'm the curious old gay at Hannah Cottage. Something of a freak in the village. It did not worry us." Ashton's eyes were filled with tears. He picked up his tea but the cup again rattled so much in the saucer that he was forced to put it down. "We had each other and were happy in ourselves. No doubt in their odd way the police think Freddie got his just deserts."

The murders of Joseph Samson and Frank Stewart suddenly looked more ominous. "Why would anyone want to kill you?"

Ashton failed to meet Jacko's gaze.

"Earlier, you were quite sure you could kill your brother yourself. That's a pretty drastic thing to say. Why would you want to?"

Ashton was still struggling with himself. "I meant it."

"I know you did, but why?" Jacko reflected that when

the actor, Johnny Wheeler, had said something similar his was wishful thinking; this man really did mean it.

Ashton had now gone boyish as if he had said something he knew he should not have said, and was now sulking. "I have my reasons."

"I know you have. But you're talking about your own brother."

"Am I?"

Jacko suddenly felt cold. What had he touched upon? "You told me you are his brother."

"Then I must be. Would I lie about such a thing? Would I lie at all?"

"You're beginning to play games with me, Mr Ashton. I believed in you. I even believed your version of how your boyfriend died. Now I'm beginning to doubt what you told me. Is that your intention?"

"No, of course not. There are some things better left unsaid."

"Then you shouldn't have started to say them. If you cannot help me I might just as well leave."

Ashton sat up in his chair. "Please don't do that." He started to get up. "I'll make some more tea."

"Sit down, Mr Ashton. I don't want any more tea. I want the truth. You believe someone has killed your lover. You have a duty to him and his memory, and yes, your love of him, to tell me exactly why you think that."

The sad eyes sparkled briefly. "It is true that I would like to kill my brother and it is equally true that I will never have the courage to do so. I am sure he feels the same about me but he certainly has the courage."

"Then why hasn't he done it?"

"I believe he thinks he has; at the moment."

"You still haven't told me why. Just now you cast some doubt on whether or not he is your brother."

"Perhaps I should not have done that. He is. But was not always."

Jacko was becoming irritated yet hung on to his patience. Ashton was trying to say something yet simply could not face up to it. He was going round and round, dropping off the edge here and there but with nothing really conclusive.

"You're playing with me, sir. I'm disappointed in you. I would like to help you but you are not helping yourself. I'm getting nowhere and I'm beginning to think the local police are right to take the view they have. I will endorse that view to them when I leave here."

"Please don't do that, Sergeant. I'm not playing with you, but examining myself. I want to tell you but am prevented."

Jacko considered that. There was no point in putting forward suggestions; there could be many; fear, obligation, perhaps his word, for he seemed to be an honourable man if confused. Was Dickie Ashton keeping his brother?

Jacko took a good look round. There were some quite valuable antiques in the cottage and he had already seen something of the silver. "Do you work for a living, sir? Or are you of independent means?"

"Neither." The word shot out. Ashton seemed grossly offended by both suggestions.

Jacko rose. "I'm not going to get anywhere. I'm afraid I must leave, and try and make up the time I've lost."

"Must you go?" Ashton was pleading again and stood up awkwardly.

"You know I must. I'm really sorry about your friend. When is the funeral?"

"He has left his body to medical research, as will I. Perhaps we are both odd enough for the medicos to explore." Ashton stepped round the table, his belly briefly silhouetted against the dull light from the window. "Can you call again tomorrow, Sergeant?"

"There is no point."

"I want time to think. I can't promise you I will have a story to tell, if I could do that I'd tell it now, but it is most likely that I will have. I need a little time to sort myself out."

"I haven't the time, sir. Please don't do this to me."

"I really believe I can help you. It's a burden I cannot shift casually. Besides, I have things to find first."

Jacko hesitated, then said, "All right. Same time tomorrow. Don't let me down." He turned at the door. "Can't you spend the night somewhere else?"

"I won't leave here."

"Then make sure you are well locked in. Never mind the heat, lock all doors and windows."

"This is the last thing I wanted to happen. Meeting like this is absolutely crazy. It's asking for trouble." Dickie Ashton was livid.

Cirillo was not in the least put out. He had suffered disgruntled clients before and there was one quick remedy for their antics. "If you don't like the way I do things, do it yourself. I'm out of pocket on this deal; there's no final payment."

They were walking along the Brighton promenade. It was dark and well after midnight, but, with a cooling breeze coming off the sea, they were far from being alone; people were enjoying the early morning and the soothing swish of the tide.

Everything about the meeting was wrong; the time, the place, and above all the reason.

"Some of the photographs you gave me are useless. They are years old. You didn't tell me he had someone living with him, you said he lived alone."

"For God's sake, you could easily have checked his identity. You're supposed to be a pro; the best. Is that your best?"

"If you want to see my best, sport, then watch your back. Nobody speaks like that to me."

Ashton was unimpressed. "Cirillo, I take out insurance against people like you." Ashton suddenly stopped and turned to face the sea. "This is ridiculous. We shouldn't be arguing like this. But it has to be straightened out."

"There's only one way to do that; I'll have to go back. I'll do this one for half fee."

"That's magnanimous considering it's your cock-up." And then, realising that he was making things worse, Ashton added in a more conciliatory tone, "Look, I'm

62

uptight, okay? I'm bound to be. It's some time since I've been in touch with my brother. I had no idea anyone else was living there."

"If I had known that in the first place I would have had to take them both out, so perhaps nothing has changed. It might be even better this way. I'll go back."

"Be careful."

"I'm always careful. You notice there is no cry of murder. The police bought what I set up."

Ashton started to walk again. "My brother might not have."

"I'd better take you home." Ewing pushed his chair back, still gazing at Liz Mitchell. She was lovely anyway, but the excessively hot weather had induced her to wear the flimsiest of dresses and her arms were brown against the silk. He went round the table to help her rise and found it difficult to restrain himself while she was so close.

"You're a surprisingly good cook, Thomas. That really was delicious. I'll help you clear up."

"Absolutely not. You'd better escape from here before I make a fool of myself."

She turned and kissed him lightly on the cheek. For a moment he thought there would be more and he was sure she was on the verge of returning his feelings.

They walked down the stairs and Liz put her arm through his. "You've been a brick. Not many men would have been so understanding. I'm just as anxious to break down this barrier as you. It's just that the break-up hit me much harder than I could have imagined. It's easing, especially when I'm with you. It's been difficult to build up trust again. You've helped enormously."

"Good."

They reached the street and Ewing unlocked the front doors of his Daimler. When they were sitting inside the car he did not switch on but remained with hands on the steering wheel staring out into the empty street.

"Is something on your mind?" asked Liz. "I think you've been worrying all evening."

"I'm sorry it was so obvious. There is something that concerns me, though. Don't take this the wrong way, but how often do you see Dickie Ashton?"

"There's no need to worry about it."

"I think you've misunderstood my reason for asking."

"Not very often. He's never tried anything with me, if that's what concerns you. Don't go boyish on me, darling, please."

He took her hand. "There is nothing I can say about this that will convince you I'm not being childish. I hope you will take this as good advice and nothing more. What happens to you is important to me, Liz. Ease out of his company. Start turning down some of his invitations."

Liz's hand went limp in his but she did not remove it. She stared ahead, unsettled by what he had said.

Ewing looked at her; she was just a splendid outline and her perfume in the confines of the car made everything more difficult for him. "I'm not being possessive, Liz. Please believe me. I would not attempt to tell you who you should meet or stay away from. This has nothing to do with you and me, except that I care deeply what happens to you."

"Then tell me what it is you're afraid of."

"I can't. Not even to you. Can you not trust me on it?"

"You're not trusting me too well, are you?"

He was sorry now that he had raised it. He switched on the engine and let it tick over. He sighed in exasperation. "I know what it sounds like but it's not like that at all. There are reasons, very good reasons, why you should keep away from Dickie Ashton if you can."

"I can't promise you that. You've given me nothing to go on. You've cast some kind of cloud over him and I wonder if that's fair."

Ashton the charmer. No wonder so few had anything to say against him in his circle of friends. Jacko had found a couple who thought very differently but he could hardly tell her that. Not yet. He had made a mistake raising it.

"Okay," he said. "You're absolutely right. I've no right to ask you without giving a sound reason. By the time I

64

am able to do that it might no longer be necessary." He drew out and headed for her home.

Liz turned to gaze at him with some concern. His final words had more effect on her than anything else he had said.

Jacko wished the weather would cool as he drove up to Chelton after a very early lunch the next day. He was a cold weather man, had never liked too much sun. At least the air could get at him but even that was warm.

He reached Chelton mid-afternoon while the heat was at its most oppressive. He parked outside the cottage exactly where he had the previous day and went up the untidy path to hammer on the door. When there was no reply he hammered louder.

He stepped back to get a better view of the cottage. There were no near neighbours to see or hear him. The cottage seemed closed up, all windows shut. He struggled through the mass of weeds to the back but it was no different there except that two bicycles were propped against the stone wall.

He tried the windows and then tried thumping the edge of one to set up a vibration to work the latch loose. It almost always worked, if not on one window, then on another. He pulled the window open and struggled through, having difficulty with the long Regency stool beneath it.

He knocked the stool over as he finally got in and set it up again. The place must be empty for Michael Ashton would have heard him. If he was alive? Jacko had a presentiment.

The cottage was stifling, the air filled with dust. Jacko stood still and took stock. Nothing seemed to have changed from yesterday. He crossed the living-room and entered the hall. At the foot of the stairs he called up but there was no reply. He ran lightly up the stairs to find Michael Ashton dead in bed.

One look was enough but Jacko made sure; Ashton seemed to have been dead for some hours. A half-empty tumbler of water was on a bedside table, and beside it an empty pill bottle. A plain label was marked in ink, Temazepam. Jacko seemed to remember a girlfriend took something sounding like that when she was ill; sleeping tablets.

Jacko crossed to a window to let in some air. The ceilings up here were even lower than downstairs. He went back to the body and put his head close to the mouth. He stood back thinking quickly.

It was a classic. Ashton had done himself in because he could not stand being alone in the house after losing his lover. That was how it looked. And even to Jacko it was understandable; even acceptable. But for one thing.

The nostrils were pinkish, almost a drinker's nose, the peripheral veins slightly angry. Jacko had not noticed that yesterday; he had considered the whole face to be pale, what he would have described as prison pallor. What he now saw was quite noticeable. The nostrils had been squeezed hard enough to leave some bruising.

Jacko suddenly felt very vulnerable. The pills had been forced down the throat while the nostrils were held. Michael Ashton had not appeared to be a strong man and would have put up feeble resistance. And perhaps he had not really cared. But that meant he had let someone in or someone had broken in. All the windows had been closed and the doors locked.

Jacko's first reaction was to call the police but he dismissed the idea. How would he explain his own presence? The body could lie here for days unless friends visited. There had been no milk outside, or papers and they were probably collected from the village post office not far from the pub.

Jacko went round wiping everything he thought he might have touched. There was absolutely no guarantee that the local police would take the same view as they had with Freddie, although it would tidy things up for them if they did.

Suddenly the blood-red Ferrari seemed not such a good idea; it had been seen all over the place and was still parked outside. But first, Jacko made sure that he dusted down thoroughly. It was not something which could be hurried.

Yet in spite of the dangers he felt were building up, he could not resist looking for anything he could find to offer some idea of why there had been two murders. He went downstairs to find a small study at the back of the house. There was a desk and some crude shelves. Nothing was locked and he used a handkerchief to open drawers and carefully search through papers.

His time was limited and he might well have missed important items but he did find bank statements and tried to remember balances. He also found a bank receipt, the type of printed form given for depositing a case or valuables for safe keeping. He hesitated, then put it in his pocket. He was asking for trouble, he accepted that, and he was already in enough.

He must get away. He locked the windows he had opened, then went to the front door. It was an old-fashioned lock, heavy, but the tumblers must have worn over the years. Any worthwhile pro could have entered that way. He opened the door and made for his car, glad to get behind the wheel and to start her up. He pulled away, feeling that he had somehow failed Michael Ashton; he had warned him but it had not been enough. If there had been a mistake he should have known it would be rectified. Poor sod; at least he had presumably linked up with his lover again.

But Jacko knew he was grasping at straws. Someone had got to Michael Ashton before him and he would never know what Ashton might have told him. Nor did he like the idea that he had been seen all around the place and had even asked directions to the cottage. If someone remembered his car number he could be in trouble. He had a military prison record, and the Metropolitan Police would be delighted to land him. If the Yard were called in the whole thing could explode.

Apart from that there was a very able killer on the loose.

*　　*　　*

Piero Cirillo checked out of his Kensington hotel and moved to the Dorchester. He never stayed more than one night in each hotel. As it was the height of summer it needed Ashton's behind-the-scene pressure to obtain accommodation at all. But Ashton had laid his plans some time ago and reservations could always be cancelled.

Cirillo went up to his room with his two cases which he always carried himself, and lay down on the bed. He was feeling tired but satisfied. He had covered his tracks and rectified the error he could barely admit to having made at Hannah Cottage. He felt he needed a little time to recover. When he considered it he had already executed four people for Ashton in quick time. He was well aware that they might not all be so easy as the last two.

If Ashton were able to see Cirillo at that moment he would realise that beneath the cold ruthlessness of the man, even he, a man without compassion and virtually no feeling, had his limits. He was just like any other man when it came to the need to recharge. A few hours' sleep, totally devoid of conscience or any form of remorse, would rekindle his killing instincts.

He put his hands behind his head and gazed at the ceiling. Everything was feeling good again. Yet when he tried to sleep the same little niggle came back. He was used to being recommended; he depended upon it. But Ashton seemed to have found him with no effort at all, and clearly knew about the killing in Canberra. He wondered if Ashton had played some part in it. By now he was quite satisfied that Ashton's contacts and interests spread far beyond the UK; he was probably into every imaginable racket, and in a big way. Ashton was a very misleading man. Cirillo would bear that in mind. Very, very dangerous.

6

Ewing was beginning to look tired. Jacko looked across the room at him and said, "I'm the one who should be shagged. I've been acting like a copper for the last few days which takes it out of me, I tell you. And I've had to shack away the Ferrari in a friend's lock-up in Wandsworth. I can't use it again. If the local police down at Chelton suspect murder and call in the Yard, I'll be in a dodgy position."

"Do you want to call it off?"

Jacko slowly climbed to his feet, went to the kitchen and brought in another beer. "What's the matter, cocker? Not enough Campari or is it girlfriend trouble?"

Ewing broke from his reverie; Jacko had been too near the mark. "My problems are nothing compared with yours. But have we really got any further? Is it getting too risky?"

Jacko pulled the ring off the beer can. "It has always been risky. But I can do without the fuzz on my tail. I have a record, and anyway, they've been after me for a long time. Isn't that how you blackmailed me into this? To take the police off my back?"

"You're beginning to sound like a politician, Jacko, evading the issue. Answer the question."

"We've confirmed a lot. I'm satisfied that Dickie Ashton is a first-class bastard. The man is evil. Why would he want to knock off his own brother? If he was his brother; there was a point when Michael did not seem so sure."

"I'm listening."

"Michael has a considerable bank balance and regular large sums were deposited every six months; in cash. How was it delivered? And why should he live as he did with so much money? He had not been fifty, but had allowed himself to look old as if he had given up in life; even with his boyfriend around. The loss of Freddie could have been the final score, and he simply did not want to go on."

"But you don't think so?"

"Oh, no. He was topped, but it could easily look the other way. The one thing I don't like that might get the fuzz thinking, is that there was no suicide note. They almost always leave a note of some kind." Jacko was wondering if Ewing had gone to sleep. "And who will be the next? And the next?"

Ewing started to wander round the room and it was obvious he was trying to keep awake. He had slept little the previous night having found no solution to getting Liz to keep away from Ashton without alienating her; that was the last thing he wanted. He swirled what was left of the ice in his glass and finished his drink. He kept the glass, still clinking the ice.

Jacko watched him, knowing something was coming.

At last Ewing said, "You do realise that as Ashton is clearly cutting off his tail, that will include you, if he ever gets to know about you. This is no amateur roaming around out there, it's a professional hit-man. And sooner or later your paths will cross."

"I know. He's already made one cock-up."

"Don't take it lightly, Jacko."

Jacko aimed his empty can at a waste basket in the far corner of the room and it went in cleanly. "It's a bit late in the day to warn me. You knew this all along. But it's okay. As long as you keep your word that when this is over I start with a clean sheet."

"You've already had my word. I won't break it."

"Except if matey knocks you off where does that leave me?"

Ewing turned, his glass tight in his hand. He could not understand why he had not thought of that before. "I'll get it down on paper and lodge it in the bank. I'll give you the receipt."

"Which is a cue for this." Jacko pulled out the bank receipt he had taken from Hannah Cottage. "Is there any way we can redeem this?"

Ewing put down his glass and held the receipt. "You stole this?"

"I found it. And don't come that stuff; if you want Ashton we've got to do it any way we can. If it embarrasses you don't ask questions like that."

Ewing scanned the receipt again. "I sometimes wish the PM hadn't given me this job. I'm out of my depth." He was tired, a little confused and had really mumbled to himself.

But the sharp-eared Jacko heard it and was shaken. He had realised from the beginning that some government source was behind the business, but had not even considered that it emanated from the very top. Prime Ministers kept out of this sort of caper and handed it to minions. He supposed Ewing was that minion. "Well?"

"It can be done but would mean bringing in the police. We don't want that. It would suit both of us if Michael Ashton's death appeared to be a suicide; if we use the police to claim the package mentioned on the receipt they might think otherwise."

"Do you know a bent lawyer who could handle it?"

Ewing was appalled; he was beginning to see odd flashes of Jacko's world.

"Come on, Thomas. Get into the world of the living," Jacko railed. "Do you want to crack this thing or not?"

Ewing handed back the receipt. "I'm sorry, Jacko. I know of no one like that. The best I can do is to turn my back on it."

"You really think I can operate this thing within the law? You've already given me a bent warrant card. Your mind isn't on the job. What's happened?"

"There's some other aspect that's cropped up. It's a little worrying. It's all right, it does not concern you."

"Everything about this business concerns me. I'm in the hot seat."

Ewing was still standing, hands in pockets, head down. He thought for a moment then said, "It's a personal matter, so in confidence then. I am particularly fond of a girl who knows Ashton quite well. I have not found a way of convincing her to stay away from him."

Jacko saw straight through Ewing's maze of conflicting thoughts. He penetrated the root of the problem Ewing had been unwilling openly to face. "You think that if Ashton finds out you are trying to fix him, he'll get back at you through the girl."

Ewing glared at Jacko as if he could kill him. Then he gradually unwound and his shoulders sagged. "They were right about you; you see the problems before they happen."

"It looks like that because you're too close to it. What are you going to do?"

"I don't know. She probably thinks I'm jealous of him and she'd be quite right. But that's far from being the reason."

"Do you trust her?"

"Of course. But she's a free spirit."

"I was in love once. What a bloody problem that turned out to be."

Ewing was irritated. Jacko had this way of facing things he himself should be facing. Dammit, he was in love with her.

"There's only one thing to do," added Jacko. "You'll have to explain your suspicions to her and ask her help. But for God's sake don't mention me."

Ewing was startled. "I couldn't possibly use her like that; it could put her in danger."

"She may not believe you unless she feels she's playing a part and can thereby find out for herself. She might come up with something useful, matey."

"I can't do that." Ewing glanced at his watch. "I must be off."

"Just don't do anything that could cock it up for me. What a bloody time to fall for a girl."

When Ewing had gone Jacko kicked out at the air. Ewing was losing his concentration at a crucial time. Jacko went into a spare bedroom and fumbled under a large, old-fashioned chest-of-drawers. He tore away the tape and a heavy package dropped on the carpet.

He sat on the bed and undid the oilskin to remove his Browning pistol and two empty magazines. He went over to the large window and pulled up the hem of the heavy curtains, easing out a whole row of 9 mm ammunition. He took as many rounds as he needed then returned the remainder to the hem. Back on the bed he loaded the magazines, ensuring the rims of the bullet casing did not overlap, and then inserted a round in the breech and applied the safety catch. He had to go down to the basement for the silencer which was among a pile of tools in a big metal box. From now on he would travel armed.

Liz Mitchell had come as close to staying the night with Ewing as she ever had. She had met plenty of men since her divorce but had recoiled at their touch. She was becoming very fond of Ewing who was not nearly as straight-laced as he sometimes appeared to be. He had a wicked sense of humour, but it had faded of late as if he had something perpetually on his mind.

She found herself wanting his company more and more, but he worked hard and long hours and was not always available. At the moment even dating him was somewhat difficult. She knew that he had lost his wife some years ago in an horrific multi-car pile-up on the M6. It was something he never talked about and she had found out from friends.

He had been so vague about Ashton, which was quite unlike him, that it worried her. She knew there was a twinge of jealousy but there was something else and it was serious. She was, in fact, having lunch with Ashton the next day but she believed there would be others there.

As she slowly undressed in her apartment, she wondered if she could help Ewing by doing a little probing herself. There was something about Ashton which clearly upset Ewing, and it was serious enough for him not to tell her. Maybe she could find out for herself; Ashton could not be that much of an ogre, surely. It might be amusing. As she thought that she shivered, and suddenly, inexplicably, felt afraid. She slipped between the sheets and tried to put it out of her mind.

The old man put down the telephone and stood still for a while. He slowly turned to look out of the huge Georgian windows to the rolling grassland with the long fringe of trees at the end. The weather was much like that in England but the heat was not so extreme. In this part of Ireland the climate was more temperate the year round. But it was still hot enough to have all the windows wide open.

He sat down on a heavy, nineteenth-century Dublin-made chair and it took his considerable weight comfortably. His lined face was grim. His features bordered on the cruel; they were rugged and hard, and pale blue eyes were deep set as if hiding in the folds of skin. It was a strong face, aged now, but the lips were too thin and it was there, and in his general expression, that the cruelty could be seen by the discerning.

John Gorley had seen most of what life had to offer and he was far from finished with it yet. In his early seventies he still cast around for something to do and if it was not risky he was not interested. He had thrived on risk even if others had suffered as a result. And he had never been a man to show compassion except, perhaps, in one area.

Gorley had lived the life he had chosen and had no regrets, not even now, after the telephone call from England. He supposed he had been expecting the news and his only surprise was that it had not come before. What was now beginning to happen was something he might well have engineered himself in his earlier days.

Gorley ran his big hands through the mass of grey hair. He was still powerful, very little superfluous on his body, and he was very fit for his age. He had lived in Ireland for some years now, although, until recently, it was inclined to be something of an accommodation address, for he travelled a great deal. Those who did not like him would describe it as keeping on the move.

There was a rare touch of sadness about him as he went into the large, beautiful drawing-room, and beyond that to the library. It was here that he kept his guns. It was relatively easy to get firearm licences in Eire, with its abundance of foxes and other wild life. He opened the glass doors of the gun cabinet and looked along the rows of shotguns and sporting rifles. The selection showed him to be both knowledgeable and wealthy. He took down a single-barrel shotgun and pressed an area of baize where it had been, and the whole panel moved along into an unseen cavity to show yet another set of weapons, fewer but even more selective.

There was something gory about the display, and something compelling too, as if each gun told its own bloody story. Not here the selection of sporting arms, but sawn-off shotguns with a well-used look about them. The selection of pistols was far from new, but most had been lethal at some time, and there was that about them which demanded use. Like the old man himself, they were far from through.

Gorley gazed at the display with affection. Over the years these weapons had served him well and they somehow gave the impression that they had been used by an expert who respected their power and accuracy.

Gorley took down a double-barrelled sawn-off shotgun, a sawn-off sporting rifle, and an old-fashioned, wooden-stock, Steyr, semi-automatic, 9mm pistol. He held the pistol in his hand musingly, feeling the balance he remembered so well. There was an inset panel at the base of the cabinet and pressure in the right place allowed a section to open and from the cavity he helped himself to ammunition.

He reversed the cabinet panel so that the legal selection of arms was showing once again, and took the weapons he had selected into the utility room where he took his time cleaning them. When that was done he loaded them. He then went back for three more weapons and repeated the process, and did this twice more. There were few left in the cabinet by the time he had finished and the day had worn on and the light was fading. He then went round the house hiding the guns in strategic positions while keeping the Steyr with him; he would go to bed with it.

Having taken care of his own safety as much as he thought possible, he turned most of the lights on in the house and returned to the drawing-room for a large whiskey and water. He sat down thoughtfully and considered what else he might do. How much had he forgotten? Just how rusty was he? He smiled; he felt good.

Gorley lived alone in the big house yet seldom felt lonely. If he wanted a woman, and age seemed not to have diminished his appetite for them, his money would ensure that he got one, and the type trained not to be curious.

Gorley was self-sufficient; until, that is, the telephone call made him wish he had some back-up. But he could handle it. He had better warn some of the others; the remainder did not matter. He reached for the phone, dialled a number, listened to a woman's protests about the time of night, and said, "Stop bleating. It's started. He's got Michael. Do what you have to."

He made one more call, considered making another and decided against it. The others could take care of themselves. He placed the Steyr within easy reach on a small table by his chair. When he had finished his drink he went round the house closing the windows and doors. It was then hot in the house, but the night air would soon cool things down. When he went to bed he set the burglar alarm; he had passive infra-red, door and window points, burglar locks, pressure pads, acoustic alarms, all over the place.

His alarm system had not gone unnoticed with the locals and the Irish, by and large, kept away from him. A naturally friendly race, they found John Gorley wanting and could not abide his lack of a sense of humour. It did not worry him; what people thought of him never did.

Maria Rinaldi put down the telephone, her hand trembling. She gazed into space with frightened eyes and saw nothing of the twinkling lights spread widely over the

Tuscany hills as if trying to pinpoint each hill and valley. It was, in any event, too dark to see the beauty from the villa windows.

From upstairs her husband, Rocco, called out to her, "What's the matter? Who could call at this time of night?"

"It was a wrong number." The message had been short enough for her to say that.

"Then why haven't you come back to bed?"

Rocco would not allow a telephone in the bedroom and she was supposed to disconnect it downstairs before going to bed each evening. His reasons were sound; he ran a successful jewellery business in Florence and after a hard day and a long journey back to the villa by road, he simply wanted to leave his work behind. His philosophy was simple; anyone who rang late at night was trouble and in this instance he had unknowingly been right.

"It's woken me up. I'm getting myself a drink of lemonade. I'll be up in a moment." Her Italian was good but had an unmistakable English accent.

She did not switch on any more lights because the moths would fly in, but high up in the hills there was enough natural light for her to go to the large, modern kitchen with its artificial onions and grapes hanging from hooks, and the faint smell of fresh coffee coming from the Gaggia on the counter. She opened the refrigerator and took out a flask of fresh lemon juice she had made herself.

Maria sat at the bar table near the end wall. She was a dark-haired, small but attractive woman in her early forties and had enjoyed a happy married life these last fifteen years. Prior to that she had been anything but happy and now the old ghost had returned. Her inclination was to pack her bags and flee but Rocco deserved more than that and where would she flee to? She had already fled to this lovely secluded spot.

Maria loved Italy, the warmth of the Italian people, and their way of life, the beauty of the Tuscany hills, and the romance and art of nearby Florence. She had everything she wanted and was rash enough to think she had it for good.

She managed to stop bursting into tears because she thought Rocco would hear her. Shadowed in the dull kitchen light, her image reflected her sombre thoughts. She had managed to put it all out of her mind, and now, one single brief phone call had brought it all back and terror with it.

Maria sipped her drink and wondered what she should tell Rocco. He had a right to know because he also could be in danger. Yet could she tell him anything at all? And if she did would it make sense? What would be his reaction when he realised the position she had put him in?

She finished her drink, the sharp tang still on her palate, and she rinsed the glass at the sink. She could not face going upstairs and lying down beside Rocco, yet she knew that it would be worse if she did not. She tried to get a grip on herself and mounted the stairs, her terror rising with each ascending footstep.

In New York Julie Ashton took the call at 6pm local time. The message she received was as brief as the other John Gorley had passed on. She, like the other, had had little time to answer but she knew the voice and shuddered. She was not even sure where the call had come from but did it really matter?

She was an elegant woman in her mid-sixties, and lived in a Brooklyn apartment. It was spacious, generous cash payments came through regularly so she was well cared for financially, and she was living a reasonably satisfying life with a circle of friends who kept her occupied. Life could be worse, and indeed had improved considerably over the past years. There was no man in her life, nor did she want one. She considered herself too old but in any event, had lost interest in men years ago.

She calmly thought over the implications of the call, briefly shuddered again, then looked to the future as she had always managed to do. Security had always been a priority and she had enjoyed financial security for a very long time. She did not think that would change but would she still be around to enjoy it?

Julie dialled a number on the telephone and said without preamble, "You remember that apartment you were talking about? The one in New Jersey? I've changed my mind. I'll take it. I've worked it out; I reckon I can afford it. I can drop by tomorrow. How long will it take for you to fix it?"

Julie Ashton had always been a positive person and knew how to act in her own interests, although it had not always worked out for the better. But she had never been afraid of making decisions and she had made one now which she felt must be right. The thought did not remove her qualms; some aspects of life were simply beyond her. She fervently hoped that this was not one of them. Please God, no.

Rose Drew lived just outside Guelph, about seventy miles from Toronto. The bungalow belonged to one of her three daughters, now with three adult offspring of her own. Rose also had two middle-aged sons who rarely visited her; one was a waster anyway, always in trouble of some sort and had once been to prison. The other was a successful business man in Toronto who made sure she lived in reasonable comfort. But comfort was relative; so far as Rose was concerned her standards had plummeted over the years.

A bitter woman, she did nothing with features that were once pleasant, even pretty. She had let herself go and had convinced herself that she was an old woman long before it became a fact. Difficult to live with, her daughter was always berating her sisters that it was their turn to take something of the burden. It was a familiar story and nothing changed.

Rose had received no telephone call. It would have made no difference to her outlook if she had. A frail woman, her hair was rather unkempt as if she had long lost interest in how it looked; her eyes were weak and introspective because life had been cruel and self-pity had followed.

As she half-watched a video on television she would have been immensely surprised had she known that Richard Ashton, a name with which she was not familiar, in London, was contacting a London detective agency to find the best Canadian equivalent in order to track her down. And she would have been scared out of her perpetual misery if she had learned that once that was done someone would follow to kill her.

7

Jacko took Georgette Roberts to the Hot Pot where she was ogled from the time they entered. He did not take her into the back-room where the heat was overpowering, but to a table he had arranged at the rear of the main club room. It was almost as bad and was certainly stifling. A newly installed ceiling fan stirred hot and stuffy air and broke cigar and cigarette smoke into tiny clouds of cumulus.

Georgie was watched all the way to her table and had Jacko not been with her there would have been some risqué comments from the sweating clients. She had all the accoutrements of a fashion model, work she had once tried and did not enjoy, but she was actually a solicitor which suited her fine.

Her looks were a disadvantage to her work. She could not help being stunning but few would take her seriously as a lawyer. It was an aspect she found so frustrating that she had even tried to tone her looks down but there was little she could do about her figure and the present heat-wave demanded light clothing. In the end she had given up and struggled on and had even considered going back to modelling where the rewards, as matters stood, were better.

She sat down, back to the rear, grimy wall, placed her bag on the plastic table and said in disgust, "Is this the best you can do for me, Jacko?"

Jacko took her hand and raised it to his lips, knowing that everyone was watching. "I thought they needed a treat, love. The poor souls here are deprived; they never see a bird like you except in their dreams."

"I can imagine the kind of dream; half of them look as if they are straight out of prison and will be back any moment. You could have warned me, Jacko. Even I can afford better than this."

"Georgie, the place is pricey and the food good, believe me. You'll get good attention here."

"I'm already getting it, damn you. I thought you might have changed for the better."

"You'll get a fair deal here. They all know me."

"I bet they do." Georgette smoothed back her dark hair. "And it does not need much imagination to know where you all first met."

"Don't be like that." Jacko called for two large whiskies on the rocks and they arrived remarkably quickly.

"I wish they wouldn't keep looking at my legs; they are not even subtle about it. Why are there so many men and so few women?"

"I can't even see your legs," Jacko complained. "It started off as a men's club but wives and girlfriends formed a pressure group and the management had to give way. You want to order?"

Georgie picked up the well-thumbed but impressive-looking menu and tried to ease her anger; she had no illusions about some of the things Jacko did but it was a long time since he had first come to her for legal advice, and it was difficult to be annoyed with him for long.

They ordered and were sipping their drinks when Jacko said, "You should have married me, Georgie. You could have taught me new ways and we could have been sitting in the Mirabelle instead of here."

"I don't recall you ever asking me." She was eyeing the people in the room with distaste.

"Is that a 'yes'?" asked Jacko hopefully.

Georgie smiled at him. "How can a respectable lawyer marry a villain like you? What do you want from me, Jacko?"

"I'm a retired villain. I eventually took heed of what you used to tell me. Strictly on the straight and narrow."

"I'm your lawyer, Jacko, not your potential probation officer. Just cut it out and answer my question. I have clients waiting for me."

82

Jacko could not stop himself from smiling. He tried to cover it by raising his glass.

Georgie kicked him under the table. "That was for your dirty mind," she said as he gasped with pain. "Legitimate clients, Jacko. And I don't count you as one. Just answer."

He was saved by the arrival of the first course and he was right about the food which was surprisingly good. They talked of past times while they ate but the moment had to come when he confronted her with what he wanted.

He waited for the coffee and Georgette had a cooling Marie Brizard frappé. He produced the bank receipt and handed it to her. "Any chance of redeeming this?"

She glanced at it then handed it back. "Of course. Just give it to the person to whom it belongs or get his written authority to collect it."

"That's a bit difficult, love. He's dead."

"What about heirs and successors?"

"I don't think he had any."

Georgie looked suspiciously across the small table. "How do you know?"

"He told me. Look, it's no big deal is it? I don't think it's money or valuables. I'm not after the family heirlooms, it's not my style. You know that."

Georgie offered a long sceptical look from disconcertingly lovely eyes. "How did you get that, Jacko?"

"He gave it to me."

"After he was dead?"

"Come on, Georgie. He wanted me to redeem it for him."

"Then why didn't you? Why come to me?"

"Because he snuffed it before I could do it. That same day. I was lumbered and didn't know what to do."

"This is delicious." Georgie put down the glass of Marie Brizard, but her tone was as cool as the drink. "Don't do this to me, Jacko. And don't disappoint me."

He laid the receipt out flat between them, smoothing it down. "You think I would put you in a compromising position?"

"Look me in the eyes, Jacko, and say that again."

"This is important, Georgie."

"And so is my career. Okay, what exactly are you asking me to do?"

"Isn't there some legal way of collecting what's on the receipt?"

"Of course. If he's dead it will go into the estate and in due course be handed over to whoever."

"It could be dangerous for whoever to get it. People might suffer."

"Do you know this or are you guessing? What's your game, Jacko?"

"If I tell you the truth you won't believe me. If I lie to you you'll see through it. What shall I do?"

"Try the truth first." She pushed her empty glass across. "May I have another one of these?"

"Sure." He called for the drink and leaned closer to her. "I can't tell you all of it. It's pretty hush-hush stuff. I had an appointment with someone yesterday, out in the country. I had seen him the day before and had arranged to go down again. There were certain issues he intended to explain which would put some light on another matter. He was dead when I returned. This was what he intended to give me."

"Dead? So quickly after seeing you? Natural death?"

"That's how it looked. He was murdered."

Georgie did not notice the waiter place the drink at her elbow, and almost knocked it over. She steadied the glass by the stem and gazed steadily at Jacko, trying to read his mind; she had yet to succeed; Jacko was good with a mixture of truth and lies.

"I suppose the police know about the death. I mean, you did tell them? You or somebody?"

"I didn't tell them. He might still be lying there but there is nothing I can do. I could be a suspect, very much so."

"Oh, God." Georgie sat back. "Is there ever anything simple about you? Why don't ordinary things happen to you like everybody else? Are you having me on?"

"No. Georgie. The guy was croaked but it might not come out like that. And it wasn't me. If I can redeem this I might have some answers."

"Then why don't you hand it over to the police?"

"I've told you why."

"Then post it to them from some remote place."

Jacko stared at what was left of his drink. "I knew this would be difficult but it's now starting to sound stupid. I mean, you won't believe me if I say there are good reasons why the police should be kept out of this."

"That's right. I won't."

Jacko considered arranging for her to see Ewing but he did not think the PM's aide would be too pleased. He said, "I'm sorry, Georgie. I can promise you that I've done nothing wrong and what I am doing is for the highest possible motive."

"Come, Jacko, you nicked that receipt. Don't take me for a fool."

"Yes I did. And it was a bloody good job that I did." He waved the piece of paper. "This isn't for me. I won't gain anything by it. I'm doing this for someone very high up and that's more than I should tell you. Don't you think I have enough money? Do you think I'd try to use you for some paltry swindle from which I'd profit? I love you too much. But I need help."

Georgie was touched. She wondered if he knew exactly what he had said. It was unusual to see Jacko so emotional.

"Thanks, Jacko."

"What for?"

"Never mind. It's nice to be wanted even for the wrong reasons. Your story is so unlikely that there might be a grain of truth in it."

This muddled him a little. "You're not still with that yuppie berk I warned you against?"

She smiled. "No, I'm not with that yuppie berk. I'm waiting for you to go straight."

He thought she was pulling his leg; anything else would be ridiculous. "Can you help?"

She took the receipt, folded it and put it in her handbag. "If I can without breaking the law. I need to ask one or two people."

This worried him. "You won't go flashing it around?"

"They'll never even see it. I can't promise anything except that I will do my best. Is there any danger to you in all this, apart from a police enquiry?"

"No. To other people maybe, but not to me. I wouldn't have taken it on."

Now she was really concerned. He always made light of his own dangers and he was the sort of man who went looking for them. One day he would look once too often, and she surprised herself to find that she dreaded that day. "Is there anything else I should know?"

"There's a whole lot but I can't tell you. One day, maybe."

As she watched him, she thought he looked like a power unit switched off. His self-effacement, his apparent inability to take most things seriously, could sometimes give a false impression of indolence. She knew Jacko to be highly intelligent but there was nothing outwardly to suggest it. He could be emotional, erratic, and brilliant on his day. He was at his best when he lived by reflex action, responding the right way to something without knowing why. Jacko was a one-off and therefore precious. She hoped his luck would never run out.

He reached across and took her hand. "Don't take it away, I'm showing off in front of the boys." He had a half-sloppy, slightly crooked grin on his face which she found disarming. He was trying to thank her.

She was forced to say, "I might not succeed, Jacko. And even if I do it could take time. Look after yourself, okay?"

8

John Gorley woke to a fine morning, opened up the house and switched off the alarm. He had a headache, something almost unique in his experience, but even with the high ceilings he had found the house stuffy and too hot with everything closed up.

Over breakfast, he began to have second thoughts about staying in the house. It did not make any difference how many guns he had: if someone crept up to him from the rear there was little he could do to avoid a bullet.

If he had someone he could trust living with him it might be different but, due to a mixture of gradually losing his friends, some dying off, others going their own way in retirement, he had lived alone for some years. And until now he had never felt lonely. He was self-sufficient but he could not stay awake twenty-four hours each day. Closing up the house last night had made him face his vulnerability. For once, he was indecisive.

He considered his position. He could move on, make life difficult for his tracker, but that might turn out to be merely a postponement. He could sleep in the nearby stables and rig the place for defence; he no longer kept horses. Or he could take the attack to the heart of his problems.

This last option held attraction, at the same time filling him with a great sadness. Yet he had never balked or been troubled by conscience concerning what must be done to protect his own safety. Nevertheless, for just a short while, he held some regrets over what must be done. And then they were brushed aside for ever.

He finished his breakfast slowly and afterwards put the

guns he had placed around the house back in their racks. But he kept the Steyr with him.

Mid-morning, John Gorley packed a bag and booked a flight to London to depart from Cork Airport. He would have to leave the Steyr behind because it would not get past airport security, but he had its twin in London. When it was time to leave he locked up the house and left without telling a soul. Although his departure did not go unnoticed.

Jacko lacked the information and addresses Cirillo had. He continued to call on old university acquaintances and friends of Ashton but merely received the mixture as before. His best contact had been killed and he could not raise anyone as interesting as Michael Ashton had been.

Realising that an assassin had been hired by Ashton and that he would certainly have a clearer line to follow, Jacko could see that any useful contacts would be eliminated long before he heard of them.

So he decided to follow Dickie Ashton to see where it might lead him. It was too risky to do all the time, and anyway, impossible for one man, so he kept most of his surveillance to the evenings. He used hired cars, taxis, and public transport.

He did odd lunch-time work and once saw Liz Mitchell with Ashton without realising who she was. He remembered thinking that she was a dish and that Ashton, if not his money, knew how to pick them. On these limited day-time occasions he used a camera. After three days he considered he was wasting his time but decided to give it one more day.

Meanwhile, John Gorley flew to London the day after Piero Cirillo caught the ferry to Cobh taking with him a hired car. Cirillo carried no passport and on arrival in Ireland announced himself as a British citizen and produced a driving licence to prove it.

Gorley had a pied-à-terre in Highbury. It was not in his name but he had owned it for many years. The area was one he had chosen carefully. He seldom used the apartment; most of his travel took him to the United

States or Australia. He had a similar small apartment in Nice under yet another name.

As soon as he was unpacked he rang Dickie Ashton's number. A maid answered and he put down the receiver straight away. He took the replacement Steyr from behind a refrigerator, left the apartment, and took a bus to the West End and meandered around Piccadilly finding the town heat unbearable after the openness of Ireland. It was so sticky and oppressive and filled with petrol fumes and noise that he caught a cab back to the apartment.

Jacko picked up Gorley's trail in a situation that could so easily have been reversed. Jacko had mastered the rules of observation on the Belfast streets – no better place to learn about survival. Following someone could mean that someone else was following you. And Gorley was more out of practice than Jacko.

Ashton climbed out of his Rolls, the chauffeur holding the door open for him. Jacko was at the end of the street which was quite busy, and as he watched Ashton mount the steps to his town house, on his peripheral vision he noticed a big man, leaning over a parked car as if to open a door, swing his head round to watch Ashton disappear into the house.

From then on Jacko was interested in the big man who he could now see was fairly old, but sharp and fit. Jacko took two careful shots with a pocket camera then sank further back, but the old man seemed to be fully occupied with Ashton's house as if he did not care if he was seen. There was a moment when Jacko thought he would walk down towards the house but he obviously thought better of it. Yet even when the chauffeur drove past him in the Rolls to the mews garages at the back, he made no attempt to hide his interest in the house.

It was one of those times when Jacko, because of parking problems, had used a cab to get to Ashton's town house and now he wished he had a car readily available.

Jacko swung round the corner, crossed the road, and walked towards Gorley who was some fifty yards away.

There were plenty of people about and he weaved in and out increasing his pace, hopping round people until he bumped into Gorley.

Jacko struck Gorley quite hard, grabbed him, and in a stronger cockney twang than usual, said, "I'm sorry, mate. My fault; in too much of a bloody hurry." He held on to Gorley's arm and added, "You all right?"

Gorley straightened himself; Jacko had winded him but not enough to prevent him saying, "You young sods are always in a hurry. I'm all right. Now piss off and watch where you're going."

"Sorry," said Jacko again, and continued on to search for a cab. So the old boy was armed. Well, well. It was the only lead he had right then. It took time to find a cab and he thought he had lost his man but when the cab rounded the corner Gorley was still there, hailing a passing taxi. Jacko told his cabbie to wait – and bugger the traffic – and promised a bonus. When Gorley finally found a cab, Jacko followed.

As Jacko sat back he considered it a strange episode; it was as if the old man had not cared whether he was seen by Ashton or not. Perhaps Ashton did not know him but anyone as open as the old boy had been must arouse suspicion. Just who the hell was he?

The journey back to Highbury was not easy and Jacko's cabbie complained all the way. When Gorley's taxi eventually pulled up Jacko shouted to his cabbie to drive on and take the first corner. When his cab pulled up Jacko shoved some notes into the driver's hand and hurried back.

Gorley was not in sight but the cab was just pulling away. Jacko marked the spot and walked slowly towards the house where the cab had stopped.

There was a display panel of tenants. He chose a name at random and there was no reply. He tried the next and a woman's voice answered. He apologised and told her he had pressed the wrong buzzer. Two more tries and a voice he recognised answered irritably. In spite of the voice distortion through the poor quality speaker he knew that it was his man. "Mr West? This is the police. Can I come up?"

Jacko expected an argument but instead the man called West released the door catch and Jacko pushed his way in. There was a small elevator in the hall but Jacko took the stairs; elevators were bad places to be trapped in. The apartment was on the top floor, the sixth, and he stood for a while to regain his breath before ringing the bell.

While he waited he recalled that the man had been quite well dressed, while this small block was verging on the run-down middle-class.

A voice called out, "It's open." That was trusting. Jacko pushed the door so that it was flat against the wall. There was no sign of anybody. Jacko stood just inside the hall and in front of him was a partially open door through which he could see part of a settee.

"Come in. And close the door behind you."

It was the old man's voice all right, but he was still out of sight. Jacko touched the Browning in his pocket, slipped off the safety catch and moved further down the tiny hall. He pushed the living-room door open with the back of his hand and kept the other near his hip pocket.

"What's the matter with you? Afraid of an old man? Come right in."

Gorley was against the door wall and had the Steyr in his hand.

"You got a licence for that thing?" Jacko asked knowing it was too late to draw his own gun. He went in and sat down to face Gorley.

"I'm not sure. I might have one somewhere. But that won't matter to you. Have you got one for yours?"

Jacko had to admire the man; he had checked on Jacko as Jacko had checked on him. He could see that the man was completely familiar with the gun and hard to the core; not a man to compromise or hesitate. "Are you going to top me in your own pad? You haven't even got a silencer on the damned thing. If you put it away I'll introduce myself."

"You already have, sonny, so what's your game?"

"My identity card is in my inside pocket. May I take it out?" As Gorley hesitated Jacko added sharply, "You know damn fine that my gun is in my hip pocket. I can't get at it without standing up."

"You might have moved it. Okay, go ahead. You know the rules."

Jacko took out his police card and handed it over.

The man he knew as West kept his distance and his gun hand steady while he studied the identity card. He crossed to the telephone, put the open card beside the instrument and lifted the receiver. He dialled without the Steyr moving and said, "Put me through to Detective Sergeant Willis of Special Branch." He did it as if he had done it many times before. After quite a long wait he said, "Out? No message, I'll ring back later."

Gorley tossed the warrant card over to Jacko who hid his relief; if Willis had been in it would have been more difficult. "I've seen better forgeries than that. You're no cop. Who sent you after me?"

"Nobody. I've not seen or heard of you before though in view of you having a gun I very much doubt that your real name is West. Don't you think it's time you put that thing away. I mean, look at it, it's antique; you could hurt yourself with it."

Gorley smiled, but from affection for the gun. "Put your hands on the arms of the chair and keep them there." When Jacko had complied Gorley sat opposite him at the same time facing the door. He put the Steyr down on the phone table beside him within instant reach.

"You're in serious trouble," said Jacko. "Holding a police officer at gun point could get you life."

"Balls," Gorley responded. "Let's get down to it; I know who sent you to kill me but I want to hear it from you. I just want to be sure."

"No one has sent me to kill you. I say again, I don't even know who you are."

Gorley glanced at the Steyr; his thin lips tightened. "I'm not going to give too much time to this. And don't kid yourself I won't hit you here. This place is un-occupied for most of the year. I hardly ever use it. Nobody comes but me. I could leave you here until a safe time to move you. Just bear it in mind when you give the answers."

Jacko was quite sure he was not dealing with a nutter; but who was this man who was confident he could get away with murder? It appeared to be no new game to him. "I still haven't been sent to kill you or anyone else for that matter."

"You mean it was a coincidence you bumped into me?" Gorley's attitude had hardened, his tone dangerous.

"No. Not bumping into you; I did that deliberately. But we were both watching the same man. I noticed you. Had you been doing a better job I might not have seen you. I decided to find out if you are armed and followed you here to ask your interest in Richard Ashton. I was on surveillance."

"So you are sticking to the cop story. Okay; why were you watching him?"

"That was my question. I asked first."

"But I have the gun. And this is my apartment, and you are my unwelcome guest."

"He's had threats on his life. I was keeping an eye on him. When I discover someone else doing the same, and is armed, I am apt to draw conclusions. It is not me who is out to kill you but you who are out to kill him."

"That's a dangerous thing to say in your present situation." And far too near the truth. For once Gorley was not quite so comfortable.

"My situation hasn't changed since I came through the door."

"Hands on your head and down on your knees." Gorley picked up the Steyr.

Jacko knew what would happen next. He was dealing with a pro and could see no way out. He placed his hands on his head and slipped to the floor on to his knees.

"Lie flat and keep your hands where they are."

"There's not enough room."

Gorley removed a small table and stood well clear.

Jacko lay prone, his hands still on his head. Gorley stepped round him and then straddled him, still standing.

Jacko could not actually see Gorley but he knew what was going on and he frantically sought a way out. He knew the worst when he felt the barrel of the Steyr press against the nape of his neck and a hand groping for his gun.

9

Piero Cirillo motored along the Irish country roads hating every minute of it. He rarely saw another car which would normally have pleased him, but with his bad sense of direction and few road signs he was not really sure if he was going the right way.

He stopped from time to time to study the map on the seat beside him, but the distances were surprising and the high hedgerows, and often narrow lanes, were another kind of prison. When cars came from the opposite direction and, as often as not, the driver raised a finger in token greeting, Cirillo was left with the unreasonable sensation of being recognised.

It all came back to his uncertainty on country roads and his reluctance to ask other motorists for directions. It was a weakness with which he had managed to live; once his target was identified his mood would change.

Cirillo would have been happier had he known that the body of Michael Ashton had just been found. The village post mistress had missed his regular visits for newspapers and supplies and had raised the alarm.

The local police broke down the cottage door, and after overcoming the sickening smell, searched the house to find Ashton where Jacko had left him. They called in the Regional Police who were guided by the locals' appreciation of the situation. There was no note but everything else pointed the same way; chummy had found it impossible to live without his companion. Open and shut. The police were glad to get away. Cirillo had done a good job.

Meanwhile, he pulled into a lay-by to examine notes he had made from Ashton's directions. He had taken pains over getting them right, but somehow, on these Irish roads it did not seem to matter.

He finally found John Gorley's small estate; there were about five luscious acres, and the big Georgian house was roughly in the middle of them. There was no other house in sight, nor had he seen one for miles.

There was a big forecourt set before the large wrought-iron gates and he tucked his hired car to one side, well off the road. The whole area was isolated, parkland seeming to stretch for miles. Cirillo climbed over the padlocked gates to follow the avenue, flanked by a variety of trees, which led to the house.

After two hundred yards the tree line finished and the avenue no longer enjoyed protection. Cirillo stood by the edge of the line of trees to identify the problems. There were plenty of trees, he located a distant orchard, but none near the house. It was impossible to reach the house without covering open ground.

The location was ideal. The square-shaped house was majestic on its central, unobstructed stage, the paned windows staring out as they had done this last two hundred years. Cirillo was impressed not by the majesty of the sight but by the security it provided.

He was not absolutely sure that he had the right house; as often in this country with the larger rural houses, no names were on display. But his gut feeling told him that this was the place. He started to walk down the unprotected avenue to the house.

As he neared it he knew it was empty. Its shutters were drawn and it simply had that familiar feeling about it. He rang the bell without expecting a response and after a while went round the house trying to find an unshuttered window.

It was easy to locate the alarms, high up, one front one rear. But other than making a racket and warning the person inside, what purpose did they serve? There was no neighbour near enough to hear anything. If it was connected through to the nearest police station just where the hell was it? It could be miles away. He was sure that he could break in right now and nobody would know.

There were no windows he could peer through, not even at the rear where a Victorian wing had been added. He found that frustrating. He went round the back to the stables to find straw and two sacks of potatoes and empty, untidy cubicles for horses which had not been used for years. In one section were double doors and plenty of space to take his car which he could park beside the old Bentley, gleaming in solitude.

Cirillo decided to stay a couple of days and he had slept in far worse places than stables like these. It was a waiting job; there was nothing new about that. He returned slowly to the gates searching his pocket for the gadget which would pick the padlock. He did not hurry. He had food and water in the car, adequate armoury and a strange patience peculiar to his deadly calling.

Jacko felt his gun being removed from his hip pocket, heard the faintest of clicks as the hammer of the Steyr was pulled back, and swung round on an axis kicking his legs out hard. It was no more than a fifty-fifty chance with a gun pressing on his upper spine.

Spinning took his head from the line of fire but only for as long as Gorley needed to adjust his aim and squeeze the trigger. His thrashing legs caught one of Gorley's and the old man staggered. It was enough. From his prone position Jacko contorted to kick Gorley in the crutch. It doubled the old boy up and he was clearly in agony as Jacko climbed halfway to his feet. But Gorley still held on to his gun and was struggling to raise it, eyes watering, lips compressed from pain.

Jacko pushed hard and Gorley toppled over. By now Jacko had grabbed the Browning. "Drop the gun or I'll blow your bloody head off, you mad bastard."

Even then Gorley would not accept defeat. He was ashen with pain but still managed to raise the Steyr in a shaking hand which he struggled to steady. Jacko brought the Browning crashing down on Gorley's wrist but it took

97

another blow before the Steyr fell to the floor. Jacko pushed Gorley away and grabbed his gun.

"Sit down and be your age," Jacko snapped. He made no attempt to help Gorley to a chair, not trusting him even doubled up.

Gorley managed to get on to a chair and he sat, bent forward, arms between his legs. "Christ," he said at last. "Did you have to kick so hard?"

"You were about to top me, you silly bugger. You know what the chances are with a gun on the spine. You knew what you were doing. Don't complain to me."

Gorley straightened a little, face still contorted. "I was trying to take your gun, that's all."

"Cocking your own at the same time? Don't give me that. Anyway, you've answered one of your own questions."

"Which one?" Gorley was staring balefully across the room.

"If I had come to top you I'd do it right now. I'm not feeling too friendly towards you, matey. And I'd get away with it as self-defence. Use your bloody brain or has time addled it?" Jacko was quietly seething, knowing he had survived a near thing.

Slowly recovering, Gorley gazed towards a row of bottles on a small sideboard. "Okay, we'll drink on it. I need it."

"And so do I, but I'd be crazy to drink with you; you'd try to smash the bottle over my head. You stay where you are."

"So what happens now?" Gorley was beginning to concentrate again, already scheming.

"If you try anything again, I'm going to shoot your ears off. I can do it so don't think about it. What were you doing at Richard Ashton's place?"

"You told me I was there to kill him. Well, why didn't I? There was plenty of opportunity."

"Too many witnesses. It looks as if I'll have to take you down to the Yard; I'm not going to get anywhere with you here."

Jacko crossed to the telephone but before he raised the receiver Gorley said, "You're bluffing. Go ahead and ring."

Jacko smiled slowly. For once Gorley was not so sure of himself. "What's the matter? Afraid of what your prints might throw up?"

"Okay, I believe you. You're not here to kill me."

"That doesn't get anywhere. Take your wallet out and toss it over to me." Jacko grinned. "You know the form."

Gorley did not move. "If you want it, get it."

There was a television set in one corner of the room. Jacko made his way round to it without losing his concentration on Gorley. He switched on, found the channel with the most sound and turned up the volume. He had to shout now, for Gorley to hear. "Throw your wallet."

Gorley held up two fingers and Jacko fired. The shot was like a crescendo in the music and a lower window frame splintered as the bullet lodged into it. Gorley went crashing to the floor, hand up to the side of his face, blood seeping through his fingers. He lay glaring up at Jacko, now really wondering what he was up against. "You dumb bastard, you could have had my eye out."

"I wasn't aiming at your eye. Don't tempt me. The wallet or the other ear will be halved."

Gorley reached inside his jacket, hand shaking. He tossed across his wallet and Jacko caught it neatly.

"Back on the chair."

Gorley knew he should have seen the change in Jacko coming; he was rusty, but he was also making excuses; he could not fathom this young man, his shooting had been uncanny. The top of his ear was bleeding and his hand was covered with blood but the man before him showed no remorse as he shook out the contents of the wallet on to a chair.

The television was still blaring out and Jacko seemed in no hurry to turn it down. Jacko riffled through the contents which comprised mainly of bank notes, many of them Irish punts. There were several credit cards and Jacko viewed them with interest. John Gorley. "Well I was right about West not being your name. It raises the point of whether or not this pad belongs to you at all."

"It's mine."

"Why the deception? You on some kind of tax fiddle?"

"I don't like people knowing my business. Especially bogus cops like you."

"What's your interest in Richard Ashton?"

Gorley thought it over carefully. "He's my son."

Jacko was rooted. "Your son? So why didn't you visit him? You saw him for God's sake."

"That, I don't have to answer. I've gone as far as I'm willing, and have told you that because we were getting nowhere."

Jacko turned the television down. "You were going to kill your own son?"

"That's your hang-up, not mine. I never said that."

"But why didn't he recognise you? You're lying. You've been lying all along."

"It's true. He simply didn't see me. He went straight into the house."

Jacko did not trust Gorley and it was going to be difficult to get at the truth. "But what the hell were you doing there? A father would have approached his son, not just stand there gawping."

"We don't get on too well these days."

"So you went along just to have a look at him?"

"Fathers sometimes worry about their sons."

"And the gun was to protect yourself in case he attacked you?"

"None of this is your business. Let's call it a day and go our separate ways. You think I'm lying? Okay. I know that you are. So we're a couple of lying bastards. I didn't come to kill my son and you didn't come here to kill me. Let's leave it at that."

Jacko crossed to the phone again. He dialled Ewing's special number, keeping the earpiece close to his head. When there was no reply he spoke as if there was one. "I have Ashton's father here but he calls himself Gorley. He has a gun and I believe he intended to kill his son. He might be a handful to bring in. Can you get a squad car round to pick him up?" Jacko listened to the crackling on the line, mumbled a few more words and hung up. He wasn't sure whether or not he had convinced Gorley.

Time passed in an uneasy silence and finally Gorley said, "Look, the answers you want are in Ireland, where I live. You can come back with me. You won't get anywhere by taking me in but I will tell you this much more; you got it the wrong way round . . . it is my son who wants to kill *me*."

Jacko thought of Michael Ashton. For once he believed Gorley was saying something nearer the truth. "Why would he want to do that?"

"It's a very, very, long story. I could tell you anything. But at home I have documentation that might interest you."

"You mean you'd be a good boy all the way back and wouldn't try to slip me?" Jacko smiled sceptically.

"Figure it out for yourself. There's not much I can do on a plane. If I had come to London to kill my own son, there's no way I can go ahead with it now with you around to identify me. You don't have to trust me but I've run out of options. You're the wild card I couldn't anticipate." ·

Short of torturing Gorley, Jacko knew he would get no further. He stood watching the old boy dabbing his damaged ear with a handkerchief; the blood was congealing but it was an ugly mess. Gorley had been shocked but he was tough and had recovered; he now knew what he was up against. Gorley had dug in.

Jacko pointed to the contents of the wallet. "There are no addresses here, no real information of any kind except credit cards and some Irish money."

"I'll write down the address, but first let me tell you something. You say you are keeping an eye on my son because his life has been threatened. If it had been, and that would come as no surprise, there's no way he would go to the police; he would deal with it himself. As I would if it were me. That's why I know you're not a cop, or if you are, you're in one of those strange departments. You were watching him for a quite different reason. We can do an exchange of information. I'll fly back tonight. If there's no flight to Cork I'll get one to Dublin. I have some pull with Aer Lingus. You can come with me or you can follow tomorrow."

Jacko did not believe a word yet, without back-up, there was little he could do. He could not hold Gorley a prisoner and he could not get any more from him. He had to let him go. He could have accepted the invitation to go back with Gorley but, short of using a ball and chain, there was little he could do to stop Gorley giving him the slip. And he wanted to give what he had to Ewing as soon as possible.

"Write down the address," he instructed. "I'll come over tomorrow." It was a charade. He was losing a strong source of information and could do nothing about it. Yet he had learned enough to make enquiries and to help cut through Gorley's lies.

Gorley printed the address in large letters on a page from a pocket notebook and handed it over. "The telephone number is there, give me a ring on landing and I'll pick you up at the airport, even if it's Dublin." He gave a little smile. "I guess if the flights are full, which they always are at this time of year, you, too, can work a little influence. Now can I have my apartment back to myself? I want to get this ear fixed up."

But Jacko was thinking that if he flew over he would not be able to take his gun and he did not think much of that. He went back to the phone and asked for international directories. He waited some time then asked for Gorley's Irish telephone number, having read the address out Gorley had written down. He was surprised to find the number checked with the one Gorley had given him.

"Satisfied?" Gorley snarled. "You don't believe a bloody word I say, do you?"

"I trust you as much as you trust me. I'll see you sometime tomorrow." Jacko took the clip out of the Steyr, ejected the round from the breech, then tossed the lot on to the floor and left Gorley to fix his ear; if there was one thing he was certain about, no matter what pain he suffered Gorley would not go to a hospital.

* * *

Unable to raise Ewing by telephone, Jacko went to his London address late at night to wait in the shadows for his return. It was uncomfortably humid and the sound of nearby traffic carried on the heavy air. It was almost midnight before a taxi pulled up and Ewing climbed out with a striking looking woman Jacko at once recognised as the woman he had briefly seen with Ashton.

Jacko slid back into the shadows, concerned that the woman knew both men.

It was an hour before another cab pulled up, the front door of the house opened, and Ewing helped the woman into the taxi. Ewing stood outside until the cab had turned the corner and it gave Jacko sufficient time to cross the road calling softly to Ewing as he approached.

"What on earth are you doing here?"

"Waiting for you while you've been entertaining a friend of Dickie Ashton's." With the wait and the indifferent reception from Ewing, Jacko was in no mood to spare feelings.

Ewing, himself concerned, was almost as tired as Jacko. "That was unnecessary," he snapped. "What's upset you?"

"What's upset me is that you gave me an emergency number to ring you and you're never bloody there. I've been trying to reach you for hours."

"I'm sorry. I do have other work to do."

"Sure. I can see you're on the job." Jacko regretted saying it immediately. Even in the dull street light he saw Ewing pale a little, and he saw something else which made him realise that the woman was very much part of Ewing's problem. "Forget I said that. I'm on to something hot and you weren't around when I needed you most."

They were standing on the pavement at the foot of the steps leading up to Ewing's still open front door, through which a wedge of light caught them in its widening arc and threw long, faint shadows.

Ewing scanned the street; a young couple was approaching. "You'd better come in," he said wearily.

They went up well carpeted stairs to a second-floor drawing-room, pleasantly, but not too expensively furnished, and Ewing closed the door behind them. "Drink?"

103

"Scotch and water." Jacko selected a chair facing the main door; he hated having his back to doors. "Cheers." He raised his glass. The whisky was just what he needed. When Ewing was comfortable Jacko told his story while Ewing was transfixed.

At last Ewing said, "I now understand your frustration, both with Gorley and my absence. I am sorry, Jacko. But I do have to try to live something of a normal life. Liz Mitchell is the girl I told you about. I've warned her about Ashton without mentioning specifics. She thinks I'm jealous but I also think she believes there is more to it than that."

"It's dangerous, Thomas."

"Yes, I know." Ewing sat forward, sufficiently dejected for Jacko to feel a bit sorry for him. Ewing looked up, drink between his hands. He broke away from the subject. "Do you believe Gorley is Ashton's father?"

"I hardly believed anything he said, but that was a strange thing to say if it wasn't true. And it certainly seems that Ashton is having some of his family knocked off; perhaps all of them. But we don't know who they are or where they are. I must try to get to Ireland; at least the address is genuine. I need a private plane."

"What! What's wrong with the regular service?"

"Even if you fiddle me a seat at the height of the season, there is no way I will meet a bloke like Gorley without a gun. It will be almost impossible to get one through the airport security check."

"A gun? Good God!"

"Don't go naive on me, Tommy boy. A gun like this." He produced his Browning and Ewing almost shuddered. "You've landed me in a rough game. Unless you can fix me one the other side; I have no contacts in the Republic."

"I can't fix you one. Good Lord!"

"If I hadn't carried one, Gorley would have blown my head off. I'm sometimes sorry I didn't let him go ahead and kill his son; it would have saved us all a lot of grief. A gun in Ireland or a plane. Which is it?"

*   *   *

104

The flight details were made during the night although some of the paper work and clearance at Cork Airport could not be finalised until early in the morning. Jacko was surprised to find he had an executive jet allocated to him, and to discover that many of the lighter planes could not safely cover the distance to Cork with an adequate reserve of fuel.

There was building development in the Kinsale area and he quickly arranged a cover as a British business man, if cover were needed.

Jacko enjoyed the flight over the wide stretch of St George's Channel. The pilot followed the coast line for a while, then banked in for Cork Airport, at that moment hidden by mist. The plane came below the barrier of haze and they landed some few minutes later at 10.30am.

Jacko had no problem with Customs and arranged a car hire at the desk. He obtained rough directions and set off almost due west.

It was his first official visit to Eire; not too long ago he had crossed the border from Ulster on an undercover job but strictly against orders. Now he felt free on the almost empty Irish roads, his reaction quite different from that of Cirillo. Jacko was happy as he sped along, enjoying and returning the acknowledgement of other motorists once on the rural roads.

He had one or two problems before reaching Gorley's impressive house, but his sense of direction got him out of trouble each time and he rarely referred to the map after his initial scanning at the airport.

He reached the big double gates and parked in much the same position as Cirillo had done. There was no bell at the gates and the padlock hung loose, suggesting Gorley was in; he had deliberately not rung from the airport to let him know he had arrived. He still did not trust Gorley and as he swung the big gates back, he gazed down the avenue towards the big house. A white Mercedes was parked close to the house just beyond the front entrance.

He climbed back into the car and went down the

avenue slowly, scanning the windows of the house and the tree lines at its flanks and rear. He did not know the Republic was peppered with these commanding Georgian properties and he was impressed. And wary.

If there was anyone in the house he must have been seen or heard, as the engine was rough, but there was no reaction. He eased out the Browning and laid it on the seat beside him. He continued on to the gravel apron which went three-quarters of the way round the house. None of the windows was shuttered; the place looked opened up and the double wooden front doors were wide open showing a shadowy inner hall. The Mercedes was just ahead of him.

Suddenly, not liking the confines of the car, Jacko climbed out and crossed to the Mercedes. All doors were locked and it was quite empty. He walked quietly to the side of the doorway with his back to the wall, gun in hand. There were just two wide steps leading to the doors and he climbed up the edges to reach out and to ring the bell.

The electric bell was clearly heard somewhere towards the rear of the house, the long hall acting as an echo chamber, but nobody responded. Jacko felt he was about to walk into a trap. In a small alcove by the cantilever stairs he saw the small red light of the burglar alarm box but it was unlikely to be on with the doors wide open.

It made no difference whether he entered by the front or the rear; at some point he would have to mount the stairs if he went in at all. He had travelled too far not to go all the way. He ran across the empty hall and mounted the curving staircase with his back to the wall all the way up. He stood on the landing for some time hoping to hear something move.

The carpeting was rich so there was no footfall as he moved along to the nearest room, but in a house of this age, a board occasionally creaked. There was nothing he could do except to wait a while before continuing.

Jacko searched every room in the house from top to bottom, refusing to hurry or drop his guard. It was tedious work and took time but at the end of it he was quite sure the place was empty. So far as he could see nothing had been disturbed.

So where was Gorley? Jacko went into the roomy kitchen for the second time. The kettle was barely warm but had obviously been used. As he gazed around trying to put together Gorley's movements, he suddenly thought he might be making something out of nothing; Gorley could be anywhere in the grounds.

He saw the stable block through the kitchen window. Two of the old double doors were open and he heard the purr of an engine, then a Ford Granada emerged gathering speed as it approached the house. Jacko ran towards the front doors hearing the car skid to a halt, heard two muted explosions, recognised the sound and ran as hard as he could.

When he reached the front he saw the same car racing up the drive, tail swinging as it rounded the bend at the tree line. He raced to his car but instinct and training compelled him to look down in case it had been wired. The two offside tyres had been shot and the air was still escaping. By the time he could break into the Mercedes and fiddle with the ignition wires the Granada would be miles away. He ran back into the house to find the telephone wires cut, the jacks removed and the sockets badly damaged. He was marooned.

10

Jacko swore profanely for several minutes and had difficulty in calming down. He had not seen the driver who had been hunched up with a cap pulled down over his eyes, but was satisfied it was not Gorley. He wandered over to the stables, as cautious as ever, with a sickly feeling in his stomach.

Jacko went through the same routine; it was slow but far safer than hurrying. The stables housed an old Bentley. At the other end was a tractor and shelves of tools and cans of oil and two drums of petrol. Upstairs, the floorboards were covered with potatoes and little else. The stables were as empty of people as the house.

He went round the back and the long grass suggested nobody ever came that way. He returned to his car, changed the rear wheel with the spare but was left with the problem of the deflated front wheel. He remembered passing a small garage but that was miles away; he needed to get away from the house.

He went back to the stables and into the tractor section. Gorley was the type to be self-sufficient and this must be his workroom. There were some spare wheels and tyres stacked neatly at the back but none that would fit his particular model. But he did find the tools he needed.

He jacked up the car, removed the wheel and rolled it over to the stables. He managed to jemmy off the tyre and sealed the surprisingly small hole with a patch from one of the supply tins Gorley kept. It was no surprise to find that Gorley seemed to cover all eventualities. Finally, he inflated the tyre with an electric pump Gorley kept plugged in, and slipped the bullet into his pocket; its nose had been flattened against the metal of the wheel.

With the car now ready, Jacko went back into the study. It had all taken time and pursuit had long been out of the question. But where was Gorley? During his search he had been careful to touch nothing but now he pulled on a pair of thin cotton gloves and began to search as he had done at Michael Ashton's who had presumably been Gorley's son.

Jacko did not attempt finesse. Gorley was missing, the house was wide open, and he was in a hurry. The executive jet was waiting for him at Cork Airport and Ewing had stressed the importance of speed and the exorbitant cost of airport fees. Well, Ewing hadn't had his bloody tyres blown out by someone who knew how to handle a gun.

The big desk revealed nothing but bills and accounts and general stationery. But a small safe did. It was at the back of a wardrobe in one of the bedrooms and had a combination lock which Jacko blasted with a couple of rounds. It needed a third round before the dial fell away and he was able to open it.

There were some interesting foreign bank accounts in the separate names of Gorley, Steed and Hamble. If they all belonged to Gorley he would never want for money again. Even the account in his own name was sufficient for a lifetime. Gorley, who lived in isolation, and who wanted to kill his own son, had all the resources he needed. Where was he?

Yet it was not the disclosure of money that interested Jacko so much – it was already evident that Gorley was not short of funds – but a birth and marriage certificate in the name of Adams. Both were kept in a tatty, unsealed envelope, and were themselves well ruffled as if they had been screwed up and straightened out again; the ink was faded.

Joseph Archibald Adams had been born in Coventry, England on 24 July 1917; a sheet metal worker. He had married Rose Carter in Birmingham on 4 April 1940. In another envelope, cleaner and in better general condition, was a Canadian birth certificate in the name of John Ashton, together with a marriage certificate in the same name having married Julie Marvin in Paris

109

on 12 February 1956. Ashton's occupation was listed as 'Co. Director'. These documents were new enough to be copies and were in pristine condition. Jacko pocketed both envelopes and returned the remaining documents to the safe. He dropped the shattered combination lock into the cavity and closed the wardrobe doors.

There was no point in going over the house again; Gorley was missing or had been killed by the man who had shot his tyres out. But he had come too far to let it drop now. With gun in hand Jacko strode out to the nearest tree line. He knew he was wasting his time; if Gorley was hiding in the trees only dogs would find him. And if he was dead in them, he would most likely be well concealed. Jacko needed another full day to search this land thoroughly and the pilot would not wait much longer.

He called out as he searched, shouting for Gorley and telling him Willis had arrived as promised. If Gorley heard he gave no indication and after a while Jacko had to give up and drive back to the airport. He left the front doors open just as he had found them.

He was so preoccupied that he barely greeted the impatient pilot who had filled in his time in the small airport lounge. Jacko had memorised the number of the car that had raced away from him but he now put it out of his mind; it would be a hire car as his own had been, and the name would have been false just as his was.

He pulled out the two envelopes and studied the birth and marriage certificates again. If Ashton had been born in Canada then the Canadian birth certificate could possibly be that of his father. The name was right and the date fitted in. Dickie Ashton would have been born about 1943.

All Jacko could do was to hand these over to Ewing who would have to follow his own line of enquiry without raising suspicion. It was not easy with the important contacts Ashton had. But in the back of Jacko's mind was the disappearance of Gorley. He had been home, presumably an assassin had come after him, or had even been waiting for him, and yet he could not be found. Jacko was tired of chasing the tail of a professional killer and losing out each time. He had come closer. But still not close enough.

They landed at Gatwick Airport and Jacko crossed to the airport building. His Browning was tucked into his waistband in the small of his back under a loose jacket. If Customs searched him Ewing would have to sort out the mess. He had one grip and went out through the green door without trouble. He collected his car and drove back to Notting Hill.

Once inside he was grateful for the air-conditioning; he was hot, sticky, puzzled and very tired. He replaced the three rounds he had fired then ran a bath, felt slightly better after it, dressed and went out to the car. He drove to his warehouse in the East End to hit the back-end of the home-going commuter traffic, but once on the dock-side streets it was easier going.

He pulled up outside a shabby looking warehouse, unlocked the huge padlock, then the two mortice locks and swung back the heavy door. He went inside, closing the door behind him, and immediately switched off the alarms. It amused him that the alarm was connected to the nearest police station. Once beyond the inner hall where a watchman's cubicle still rested, some of the glass broken and now not used, he stood to gaze at rows of clothes and costumes hanging from mobile metal frames.

This was one of his legitimate businesses, hiring out period and modern garments for TV and film companies, and also, to a lesser degree, for private hire. Although the business itself was legitimate there were times when he had used some of the uniforms as efficient disguises.

There was a girl on daily, two if business warmed up, and he himself would help out if a big order of assorted clothes was needed. From 4.30 daily, the place was closed.

Jacko walked down the aisle of clothes, the fluorescent lights picking out costume jewellery and glinting medals and braid. At the end of the long room were two locked offices. He opened one and went over to the copying machine which he used for circularising his various enterprises. There was a large, battered desk, and a fax machine on the opposite wall to the copier.

Jacko made two copies each of the birth and marriage certificates he had taken from Gorley's house.

He removed the supply of paper from the copier cassette, placed the one set of certificates at the bottom of the cassette, then replaced the blank paper, topping it up so that it would not need refilling for some time. He closed up, went back to his car, and drove home. It had been a long day.

Jacko rang Georgie Roberts early the next morning and they arranged to meet on the corner of St James's Park opposite the Citadel, the war-time Admiralty HQ. He kissed her lightly on both cheeks and she took his arm as they wandered into the park.

The place was crowded with off-duty office workers, and scantily clad tourists making the most of the hot weather; the dry grass was strewn with bodies. They eventually found a reasonably secluded spot and Jacko dumped his hamper basket on the ground. He took out a clean sheet and spread it out. "There you are, Georgie, home from home. A palace."

Georgie tucked her long legs under her and said, "Jacko, you really have the most endearing way of making a girl feel wanted. You take me to such exquisite places."

"There'll be nothing wrong with the food either, Georgie." He began unwrapping sandwiches he had prepared himself.

"There wasn't before. The problem was we had to endure a sauna to eat it. Now what luscious surprise have you got for me?"

"Cold fresh salmon. Who wants a hot meal in this weather. The wine is in the thermos; it was well chilled before it went in."

Georgie burst out laughing; she hoped the thermos had not contained soup before. But she had to admit that the sandwiches were superb, the salmon top quality. He had even provided a sweet in the form of small trifles.

112

The place was packed out around them but they sat and ate and joked and soaked up the blazing sun. When there was nothing left to eat or drink, Georgie said, "I wonder if you will ever ask me out for myself? There's something you want again, isn't there?"

"Yes, there is. I'm sorry, Georgie, I know it looks as if I'm using you, and I suppose I am. But I've never had the guts to ask you out for yourself. I've always been afraid of being refused. I mean, look at you, and then look at me."

Georgie tilted her head and shaded her eyes from the sun. She smiled at him. "For a tough guy, you are sometimes a pussycat, Jacko. You'll never know the answer unless you ask. What is it you want this time?"

He pulled out copies of the two sets of birth and marriage certificates. "Can you check on these for me? To see if they're genuine."

Georgie studied them. "The Canadian one will take a little time but the English ones you could check out for yourself quite easily."

"I'm not so good at that sort of thing. Anyway, I'm not asking as a favour but on a purely professional basis. Bang in the bills and make them heavy."

Georgie studied the certificates again. "Was the man dead this time? Or did you just take them anyway?"

"He's missing. He was . . . "

"I know; he was going to show them to you but he didn't turn up so you stole them."

"Technically it's stealing. But if you knew the full story you would not think so."

"And you can't tell it to me?"

"It's best you don't know. For your own protection."

"Oh, Jacko. Here we are where anyone can see us so who's to know what you have told me?" Georgie opened her handbag and pulled out the bank receipt he had previously given her. "I must give this back to you. I can find no honest way to redeem this receipt. I've really looked into it and it must go through the estate. I'm sorry."

Upsetting her was the worst, and he was deeply sorry for that. "You think I'm asking favours yet won't take you into my confidence?"

"Well, aren't you?"

When Georgie looked like that he did not know what to do. He could no longer think clearly. She was hurt, he could see that. He began to re-pack the hamper. As he worked he started to tell her, omitting only Ewing's name.

While he talked, Georgie took over the packing. She showed no reaction to what he was telling her and she did not look at him again until the lid of the hamper was closed. There had been times when she knew he was lying, often with the best of intentions, but this story was too bizarre to be anything but true. Besides he had a way of telling lies, as if he intended that she should know and should not take what he was saying too seriously.

When he had finished she shifted her position on the sheet and fiddled with the hamper lock. A rare period of silence made them both uncomfortable, but Georgie was carefully thinking over what he had said.

"I believe what you have told me is true in that it has happened to you. But how can you be sure that this high-ranking man you will not name is telling *you* the truth? And why on earth should he approach you in particular?"

"Since Joseph Samson was knocked off he can trust no official source. I thought I had explained that. Ashton has too many friends in official places. I can see that myself. There is no doubt that a professional hit-man is on the loose. My own enquiries support everything I've been told. It's dynamite, Georgie, believe me."

"But why you? There's something about it I don't like."

Jacko smiled bitterly. "It's a long story involving a top politician; something that happened some months ago. A friend, with my limited help, got out of a very tight situation against the establishment. My friend is on honeymoon." Jacko gave a wider smile. "I was his best man. If he had been here they would have asked him."

"So you're second choice?"

Jacko shrugged. "If you like. But with my background I'm least likely to be suspected."

"Because you're a villain?"

Jacko squirmed. "That's a bit strong, Georgie."

"No it's not. You've got to face yourself sometime. Isn't that the main reason you don't ask me out for my own sake? Because you're bent?"

"Bloody hell, Georgie, you're laying it on. What have I done?"

"I'm trying to make you face the fact that they will consider you expendable. It must have crossed their minds. They won't want any more of their own people killed. You won't matter."

"I know that. I'm not stupid. I'm being paid well for the job."

"But you don't need the money do you? So you're doing it because it appeals to you. You need the danger."

Jacko knew that Georgie was not simply needling him but was quite angry. And she had hit the nail on the head.

"One of these days you're going to finish up dead, and then who the hell am I going to picnic with?"

Jacko could not miss the catch in her voice and realised that Georgie was close to tears. It moved him in a way nothing had before. And it seemed to paralyse him for he could neither speak nor move. He felt immensely clumsy and his natural wit deserted him.

Georgie quickly recovered and Jacko wondered if he had imagined her concern. Quite composed again, she pointed out, "All I'm doing is trying to make you face the situation you have got yourself into. You can't pull off something like this on your own."

"Look, if I reach a point when I feel I'm really up against it, I'll quit. Okay?"

"Four murdered people that you know about and one missing, and you don't think you've reached that point already? No, it's not all right. Give me back that receipt." She held out her hand but he hesitated.

"When I first gave it to you I thought you might find some legal way to redeem it, or at worst, bend the law just a little. But you now intend to break it, don't you? For God's sake, Georgie, you could get yourself disbarred."

She shook her head. "I've thought of a possible way. Give it back." She put the receipt in her handbag with the other documents he had given her. "I must get back. I'll be in touch as soon as I can, Jacko." She stood up, Jacko followed and she started to fold the sheet, finally tucking it in the top of the hamper.

When she had finished Georgie cupped his face in her hands and kissed him firmly. When she stepped back she said, "I really don't know what I see in you. Are you going to walk me back?"

Jacko took her arm and they crossed the dried grass. He had always liked her company but never had he been so aware of her as now; it disturbed him, and he was disturbed more when she said, "You really must watch out, Jacko. I know your background, your qualifications for this sort of work, but you don't really know what you are up against. There are no safeguards that I can see. I think you are up against much more than you realise, and I don't think anyone is going to care what happens to you. Please be very careful." She squeezed his arm and smiled up at him; "For my sake."

Jacko handed over the second set of copies of the birth and marriage certificates to Thomas Ewing that same evening and asked him to have them checked as he had asked Georgie. He was not absolutely sure why he was using them both except that he saw it as some sort of insurance and a check on Ewing; he knew that Georgie would pull out the stops.

When Ewing had gone Jacko rang Gorley's Irish number on the chance that Gorley had returned but the number kept ringing out with no reply. He rang three times more with the same result and then raised an operator to check the line. The number rang out for her but nobody answered. So Gorley, or somebody, had gone back to the

116

big house and had repaired the telephone sockets, or at least one of them.

The only reason why Jacko did not fly back to Ireland right then was simply the problem of obtaining a seat on a flight. He knew that Ewing would not agree to a private plane again so soon, particularly as he had failed to make contact with Gorley. There was little he could do until he had information back on the certificates so he went to Gorley's London apartment instead.

He left it until it was peak television time. It was still broad daylight, the streets far from empty, but he had no difficulty getting into the house and took the stairs two at a time. Opening Gorley's apartment door was far more difficult; there were two locks, both of them well chosen. At last he was in and he closed the door behind him, wedging a chair under the handle.

The apartment was far less informative than the house in Ireland but persistence revealed the Steyr automatic and some spare clips taped to the back of a small kitchen refrigerator. Gorley seemed always to be prepared like with the array of sporting rifles he had in his Irish house; Jacko had failed to locate the other, more sinister arms behind the main display. But at least the gun Jacko now taped back to the refrigerator indicated that, although Gorley's London apartment was blown, he had no intention of giving it up, which surprised Jacko.

He went to the window and looked down into the street through net curtains that needed replacing. He could see across the street but not immediately below. It all appeared so ordinary. He stepped away, went to the apartment door to remove the chair, and heard the stairs creak.

The footfalls were barely audible. He quickly whipped away the chair, returned it to its original position, and squatted behind the settee which was at an angle to the door. He eased himself on to his stomach, made sure he could see the door through the legs of another chair, eased out his Browning and quietly attached the silencer to it.

His view of the door was not complete but enough. He strained hard to pick up the original movements but whoever it was was being cautious. He waited so long that he began to wonder if he had heard anything at all. But he continued to wait.

It was some time before he saw the door handle turn very slowly. Then the door opened a fraction and remained like that. There was a long pause before the handle was gradually released to its original position. But the door itself remained a fraction open, though not enough to see through.

To anyone not watching as closely as Jacko the door would have appeared not to have moved at all. Jacko waited for the rush but none came. Suddenly he had lost the initiative as if someone knew he was waiting. There was no way of telling whether or not there was still someone the other side of the door.

Jacko moved position very carefully so that he could now see the keyholes. Gorley was a cautious man; the inside keyholes had covers and they were closed. The door was not sufficiently open for anyone to see through the crack, but whoever might be there clearly did not like the idea of finding the door unlocked.

Jacko now had a good idea who might be the other side, but a move for the door could be as dangerous for him as opening the door could be for whoever was outside. It was stalemate.

Jacko continued to wait. Minutes later he saw the door move another fraction but still not enough to see through. So someone was still there and suspected that not only was the apartment occupied, but was dangerous. Jacko realised he should have relocked the door after entering.

Yet as he waited, now not daring to move or make the slightest sound, he learned one thing; this must surely mean that Gorley was still alive and the search for him had switched to London.

Jacko was watching the base of the door where it was easier to follow movement. The door began to close, as slowly and surreptitiously as it had opened. The handle turned with the same slow precision until Jacko was certain that the door was now fully closed. He had to wait a little longer should it be a ruse.

He waited about three minutes and then climbed rapidly to his feet and rushed for the door.

11

Dickie Ashton leaned on the fence and gazed over the dried-out pasture. He wore a cotton shirt and shorts displaying tanned legs and arms. He rested his chin on his arms as he watched the donkeys quietly grazing, leaving clumps of nettles scattered like mini-oases in a semi-desert.

"It's a wonder they find anything to eat at all. I've had to bring in bales of straw; you see, scattered round the perimeter. But they prefer nibbling at what's left in the soil. They have a go at those old tree stumps, too. Never known a summer like it."

Liz Mitchell, leaning on the fence a few feet from Ashton, was surprised by the concern in his voice. Her expression was hidden behind huge sunglasses which reflected twin images of him as she turned to study him. At that moment she knew that he was much more aware of the donkeys than of her. Was this the same man Thomas Ewing was so worried about?

"Have you names for them?" Liz asked. She was wearing a loose silk shirt outside finely tailored cotton slacks; her hair was tied in a ponytail because of the incessant heat.

"Of course. It's difficult to remember all of them but the girls who look after them will know. We have thirty-two but it's early days and they're still coming. We rescue any animal in distress we hear about." He turned to Liz with a wide smile. "Worth every penny."

Both his tone and expression were spontaneously kind which confused her. Ashton was a man of many surprises. What had Thomas really got against him? "What's the name of that one?" she asked, pointing to an almost perfectly black mare with a white muzzle.

"Oh, that's Snowdrop, and the grey one beside her is Gigi. Aren't they splendid?"

Liz nodded; they were, of course; all of them. And it was obvious they could not be in better hands. She turned back to watch the donkeys; two were wandering up to the fence and Ashton produced some sugar cubes from his pocket. Was it possible that Thomas was wrong about this man who used so much of his own money on the preservation of animal life? Donkeys were not his only concern for he also financed a hawk conservatory, dog homes and contributed to the Wildlife fund.

As she watched him feed the donkeys she reflected that he did not always present this image. She knew he could be tough, and presumably had had to be to make the millions he had, but it seemed to her that far more people liked him than not, for she had made careful enquiries, hoping they had been careful enough.

"Let's go and have some tea on the terrace," Ashton said suddenly as he threw a pocketful of sugar cubes into the air for the animals to chase.

The terrace faced south in the full glare of the afternoon sun and was scattered with tables and chairs overlooked by the immensity of the Queen Anne house. He called into the house to order tea and they sat under the awning of one of the many sun-umbrellas.

When they were seated together enjoying their tea, looking out across the vast lawns and shrubberies, Ashton asked, "Does your boyfriend know you're doing this?"

"Having tea with you? Of course. Why not?"

"Doesn't he mind?"

"Why should he? Am I doing something wrong?"

"But he doesn't know that you are not. He must be very trusting."

"He is so occupied right now. He would not expect me to lock myself in all day. And you are a very interesting companion, Dickie. There are not many men who can take this sort of time out from business to let me see one of his ventures. Why did you? Why me? Why not several of your friends?"

Ashton sipped his tea and smiled. "Perhaps I have designs on you."

"You've been remarkably reticent if you have."

"That's because I know you belong to someone else. I'm old-fashioned like that, honourable if you like. But things might change between the two of you."

"But you could have any woman you want."

"That's clearly not true, Liz, or we might be having a relationship right now. You say I'm reticent; I could interpret that as an invitation, but I know that it was not. What you mean is that I can buy any woman who doesn't mind being bought. I've tried it. It doesn't work for me."

Liz studied him behind her glasses. She did not know which way to take that. It was somehow so old-fashioned for someone with his kind of power. She could not decide whether or not he was quietly laughing at her or was really a chivalrous man. He had made no 'pass' at her. "So you've become a monk?" she said, trying to draw him.

Ashton laughed. "I'm not celibate, if that's what you mean. But I don't play the field either."

Liz poured more tea. "You are being remarkably frank, Dickie. Is there a reason?"

"Certainly there is; I'm trying to get to know you better and show you something of myself. I like you, Liz, which is something of an understatement. And I know you couldn't give a damn about my money." Ashton smiled again. "And I'm a patient fellow when it really matters."

Liz sensed that the mood had changed in a way she did not like. "Don't be too patient."

"And I'm an eternal optimist." He laughed quietly and winked at her. "Don't let it worry you, Liz; things have a way of working out."

Now he was flirting and was spoiling things. She finished her tea and as she put down her cup he said;

"What does Thomas do for a living?"

She was wary now. Everything had changed in a few minutes. Outwardly he was just the same but the purpose was different and she wondered if he had asked her down to pump her. "I really don't know. I have never asked him."

Ashton laughed outright. "Good for you, Liz. That's one way of telling me to mind my own business." He was still chuckling when he added, "He must have sent you down to spy on me."

Liz felt a chill. There was a moment, as he spoke, that she saw quite another person and it frightened her. Yet as she gazed at him now he gave every impression that he was really teasing her. "*You* invited me down," she reminded him.

"Of course I did. Don't take my leg-pulls so seriously. I had you marked as someone with a fine sense of humour. Surely I'm not wrong?"

"No, you're not wrong, but it's a strange subject to joke about. Why on earth would he want to spy on you?" As soon as she spoke she realised it was a mistake; she should have left it alone.

"To suss out the possible opposition, of course. But I now realise I was never in the running. I'm sorry if I've teased you and apologise for my bad taste. It was only meant in fun, Liz. Believe me."

Liz could see that for Ashton it was back to normal but it was not for her. And she believed that somehow it would never be the same again. "He's an aide to the Prime Minister," she said as if she accepted his explanation. "But what he actually does I really have no idea." She was annoyed with herself for saying that much but had decided that Dickie Ashton already knew and it was better to let him think that she had nothing to hide. She suddenly wanted to get back to the donkeys but realised she would have to play out the rest of the time.

Cirillo was aware of someone running parallel to him, getting in the way and generally messing things up. And some of the people he had to deal with had turned out to be wily and seemed to know about him.

Ireland had been a disaster. The man Gorley had arrived, left his car on the drive, opened up the house leaving the doors wide open, and had not been seen again. Cirillo had watched from the stables, hoping that Gorley would drive up to them to garage his car when he would have comfortably dealt with him.

So Cirillo had finally been forced to enter the house and to search for Gorley room by room. He had found nobody. It had been uncanny. Every damned room was empty, every wardrobe, every conceivable place where someone might hide; the man had walked into the house and had disappeared.

Cirillo had felt vulnerable. Somehow, Gorley must have known he was waiting in the stables and had then done the great disappearing act. He had ripped out the telephones as a precaution and soon after that heard another car approach and had dashed back to the stables where his own car was still parked.

He watched a man get out and gaze up at the house with the same sort of caution he himself had used. It was not his target but he had seen the fellow somewhere before. It did not matter at this stage; Cirillo did not perform gratuitous killings; this man was not on his list and he would only touch him in self-defence or for money.

The man carried a gun; perhaps, if he found Gorley, he would finish the job for him. He waited so long that he knew that Gorley had not been found in the house and the next logical step was for the man to search the stables. It was then that he had sped out, punctured the tyres and raced off. Wherever Gorley was he was not likely to put himself on show again; he must know someone was after him.

Now it was happening again. On returning to England Cirillo reported to Ashton who advised him to try the pied-à-terre. From the moment he entered the street door he sensed something wrong. It was a more positive warning than the one he experienced in Ireland; that had been spooky, this made the hairs on the nape of his neck bristle. Like Jacko, he relied on such feelings.

When he reached the upper landing he was convinced someone was in the apartment and that there was danger. The moment he so carefully turned the door handle and later pushed the door just a fraction to find it unlocked, he accepted that something was radically wrong.

He sank to his knees and was not surprised to find the keyholes blocked. He stayed in that position for some time. Someone was waiting the other side of the door and he was in a no-win situation. Whether he burst in, pushed the door back first, or crawled in on his belly, would make no difference. He did not think it was Gorley in the apartment; Gorley would not leave it unlocked. It was that conviction more than any other that made him decide to back down. It was a professional decision. But he needed to know who he was backing down from.

After closing the door again, mainly because a draught might move or bang it before he was away, he went down the stairs very quietly and out into the street. His car was parked in the next street but there were plenty to hide behind and he walked behind the row on the opposite side of the street to the apartment.

Jacko emerged three minutes later and from a distance of thirty yards Cirillo recognised him at once; shape, stance, purpose. Cirillo decided he must find out who this man was and what part he was playing.

Jacko slowed down as he reached the front door. He went out on to the steps and gazed up and down the street. The only person who caught his attention was a man further up on the other side of the road who was polishing a car windscreen; on a bright summer day? And on a car which, from this distance, appeared to be highly polished.

Jacko, who had tucked his Browning into his waistband, strolled slowly up the street. He could see that the man wiping the windscreen was surreptitiously watching him, and as he drew closer he knew that he had seen him somewhere before. It had not been in Ireland for he had had no clear view of the man who had shot out his tyres. But this was not the first time he had seen him. He continued on, keeping to his side of the street.

Cirillo continued polishing, hoping the car owner would not appear. As Jacko drew nearer Cirillo started to clean the body of the car so that he could keep his head below the level of the roof and get the odd glimpse through the windows. Jacko was now crossing the street at an angle and coming straight at him. Cirillo carried on working, at this stage keeping his gaze away from Jacko altogether.

"You must be a car fanatic," Jacko said pleasantly as he approached.

"She's my baby; I like to keep her clean." Cirillo smiled.

"With a handkerchief?" Jacko had not missed the Australian accent laced with Italian.

"Just getting the dust off. It's about the only dirt she collects in this weather." Cirillo straightened and shook out the handkerchief. "You know how it is; you see a speck and then start on the whole bloody car. You live round here, sport?"

"As sure as hell you don't. You're a long way from home." Jacko pointed to the building he had just left. "I live over there. Top floor. And you?"

"I'm over on holiday. Staying with friends across the street. It was raining when I left Canberra; look at it now; the sort of weather we usually get in Oz."

"How long are you staying?"

"Depends. Until the money runs out."

"Or until you've finished the job?" Jacko was smiling coolly.

Their gazes locked and neither man gave way. "This is the only work I'm doing. What's on your mind?" Cirillo's tone was placid.

"We've run across each other before, so let's drop the bullshit. You've just been in the house over there and you backed down. If it makes you feel better I'd probably have done the same if I'd picked up any vibes. And it was you who shot my bloody tyres out in Ireland. I'm getting just a bit tired of you, mate."

Cirillo stayed cool. But he was not used to this sort of confrontation. He was used to seeing terror in people's eyes and hearing them plead for mercy just before he killed them. This man was talking on equal terms; worse, as if

126

he had the situation under control. And he was showing no trace of fear.

"The sun's got at your head, sport. I haven't a clue what you're talking about."

"Well, let's sit in the car while I explain. We don't want to attract attention."

"Piss off. You're crazy."

"Then indulge me. You look as if you can look after yourself so what the hell have you got to worry about? Unless, of course, the car is not yours and you haven't got the keys. Prove me wrong. Sport."

"You're beginning to annoy me, mate." Cirillo looked around as if searching for a policeman.

Jacko grinned. "That'll be the day. You've knocked off four geezers to my knowledge. You want a copper, I'll find one for you."

Cirillo had tensed and Jacko could see he was not used to this type of pressure. Right now he was dangerously unbalanced but it was the only possibility of getting such a man to make a slip. Jacko made the concession of making sure his jacket was undone; so was Cirillo's.

Cirillo did not know how to handle it. There was one way, of course, but professionalism prevented him from making such a mistake in public view. His decision was confirmed as a heavily made-up woman flounced out of a nearby house and said;

"Do you mind if I get in my car?" She gazed at each in turn. "Unless you both want to come with me; that would save me time."

Jacko and Cirillo involuntarily stood back as she unlocked the car Cirillo had been polishing, lowered all the windows, and drove off with a wave of painted finger nails.

"Oh, fancy that," said Jacko. "You've been polishing the wrong car."

Cirillo was left with nothing to argue. They stood facing each other near the gap the car had left and defences were down.

"What happened to Gorley?" asked Jacko.

127

"Who? Just what are you talking about? You should be in a nut-house."

"And you should be strung up. You're a hit-man and it's starting to go wrong for you. You didn't get Gorley and you made a cock-up of Michael Ashton. The odds are stacking against you. Why don't you tell Ashton to do his own dirty work? Give it up while you can. What's your name by the way?"

"John Smith. What's yours?"

"John Brown. Let's have a tinny together, Smithy. There's a pub round the corner. Let's see what we can sort out."

"Get stuffed." Cirillo recovered his calm. "I'm walking away from this. Try to follow and I'll blast your guts out."

"That's better. It wasn't so hard to admit you're a gun-toting shit who knocks off unarmed people, was it? It must make you feel good."

Cirillo stiffened as he started to move off. He turned, his gaze bleak as he returned to the ground on which he was sure. "I don't know what your part is, but I'll find out and then I'll kill you. I'll do it for free, just for the satisfaction of it."

"There's no time like the present," Jacko goaded. "Or are you hesitating because you know I'm armed? Duck the next time we meet, Smithy. Which shouldn't be too long."

Jacko turned and crossed the street feeling the hatred behind him but knowing that nothing would be done on such public view. Smithy would wait; so too would he. The matter between them would have to be decided, but at least they had met.

When Jacko glanced back, the killer had gone. It would be pointless to try to follow; the man was a pro and anyway, the car number would be meaningless. He would have to wait for another day. But his hair was prickling a warning.

12

"I really cannot believe what you are telling me," Ewing ejected angrily. "You actually had the man there and you let him go? Jacko, how could you?"

"You'd better believe it," Jacko replied easily. "He knew he was the man, and I knew he was the man, but I have no proof and as sure as hell, he wasn't going to provide it. What do you want? A shoot-out on the London streets? Even he didn't want that."

Ewing was exasperated. He gazed at his Campari soda as if he was going to throw the glass into the fireplace; instead he drained the drink and crossed to the sideboard to pour himself another. "I simply can't take it in," but he was really muttering to himself.

"Don't fret. We'll meet again."

"After how many more murders, I wonder?"

"Look, we each recognised each other for what we are. That's all there is to it. It was something we communicated to each other. You reckon that will stand up in court? Do you want me to do a photofit? Send it to the police?"

"No." Ewing shook his head wearily. "It's almost impossible to do that without it getting back to Ashton in some way."

"What the hell does it matter now?"

"Because once it becomes official, as before Ashton will find a way of being notified. He'll be able to keep ahead. At least, as things stand, he doesn't know who you are or what you are or what your real interest is. He'll find out you are not official and that will puzzle him. And he'll realise he is up against someone who is not scared of his hired gun."

"Who said I'm not scared? The man is a cold-blooded killer. He simply would not take the risk on the streets in daylight. Like all hit-men, he must have the advantage or he doesn't play."

"Perhaps he was scared too, Jacko." Ewing stopped pacing and sat near the window. "Anyway, I have some news for you." He delved in his pocket and produced some papers. "The British birth and marriage certificates you gave me are quite in order. We are waiting to hear from Canada about the others."

"We?"

"A figure of speech. Does that get you anywhere?"

"Right now, the only thing that will get me anywhere is to get Ashton in a small secluded room all to myself. Then we'll have some answers."

"And every policeman in the country looking for you."

Ashton's face was almost ashen. He was trembling with rage, hands clenched round the steering wheel like a little boy in a tantrum.

They were parked in a country lay-by. It was seldom Ashton drove himself but he could not have his chauffeur taking a look at Cirillo who now sat beside him in the dark green Mercedes. To Ashton, the meeting was both dangerous and highly inconvenient. They were meeting too often, and, at the moment, too much was going wrong.

Ashton's fury amused Cirillo, but it warned him too. He had not seen so extreme a reaction in Ashton before and the mood was volatile.

Ashton tried to calm down. He tapped his hands against the steering wheel several times before sitting back. "You should have shot the bastard," he said at last.

"Don't think I wasn't tempted. But he's not part of the package. It was broad daylight with people about and there was no way I would have got away with it."

"Couldn't you have followed him and chosen your moment?"

"He's a pro. He knows the score. And he was armed. He knows how to use one, too."

"How do you know?"

"I know." Cirillo shot Ashton a contemptuous look, resenting the doubting of his judgement.

Ashton turned in his seat, hands briefly flapping. "A pro? So who is he working for?"

"Don't ask me."

"Well, what's your judgement? Security Service, Police? What?"

"He's not a cop. I don't know who your security people use, but I don't think so. I don't think he would have worked that way."

"The other side of the law, then?"

"That might be nearer. He acted like a villain."

Ashton sat back thinking. "This is worrying. I'll find out what I can. If I come up with anything I'll let you know at once. You might regret the day that you didn't deal with him while you had him."

"So might he. We'll meet again."

"You think he's following you around?"

"No. I'd know if he was doing that. And we'd have settled the matter by now. But we're following the same trail. Our paths are criss-crossing. It's a matter of time."

"Do you think he's been doing this from the beginning?"

Cirillo was tired of the questions. "I don't know. Certainly close to the beginning; he knew what happened in Chelton and about Gorley."

Ashton said nothing for a while; Cirillo did not know Gorley was his father and he did not want him to know. But did the other man? "We must assume he started when you did. Just how has he found out about these people?" For a while he stared at the passing traffic. "You've got to stop him, Cirillo. If you don't he's going to make life very difficult for you, if not impossible. If you can find out who he is working for before you kill him, then that's a bonus."

"I thought you were going to do that."

"I'll do my share, but I'm offering you more money for the information if I don't get it."

"I want double for this guy. He's not like the others. And extra if I find out who he's operating for."

"I've already agreed that. He's now on your contract list. What do you intend to do next?"

"I'm not happy about this guy Gorley. He proved to be sharper than I thought." He turned to Ashton accusingly. "Gorley is no mug. He may be old but he's been around and knows a few tricks. He also knows someone's after him. I might go to Italy; or America. It will give Gorley a chance to show himself again. None of this is the push-over you said it was."

"If you're saying you only deal with sitting ducks then I'd better get someone else."

"You try that and I'll blow your head off and cut my losses."

Ashton smiled for the first time. "I find that reassuring. I was beginning to think you were going soft. For God's sake get this job out of the way once and for all."

Georgie Roberts met Jacko in a pub in Covent Garden. They sat at a table on the piazza under the shade of a wide sun-umbrella. Half an hour later the place was full.

"It just goes on and on," observed Georgie as she gazed at a strangely subdued Jacko.

"The weather? Yeah. It's all this greenhouse stuff. If this continues year after year I'll move to somewhere cooler."

"Has something upset you?" Georgie pushed her sunglasses on to her head.

"No, love. I'm deadlocked. I'm not sure which way to turn."

Georgie produced an envelope from her handbag. "Here are your birth and marriage certificates back. The English ones are quite genuine. The Canadian one is a forgery."

Jacko came to life. "How did you find out so quickly?"

"I have a friend at Canada House who pulled some strings."

When Georgie saw Jacko's change of expression she added, "An influential girlfriend. Although why I should take the trouble to tell you that I don't know."

"Because it pleases me." Jacko brightened. "Is it possible to find out whether the English ones, Adams and Carter, were ever in Canada?"

"If they lived there it might be possible. But unless we have a place to start with it could take a long time, Jacko. If they went as tourists you can forget it."

"Interesting, though." Jacko raised his lager. "Thanks, Georgie. See if you can find something on Adams. Don't forget to send the bill."

"And I might be able to do something about that bank receipt next week. It's just that I'm pushed right now."

He hid his disappointment and said, "You've done a great job. Thanks a lot."

Later that afternoon Jacko managed to raise Ewing on his special number and said, "The Canadian birth certificate is a fake. Never mind how I know. Dig up anything you can on Adams and his wife in Canada. No, I don't know if they ever went there. But surely, if they did, there must be some sort of record somewhere. It's urgent." Jacko rang off.

He rang Harry Bateman. Bateman would not be back for at least an hour. When Jacko finally raised him he said, "Harry? Jacko. Can you raise some boys to do some work for me? Surveillance job. Okay, I'll meet you at the Hot Pot at six."

When the two men met an extra ceiling fan was working and the place was full. They stood at the far end of the bar, neither willing to sit in the hot-house of the back-room.

Bateman was a tall, dark, good-looking man in his early forties. He dressed well, and twinkling eyes suggested a sense of humour. And yet there was a certain ordinariness about him. His features were difficult to remember although nobody knew why, for his actual presence was difficult to ignore. Bateman arranged contract killing, and was a general organiser, and, without being aware of it, often worked for the Security Service.

Bateman had his back to the bar with one elbow on it and his drink in the other hand. Many in the room would know of him but few gave him any attention. "So what's this you have in mind, Jacko?"

"A guy called Richard Ashton. I want him followed."

"Never heard of him. It will cost you."

"If you spoke to Sonny Rollins you might learn something more about him. But Sonny might not be pleased. Oh, and I'm not paying, so don't worry about the cost, but don't be stupid about it either."

Bateman gazed round the room. "If Sonny knows him he could be a high-class hood. And that could be dangerous."

Jacko laughed quietly. They were both keeping their voices down, but nobody was willing to get too close. "You could be right both times. I think Ashton had Frank Stewart put down. And Assistant Commissioner Joseph Samson."

"Shit!" Bateman's drink stopped halfway to his mouth. Then it continued on and he took a long, thoughtful swig. "Tell me more."

"Ashton is basically an investment banker. It would come as no surprise to me to find he's been laundering money from the States. A City man, he's generally low profile, and presents an overall decent figure. Spends a lot on wildlife and animal preservation and has a genuine interest in animals. Seems to have more time for their protection than any human who crosses him. Background is blurred. I'm trying to unravel it and you can help."

"A man as loaded as he seems to be can buy a lot of protection, Jacko. This sounds dodgy. I mean, knocking off top coppers, the guy must have nerve and pull."

"Oh, sure; he's got both. I'm only asking you to keep a bloody eye on him, not to top him."

"Don't make it sound too easy, Jacko."

"What's the matter with you? Have you lost confidence since Sam Towler ran rings round you?"

Bateman smiled reminiscently. He nodded slightly. "He was good, wasn't he? What happened to him?"

"He's on honeymoon. I want you to get the best team you can."

"I haven't said I'll do it."

Jacko sighed. "Don't try upping the price, Harry. You'll be well paid."

"Have you got any mug-shots?"

"Yes. And one or two I took myself of some of the people he sees. I want a photographic record. A long-distance lens will do, so I'm not asking anyone to get in bed with him."

"It'll take time to get some boys together. But I can operate with another bloke until I do. You want me to start now, I suppose."

"You're already losing time."

"You always were a hard bastard, Jacko. Anything else I should know?"

"If you run into a medium-height, suntanned Aussie with a mixed Oz, Italian accent, and brown pebble eyes, back off. He's trouble. But I want to know if you see him. If Ashton is obviously going out for the night, give me a quick bell."

Bateman looked a little surprised. "Breaking and entering isn't your line, matey. Anyway, a guy like that will be wired up to the light bulbs."

"Where's Wally the Creep these days?"

"That's better. Even so. Some of these very rich bastards have television scanners. I'll tell Wally you're looking for him. Let's get down to terms; the cost of living has gone up."

When Dickie Ashton decided to stay at his London apartment he preferred to be alone. Once his cook housekeeper had served his dinner she would go home. He would eat quietly, and put the crockery in the dishwasher for her to deal with the next day. After that he would get down to work and, if there was anything left of the evening after that, he would read or watch television. He never tired of his own company.

He had just finished his meal when the street door buzzer went. He flicked the switch and said tersely into the box, "Yes?"

"It's your father. Have you got time to see your daddy, son?"

Ashton was at once confused. His computer type mind went through all the possibilities for the unlikely call and then he smiled. He had to admit that the old man had not changed his style. "Terrific. Come up, Dad. Penthouse." He released the street door catch, hurried over to a double wall safe, took out a 7.65mm automatic pistol, and slipped it in the wide pocket of a smoking jacket which he then put on.

When his door bell rang, he peered through the spyhole, saw his father, made sure nobody was with him, and undid the lock. He pulled the door open, waited until his father was inside and the door was closed, then embraced him fiercely.

"It's been too long, Dad. Marvellous to see you. Sit down and have a drink." As he poured two large whiskies he said over his shoulder, "Have you eaten? Want me to rustle something up?"

Gorley shook his head. "Lost some of my appetite over the last few days. I'm all right, son."

When Ashton took the drink across, Gorley was sitting in an armchair with a clear view of the windows and the door, with his Steyr on a side table within easy reach.

"Just what the hell is that thing for?" Ashton stood over his father still holding the drink, and a look of complete bewilderment on his face.

Gorley was smiling. "Don't put the drink on the table; you might make a grab for the gun. And don't try throwing it in my face or I'll kick you where it hurts. Just hand it to me, Dickie."

Ashton handed over the drink and went to a chair across the room from his father. "Well this is bloody nice, isn't it? I haven't seen you for years and you pitch up with a gun. Just what the hell are you playing at?"

Gorley was now smiling widely. "You've got to hand it to me. I really taught you well. You're convincing, Dickie. The presence of the gun is to stop you getting any ideas about killing me. Just a precaution."

"You are off your rocker. Why the bloody hell would I want to kill you? My own father? To get your money? I've

136

more than enough of my own. For God's sake, Dad, what are you up to? Is the gun real? Or are you just pulling my leg; you always were a leg-puller."

Gorley picked up the Steyr with the same show of affection he always displayed whenever he touched it. "Don't give me that bullshit, Dickie. Innocence does not become you. You know this gun almost as well as I do. She's still a beaut; isn't she?" He put it down again.

"I didn't realise it was the same one."

"Yes, you did. It's far better balanced than that toy you're carrying in your pocket. Why did you send a hit-man to Ireland to kill me? It was not necessary, never has been nor ever will be. You've lost your bloody marbles, son. What's happened to your perspective?"

It was happening too suddenly. Ashton needed time to come to grips with the situation. It was typical of his father that he had taken him by surprise and it worried him. Even now he needed to learn a good deal and there was no better tutor than the big man sitting across the room from him.

"You know, Dad, physically you've barely changed. But, as much as I hate to say it, you must be going senile to come out with something like that. What the hell's got hold of you?" He noticed the damaged ear.

Gorley was still smiling and there was a trace of reluctant appreciation in his expression. He glanced towards the Steyr as if to make sure it was in reach, and shook his head slowly. "You know," he said, "I've had two guys after me. One could have killed me and didn't, the other got nowhere near me but had triggered an alarm to warn me he was waiting in the stables. If you know anything about Georgian houses many of them have an indented roof to collect rain water which then gushes through a gulley right through the attic. I'd fixed a concealed loft door ages ago, and once through that, a special, weatherproof door on to the roof itself. You can keep an army at bay from up there. Anyway this guy hadn't come from a greetings agency."

"When was this? Why didn't you go to the police?"

"The usual reason, Dickie. The same reason you don't call them in. You're a fool, son. I've done nothing but

137

help you through your life. Your whole wealthy life-style is attributable to me. All you've done is to increase the bank balance, but you had no need of the extra."

Ashton felt no remorse as he heard his father talking; it merely confirmed his belief in what must be done. "I know that, Dad. I know what you've done for me."

"Then it's time you showed a little gratitude. I don't want repaying but I do want respect. You're crazy to try what you are doing. It won't work. You have nothing to worry about; we've had stability all these years. Why change a good thing?"

"You're still talking as if I'm trying to do something terrible to you. It's you who needs to come to your senses. You've just said it yourself; why should I rock the boat?"

Gorley was still holding his drink; he gazed sombrely at it, and then bawled across the room, "Cut the crap once and for all! You stupid little bastard, can't you see what you're doing?" He eased back in his chair, still furious but trying to calm down. He drained his drink in a gulp, never taking his gaze from his son. He put the glass down, hand trembling.

In a much calmer voice he continued. "As soon as I heard about Michael I knew what was happening. Like you, I have friends in all sorts of dark corners and some not so dark. You have a problem and you know what it is. Get rid of it."

"I don't know what you are talking about. You'd better explain."

"You were riding high. A banker, a financial giant but a backroom boy. The Press aren't interested in people like you unless there is a smell of fiddle. That, apparently, hasn't reached them yet, but as sure as hell it reached someone. And someone high."

Gorley spread his large hands in exasperation. "For God's sake you could ride out a financial crisis. Someone has got a whiff of laundering; probably the FBI. But these things are difficult to prove, particularly if you have outside help, and you've time to cover your tracks. Even if the worst came to the worst, and you saw the net

138

falling on you, you would have time to bugger off abroad. You must have enormous funds around the world; they would never be ferreted out because you could keep them moving. People like us must never live in high profile."

"For God's sake, I don't. Look at me tonight. I'm not a public figure, a household name, the public have never heard of me."

"Sure. But that's about to change, isn't it? And that's the crux of the whole crazy business. You're about to go into politics. You've been adopted, spread a little cash around no doubt, and a by-election is due in a few months' time. Once elected, with your money and backroom influence, you'll aim for a position of influence. In due course, I can't see you settling for anything less than a ministry. You stupid bugger. Can't you see you are committing suicide? Why the hell can't you leave well alone? Go and give your bloody donkeys some more fodder." Gorley was shaking before he finished.

Ashton had paled and was tight-lipped as he replied, "I happen to care about this country and what happens to it. I'm sick of some of the vacillating that's going on."

"Oh, my God." Gorley sank back in his chair in despair.

"It's true, damn you. You couldn't begin to understand." Ashton was meeting his father's anger head on.

"Oh, I understand, all right. And perhaps such a shift of position wouldn't make all that much difference to what you're already doing. Except that from the moment you are elected you will be in the public eye. And if that happens you're open to every Fleet Street hack around. The tiniest sniff of your background and the yellow press will not only crucify you but you'll see most of the rest of your years in jail. How does that grab you?"

"I've thought it through."

"Of course you have and we all know the answer you've come up with. If you want to be a knight on a white charger why don't you do it behind the scenes? Become a bloody philanthropist or something. You don't have to hog the limelight and that's what you'll be doing if you have political ambition."

There was a long silence. Both men were emotionally drained as they sat restlessly, each knowing they were getting nowhere. Eventually, in a strained voice, Ashton said, "I'm pretty sure I can ride out the financial problem. There has been nothing made public. And I'm quite sure they dare not. They have nothing but suspicion."

"But you don't want an enquiry."

"There won't be one. I'm certain there won't."

"They'll still have their suspicions, though. It's easy to make enemies in politics and someone will start whispering the dirt."

"The first whisper and I'll sue the pants off them. There have been plenty of politicians who have had a whispering campaign against them, and they've survived quite comfortably."

"And when the press follow up the whispers, and start digging?"

"There will be nothing to find."

Gorley smiled with satisfaction. "Which brings me right back to what I first said. You'll never kill us all. And who's the other guy floating loose? I can tell you you're up against it with him. You should have hired him to do your killing; he'd have made a better job of it. If he's open to that sort of hire."

Ashton asked uneasily, "Did you find out anything about him?"

"Oh, yes. He has tremendous reflexes. I had the drop on him and he nearly kicked my balls off."

"You know what I mean."

"He said he was Special Branch; that there had been a threat against your life and he was investigating. I won't go into how we actually met."

"Special Branch? I've had no threats. You believe him?"

"Of course not. He's no copper. But he's specialist trained; not a man to back down. If you came to your senses he'd disappear with the rest of the problems you've created. Back off before it's too late."

"What name was he using?"

"Detective Sergeant Willis. You've always taken my advice before, why not now?"

"You're going back too far, Dad. Those days are long over."

There was another silence. Gorley picked up his gun and slipped it into a shoulder holster. "I suppose you are not so stupid as to kill me in your own pad, although you would if you could find a way around it." Very softly, he added, "You realise you'll have to include your mother? If you can find her."

Ashton did not reply. He was staring at the carpet in a miserable sort of way. His father had thrust home some solid truths, but they had merely reinforced his need of what he must do. There was no way he could back down from what he had started. People were already dead as a result. He had to go on. And he had the urge to continue. He could then cut off the old life as if it had never existed, and was well into the process. He did not want the threat of it, and he wanted to do some good while he could.

He saw nothing wrong in what he was doing. His father had always taught him to go for it, tread on people before they did it to you. Life was tough; for everybody. Amen. He wanted to go respectable and, perhaps more importantly, to command some respect. He did not see it as murder to remove the past but as clearing the dead wood; those people were not important, provided no contribution to life. His one regret was his father.

He owed everything to the disappointed big man opposite. And he loved him. The decision had never been easy yet he was doing no more than his father would have done if their positions were reversed. And he believed his father recognised this, and, in his way, approved. All he was doing was a logical advancement of what they had always done, except that now he would be accountable and on view. He had to take the step.

"Did you hear what I said?" Gorley repeated.

"Yes. It makes no difference. I'll probably be doing her a favour."

"You'd better ask her that on the day." Gorley rose. "I suppose you want to settle down with kids and all that?"

"I wouldn't want any kids of mine to be brought up like me. They must have a fair chance."

Gorley rose, at last looking his age. "I won't be hanging around for you to take me, son. And if I can get you first I will. You understand that?"

"Yes. I understand."

"I could blab my mouth off meanwhile."

Ashton smiled bitterly. "You won't do that. You'd choke on your own words. And you've too much to answer for yourself."

"So it makes what you're doing a bit pointless doesn't it?"

"It's a matter of peace of mind, Dad. Knowing it can't catch up on me. No ghosts looking over my shoulder."

"Oh, you'll have plenty of those." Gorley moved towards the door. "So it's come to this, after all these years. I've bred a monster."

"You became one under your own steam. Goodbye, Dad."

"Goodbye, son. You'll understand if I don't wish you luck?"

Ashton opened the hall door and as his father drew level with him, and as their eyes locked for just a second, he fired through his smoking jacket and the shot struck Gorley in the chest.

Gorley's knees buckled and Ashton, without remorse, took his gun out and fired again to shut out the surprise and pain on his father's face. As Gorley collapsed to the floor Ashton said, "You underestimated me, Dad. I *was* willing to kill you in my own pad."

13

"There's no blood on the carpet. I managed to keep him on his back when I dragged him in." Ashton gazed down at the dead body of his father, now lying on a rug in the drawing-room.

Sonny Rollins nodded without expression. He was on the short side but stocky and was smartly dressed in a lightweight suit. He wore a MCC tie with his pale silk shirt. His features, though plump, were strong, his eyes bland. Dark hair, touched up at the sides to hide the encroaching grey, was carefully groomed. "Who is he?"

"Don't ask."

"Okay. What made you do it on your own doorstep?"

"Because I had no idea when I might get another chance. And he was after me. It was then, or God knows when. Can you take care of it?"

"Oh, sure. I'm a bit out of practice but I can raise a couple of boys to get him out later tonight."

Ashton showed his alarm. "Do you have to use someone else?"

"There's no way I can do it on my own." Sonny Rollins was slightly irritated. "And I do it as a favour, okay?"

"I'm most grateful. Where do you intend to put him?"

Rollins gazed reflectively at the corpse as if it might make a suggestion. "It's a problem. People out with dogs have a way of finding corpses, and tides have a way of washing them up."

"Can you drop him in the Irish Sea? He'd like that."

Rollins looked up at Ashton as if he had gone mad. "Aren't there flight paths and that sort of thing?"

"We'd be flying at night and wouldn't be landing. He's not going to be washed up from there. I'll fly the plane.

All you have to do is push him out. No problem."

"Me? You're crazy."

"It's the safest way. He'll never be found. Get your men to get him to the airport and the pair of us can handle it from there."

Before Rollins could reply Ashton added, "I've removed all form of identity from him and will get it burned."

"Is that the gun you shot him with?" Rollins pointed to the Steyr on a table.

"No. That was his. I shall keep that."

Rollins was not at all happy with the way Ashton was handling matters. There was a zany touch about it, yet if he was willing to fly the plane, he supposed the Irish Sea was as good as any place to hide a corpse for all time. But he considered it bizarre for Ashton to keep the gun, almost as if it was some kind of memento. The financial interests of the two men, however, were too vast and interwoven for him to be squeamish now. Maybe it would remind him of the old days; like going back to school.

"I don't like this at all," Harry Bateman said emphatically. "If it hadn't been for this big old guy pitching up I'd have called it a night. He arrived so I hung on. I can't even be sure that he was visiting Ashton, he could have been calling on anyone in the block.

"Anyway, I was going to call it off but the big guy hadn't reappeared. The penthouse lights were still on and then Sonny Rollins pitches up just before midnight. I tell you, Jacko, there wasn't a bloody shadow deep enough to hide in with that guy around. I began to get nervous but at the same time I was interested."

Jacko topped up Bateman's drink and could see he was genuinely nervous which was not like Bateman at all. But Rollins struck fear into almost any villain around town because his influence spread so wide and because, even by underworld standards, he was completely unscrupulous.

"I was dead beat, badly needed some sleep, but Rollins hadn't come out. I had to move on a couple of times because of patrolling fuzz but each time I came back the lights were still on up there. Then an ambulance drew up, one of those small jobs; no flashers, no siren. Two men in uniform get out and are let into the apartments. They had hoods written all over them in spite of the gear. By then it was far too dark to recognise anyone." With drink in hand, Bateman got up and walked over to the windows. He looked down into the street for some time before continuing.

"Rollins came out first and stood on the steps to make sure it was clear, he has an easy shape to identify. The two hoods came out carrying a stretcher with a body strapped to it. By the difficulty they had I could see that the stiff was heavy. I realised that I was watching the back-end of a topping. Sonny Rollins gets in the back of the ambulance with the stiff and one of the men, and the other bloke drives them away. That's as far as it goes. There was no way I was going to follow Sonny Rollins carting off a corpse."

"That deserves a bonus, Harry. Nice work, mate. Thanks for hanging on. But what happened to Ashton?"

"I don't know. As soon as the ambulance went so did I in the opposite direction."

"So you don't know whether or not he followed them in his car?"

"All I know is that he did not go with them. His lights were still on when I left. I was too shagged to hang about any more. Anyway, there must be another way out of the building; it's big and the garages are round the back."

"Never mind. It depends on what they were going to do with the body. How can you be sure he was dead?"

"Years of practice. He wasn't ill when he went in." Bateman started pacing, half asleep on his feet. "It'll be easier from tomorrow; I'll have three more of the boys by then. Sonny Rollins must be getting careless. It's not like him."

"He was doing Ashton a favour. He had no way of knowing you would be there."

"Does it help at all?"

"Not a lot. It confirms Ashton is a murdering bastard but I already knew that. I must get in there. As soon as

145

Ashton goes out for the evening let me know at once. I've got Wally lined up."

"Yes, well, bear in mind that Sonny Rollins is in this thing. It would be stupid to forget that. Don't get in too deep, Jacko. We all know your reputation but with people like Rollins the odds are stacked against you."

"Would you believe me if I say that my main concern is Ashton himself? Beside him Sonny Rollins is a pussycat. Rollins came running when Ashton called him, didn't he? Rollins didn't pitch up on a casual visit. He wouldn't work that way. Give Ashton every respect, Harry. He's a deceptive bastard."

"The locks will take time. How long have we got?"

"He's gone to the theatre; let's say a couple of hours. He'll be away longer, so that should be a safe estimate."

Wally the Creep was already working at the door with a huge array of pick-locks. "You watch the head of the stairs and listen for the lift." Wally had the hands of a pianist and the body of a rake. Tall and thin with a large Adam's apple which moved up and down every time he spoke, he looked a complete misfit in a suit of reasonable quality and expensive shoes which did not fit him either. He could not play the piano but everyone stopped talking when he picked up a violin. Sadly, he had never managed to discipline himself sufficiently for concert music.

It took almost fifteen minutes to open the front door, and then Wally had to check for contacts at the top of the door which meant he could barely move it until he was sure there were none. Once in, it was easier. General alarms were of limited use in an apartment block. The main security lay in making it as difficult as possible to break in.

Wally quickly established there was no infra-red, and had there been, he had a simple remedy in two small collapsible body shields to cut off the body heat that would activate the alarms. In one way the lack of alarms did not augur well; it could mean Ashton did not keep important documents here.

146

There was a balcony at the rear of the apartment, spacious enough to hold a party but the sliding windows to it were locked, which presented no great problem, but beyond them were heavy iron grids which were chained and padlocked. It was designed to keep out cat-burglars from that side.

Wally found the twin safes and while he set to work, Jacko went round the apartment. Ashton was not the type to keep important items in bread bins or refrigerators, or taped under the bed. Jacko knew this before they broke in. He did not really expect to find anything incriminating; Ashton would use a depository, or the vaults of his own bank. Yet he intended that the enormous risk they were taking should pay off.

When he had finished going round the penthouse, a quiet expression of extreme wealth, he decided there was nothing wrong with Ashton's taste. It was similar to his own in fact, though nobody would believe it. The garishness of Jacko's furnishing and dress had long been an act; people expected it of him so he outrageously obliged.

He sat in the drawing-room, glanced at the time, and quietly watched Wally at work. One of Wally's prides was that he was one of the few top petermen in the country who rarely used explosive to open a safe.

"Twenty minutes left," said Jacko softly.

Wally did not reply, but ten minutes later he had cracked both combinations and the small doors swung open.

Apart from costly jewellery, there was little else in the safes but for two guns. Jacko removed them, using a handkerchief.

The first he viewed in surprise. He recognised it as a North Korean 7.65, very similar to the Chinese Type 64 with a built-in silencer, popularly known as the assassination pistol. This explained why Harry had heard no suspicion of shots. All markings had been filed away.

The second pistol was a Steyr. Jacko picked it up with almost the same affection as had Gorley. But it was the man, and not the weapon that Jacko had feeling for. He could guess something of Gorley's past but the man had

147

possessed humour and warmth and was a good loser, which qualities he suspected Ashton lacked. Perhaps, had he known Gorley in his younger days he would not feel the same, but he was now fairly sure the old boy was dead. There was a way of finding out.

"Shall I put them back?" Wally asked.

Jacko shook his head. "No. I want him to know I've been here." He glanced at Wally who was still standing by the safes. "Close them up."

"What about the 'tom'? You can't just leave it there."

"Wally, I'm paying you for a break-in, not burglary. Close up." Jacko grinned. "Be brave, Wally."

Wally spun the dials reluctantly, glancing back to find Jacko was looking. "That's the first time I've left the stuff behind. I can't believe it."

Making sure the safes had been properly locked, Jacko then placed the Steyr on the central table with the barrel pointing directly at the door.

"You're mad," said Wally, still aggrieved. "Why let him know we've been here?"

"Because I want to scare the daylights out of him. Frightened men make mistakes."

"Don't be too clever, Jacko. Frightened men can be trigger happy, too."

"Come on. Let's get out. And be sure you turn all the tumblers of the door locks."

When the two men parted a few minutes later Jacko caught a cab to be dropped off near Gorley's pied-à-terre. It was still light and he cautiously let himself in at the street door and went up the stairs.

This time he locked the door behind him and went round the now familiar apartment. There was a carton of milk on the tiny kitchen table and a china bowl which had traces of corn flakes; Gorley's last meal?

Once certain the place was empty Jacko went straight to the refrigerator. The Steyr was missing from the back and the Sellotape was hanging down where it had come away cleanly.

Jacko sat back on his heels. He had believed from the outset that the Steyr he had found in Ashton's safe was Gorley's but now he had the confirmation he needed. Without doubt Gorley was dead. Whatever motivated Dickie Ashton had induced him to kill his own father. It was sick. He rang Ewing on Gorley's phone, but he was out; he left a simple coded message on the answering machine for Ewing to contact him as soon as possible.

On the way home he reflected once again how the power of Ashton was shown in being able to call on someone like Sonny Rollins to clean up for him. Although Rollins created waves in the underworld he had presented a respectable profile for years, and was accepted by many who did not really know him as a perfectly respectable business man. Those who did know his past no longer lived in his world.

Ewing was waiting in his Daimler Sovereign when Jacko eventually reached home. He was halfway across the street before Jacko looked round to see him.

"I've been waiting for the last twenty minutes," Ewing complained as he drew level.

"I'm sorry," said Jacko. "I've been saying goodbye to a recent adversary in the pub down the road. Gorley is dead."

They said little more until they were in Jacko's sitting-room. It was dark by now and he pulled the drapes and switched on all the lights until they were almost blinding.

"I wouldn't have expected it to upset you. What happened?" Ewing, now well familiar with the form, poured them both drinks.

Jacko told his story about Gorley and then about getting into Ashton's apartment, using a professional safe-breaker.

Ewing was alarmed, and he was about to say so when he saw the ridiculousness of it. But matters did seem to be getting out of control. He sat in the chair that had become his favourite and said, "I find all this disturbing. Not the way you've handled it, with a man like Ashton, I think you've got it just right, and don't take that as being magnanimous; I'm well aware of the risks you've taken. But we still have nothing positive against him; nothing that will stand up in court or an enquiry. We can't prove he killed his father. Can we?"

"Not unless the body can be found." Jacko produced the 7.65 pistol now in a cellophane bag, and handed it to Ewing. "Put that in a safe place. If Gorley's body does turn up you'll find that is the gun that killed him. It's of little use without the body and I doubt that it will be found. And Harry Bateman's evidence would be kicked out of court; he has too much form, and anyway, there is no way of proving who Gorley called on, or even if it was Gorley. In any event, Harry wouldn't testify with Sonny Rollins involved. But it's the first time we're aware of that Ashton has done his own killing. The bastard couldn't afford to wait for his Aussie hit-man to do it."

"We know all this but can do nothing?"

"Men like Ashton can always buy cover. But we're moving along, Tommy, old boy. We've got the sod running."

Ewing appeared bemused. "I'm glad you see it that way. From where I sit we've simply moved into crime ourselves with uncertain progress."

Noting the tone of pessimism, Jacko said, "Something's bothering you again."

Ewing nodded. "You're getting to know me too well. Liz won't see sense regarding Ashton. She went down to his country place and saw something about him she did not like. I wanted her to stop seeing him then, but she insists it's worth hanging on. He pumped her about me."

Jacko rose angrily and stood accusingly over Ewing. "She thinks this is all a bloody game; a rich woman's game. Get the silly cow to pack it in before she becomes pigs' swill."

Ewing paled. Thrown completely off balance he retorted, "Don't talk about her like that. She's trying to help in her way, right or wrong."

"God Almighty, can't you see she's walking right into it? What sort of a fool do you take Ashton for? If he's pumped her about you, he'll use her against you. It means he knows you are somehow involved. She thinks she's being clever but she can't match someone like Ashton. Get her away from him once and for all. I'm bloody serious about this; she could ruin everything and my life is on the line."

"Do you think I haven't tried?"

But Jacko was still furious. "She had better not find out who I am or even that you're using someone. That could put the lid on it."

"You think she would betray you?" Ewing said angrily.

Jacko struck himself on the forehead. "I give up. Even you don't seem to have grasped what Ashton can get up to. Of course she'll betray me, and you, if Ashton decides that's what he wants her to do. When will you bloody well learn?"

"I'll talk to her again."

"You'd better do better than that. I warned you right from the beginning. Ashton is now feeling something of the heat; he'll protect himself. Do you know when she's seeing him next?"

Ewing looked defeated. "She was seeing him tonight. A ballet. Look, I've been desperately busy. I've spent most of the evening on committee. I can't keep her on a ball and chain."

"You'll have to where Ashton is concerned. I just hope to God he doesn't take her back to his apartment tonight. There's a little surprise I arranged for him which I didn't tell you about."

Ewing could only stare in anguish, his drink untouched.

Jacko found it difficult to feel sorry for him but went as far as to say, "I'm sorry I called her a silly cow. I know she means a lot to you. But if you want to hang on to her in one piece, you'd better get through to her before it's too late."

Ewing was distressed but Jacko was unrelenting. "I don't understand you politicians; you seem to be all piss and wind and no common sense. It must have occurred to you that Ashton will be wondering why your girlfriend is seeing so much of him. Why should she do that unless she finds his company better than yours?"

"That was below the belt, Jacko."

"No it wasn't. There are only two ways Ashton will see it; that way, or 'What's-her-game' way. She thinks she's handling it; but you'll find it's the other way round. She's dealing with a mass murderer. Can you trust her enough to tell her that?"

Ashton opened the door and said, "After you, Liz."

Liz went into the lounge and almost the first thing she saw was the gun pointing straight at her. She was startled but recovered quickly to say, "Is that there to make your guests feel wanted?"

Ashton came up behind her and saw the Steyr late. His features locked and for some seconds he could say nothing. But he was still feeling the shock as he said, "It's a toy. One of those dummies that can be bought in toy shops. It really belongs to a friend but it was stupid of me to leave it there. Sorry, Liz."

He picked it up and slipped it into a drawer then crossed the room to pour drinks, relieved that his back was towards her and suddenly wishing she would go. He had to see it through, though. As he raised a decanter his hand was steady but his mind was in turmoil. He had locked the Steyr away. With the other gun. There was no way he could check until she had gone and he could not rush her, especially as he had invited her in. But he did not want to raise her curiosity any more.

He was smiling when he returned with the drinks and Liz was comfortably seated. He had intended to sit next to her but now sat opposite, quickly scanning the room as he went to his chair.

They sat and talked about the show for some minutes but Liz noticed that something had gone out of him; he was pumping up his charm as if his mind was elsewhere; his responses had become standard.

After a while of small talk, and on their second drink, Liz said, "I really must see less of you. I'm overdoing it."

152

He pushed the Steyr from his mind. "I wasn't aware we were seeing so much of each other. Just the occasional innocent date."

"I should not be doing it; it isn't fair to Thomas."

"Then Thomas should give you far more of his time. I'm only filling a gap. Do I embarrass you in some way?"

"No, Dickie. I'm having a belated conscience. He's been busy and after two bitter years, I suddenly find it difficult to stay at home."

"Have I made objectionable passes at you? Upset you in some way?"

"Your passes have been gentlemanly and you have not upset me." Liz smiled sweetly. She was getting a delayed reaction to the sight of the gun. She was now sure that it was not a toy; it was too old and battered and had a used look about it. Only now were these thoughts coming into her mind and they were frightening her.

"I shall miss you," Ashton said with quiet conviction. "I really see no reason why you should have a conscience. I am, after all, an old friend. I knew you long before you met Thomas."

"I know. But he must have made a bigger impact on me." Her tone was teasing to take away the blunt truth of it. But she could see that he was not going to give in so easily and the last thing she wanted was a scene.

He managed a small laugh. "Evidently. I'm jealous. And it shows that money doesn't count. That explodes a myth, doesn't it?"

"Not with me. I told you before. Money does not matter."

He laughed outright. "Provided one has enough. Does it matter to Thomas, I wonder? What does he feel about it?"

Liz picked up her evening bag. "I really don't know; I've never asked him."

"Perhaps you should, Liz. If he knows you have far more than he, and you must assume he does, he might find it difficult to live with, if ever you marry."

Damn the man. Liz rose and adjusted her long skirt. "I'll make sure he doesn't see it that way."

"You might find that difficult. When a woman has more money than her man it can sometimes cause a problem. Unless he's a gold digger. I'm not suggesting Thomas is one, of course."

You bastard. But she smiled again, thanked him for the evening and walked elegantly to the door. "Don't be a bad loser, Dickie," she said as he opened the sitting-room door for her.

"God forbid. But then I cannot remember the last time I lost." His smile had a tinge of anxiety.

As he kissed her on the cheek before opening the door to the apartment, she retorted sweetly, "There's always a first time. Thank you for the evening; the ballet was splendid."

His face was stony as he rang the elevator bell. "Stan will run you home. The car is still outside." He stood aside for her to enter the elevator and as a last shot said, "I'll be in touch."

He knew he should have escorted her to the car, but the moment the elevator descended he hurried back to the apartment and took the Steyr from the drawer. Now the sweat began to show with the feelings he had been bottling up while Liz was there. His hand shook as he held the Steyr; he knew it was his father's. He opened both safes; the jewellery had not been touched but the other gun was missing.

Ashton flopped on to the nearest chair, eyes staring, lips tight with anger. There was a trace of fear in his expression, something he had not shown before. He climbed unsteadily to his feet and went round the apartment looking for any evidence of a forced entry. There was none and this tormented him more.

There had been a professional break-in which he would not have known about at all if the Steyr had not been put on view and the second gun removed. Apart from the one gun nothing had been stolen or identifiably disturbed. And the gun that was missing was the one with which he had killed his father.

Just who the hell would have the nerve to come into his apartment and do a thing like that? The skill used was

154

obvious and disturbing. It also meant that he was being watched for his absence to be known.

He crossed to the net-curtained windows, pulled back one corner and gazed down into the street. The light behind him reflected on the glass and it was impossible to see if anyone was there. And if there was he would be well hidden. Ashton realised that he had made a mistake in trying to see out. He was showing his nerves.

He poured himself a large brandy and swished it round the bowl. The break-in must have been done by the person Cirillo and his father had told him about, yet neither had known his name or anything about him except his prowess; he had now seen that for himself.

He must get the gun back. Ashton was satisfied that his father would never be found but the idea of someone else having his gun was a threat, a warning, too. He went very cold when he considered that anyone should warn him at all. Cirillo had warned him but Cirillo's threats in relation to himself were empty; he still owed the Australian too much and Cirillo would only kill for money.

Ashton paced the room with his drink but could see only one way out, an obvious way but not an easy one. Whoever had broken in must be killed as a top priority. Cirillo could do it and would enjoy doing it. But Cirillo had returned to Ireland in search of the man he knew as Gorley. It would turn out to be a wasted journey from Cirillo's viewpoint but he should be back the next day and Ashton would brief him then.

Yet the main problem remained; how was he going to find the man with his gun. He believed he could see a way and how his time with Liz might now pay off. It would not be easy. But it would have to be done.

14

Georgie had her legs curled under her on the two-seater settee, leaving no room for Jacko to sit beside her. It was a small apartment but tastefully furnished with a display of nineteenth-century watercolours, haphazardly arranged on the pastel walls. Some of her other collector's items were zany like her apprentice-made paperweights, many of them awful, but all being used to keep something or other down. She used the larger ones as door stops.

Her mood was quiet and Jacko was worried about her. She gave the impression that she had been working too hard and needed a rest. But he knew it was not that; Georgie was worried.

Jacko reached out from his chair and patted her leg. "What's the matter, love? It must be serious or you wouldn't have let me in here. Do you realise that this is the first time I've actually been in your place?"

Her brows flickered. "Really? I must be slipping."

"Don't spoil it, Georgie. It means you trust me."

"Trust can come on several levels. Reach behind you and pick up that buff envelope. You will find something of interest."

Jacko twisted in his chair to find the envelope on top of a small rosewood desk. He was about to pass it over when Georgie said, "Read it".

There were several handwritten sheets in the envelope and he took his time in reading them. A good deal of the content was confusing, but here and there the meaning was clear. All in all it was something of a puzzle and the pattern took time to form but, when it did, it was like seeing it through a soft lens. Some made sense, some did not. He read them through twice more and Georgie made no interruption. When he finally looked at her she said without expression, "I had the same difficulty. It is complicated."

He held up the papers. "Did you get these with the bank receipt?"

"Yes."

There was something in the way she answered that induced him to say, "Was it difficult? I mean, you didn't put yourself out on a limb?"

"I had to or you would not have got anywhere."

"How serious, Georgie?"

She lifted her arms above her head and stretched. "If how I obtained them ever got out the Law Society would be very interested to see me and to listen to my explanation before disbarring me."

"Oh, Georgie. I'm a right bastard."

"Probably."

"Now I feel a heel."

"That's because you are one. Self-recognition has taken a long time."

He was not sure whether or not she was joking. She was jaded and there were purple smudges under her eyes which cosmetics had not quite concealed. Georgie had gone against her better judgement and had broken her own codes of decency. And she had done it for him.

"If it helps," she said wearily, "I'd do it again for you given the same circumstances. But I'm far from proud of myself. I hope they are of some use."

He put the papers back in the envelope. "I don't know how to thank you, Georgie." And because that sounded corny, added, "I simply couldn't have managed without you." He groaned, realising that that was even worse. He waved the envelope, clearly uneasy and very upset by the effect it was having on Georgie. He had simply forgotten how to express himself. But he did now realise the tremendous sacrifice she had made for him.

At last, from the heart, he said, "I knew what I was asking was a bit dodgy, but I hadn't thought it through. I had not considered the effect it would have on you. You see, to blokes like me, doing something like that is like falling off a log. And it was in a good cause."

"I know. That's why I did it. That and because you were in danger. Forget it, it's over."

But he could not forget it, not seeing her like this. She was worried and feeling ashamed of what she had done. He was afraid to ask her exactly how she had done it but it had to be by deception of some kind.

It was not often Jacko floundered but he was ill-at-ease and disgusted with himself. "I'll buy you something nice, Georgie; something really nice."

"I don't want payment. I want you. When will you wake up to it?"

Jacko was confused. "How can a bird like you want someone like me? It's not right, Georgie. Get yourself a decent man."

"You are a decent man. Sometimes. If you want to show your appreciation then take me to dinner and we'll come back here. Unless of course, you don't fancy me."

"Don't talk like that, love; it's not you." But he was smiling now, thinking that life could sometimes be wonderful. "Where would you like to go?"

It was not until late afternoon the next day that Jacko was able to raise Ewing and they met at Parliament Square opposite the Palace of Westminster. With traffic roaring all around them they slowly paced the small green which itself was crowded. It was hot and humid and the air was clogged with fumes.

"So you think Ashton's background as we know it is fake?"

They had to raise their voices more than they wished but Ewing was soon due for a meeting with the PM's PPS. And it was too late to think of going somewhere else.

"Sure. It will take some unravelling and it looks as if I'll have to do some travelling," Jacko replied. "It's pretty clear he's trying to kill off anyone who can identify him with another life. But why now?"

"Because he's about to place himself under the microscope by entering public life."

Jacko glanced at Ewing and the two men stopped at the Whitehall side of the green. "Is that what started all this?"

"I am sure. He's passed the point of no return. He's gone too far, had too many people killed; he can't go back. And if he succeeds none of us can do a thing about it. Whatever our suspicions, our certain knowledge, at the end of the day it all has to be proved, and Ashton is making damned sure that can't happen."

Ewing took Jacko's arm and guided him on yet another circuit. "A man like Ashton is not in the least bit fussed about what people think they know as long as he is safe. Rumour, pointing fingers, they all pass over his head. And if things go a little too far, and the press try something too dramatic, he will have the money to go through the courts and to finish up with even more money in damages. Ashton won't be concerned."

"Why can't you pass a quiet word to his local party; get his adoption annulled?"

Ewing laughed. "You're a better villain than politician, Jacko. Local parties don't like interference from above. They are inclined to dig their heels in. There are a couple of examples not a million miles from here. And what on earth should they be told? The truth as we see it or, if you like, know it? We would be back to the proving grounds, and Ashton would produce his cheque book and the finest slander prosecutor in the country. And he would win hands down. We have to continue searching for hard evidence, Jacko. And I think we're at last making progress."

Jacko was not so sure. "These notes we have are far from conclusive and some are obviously the guesswork of Michael Ashton. One aspect becomes fairly clear but Ashton's early life and that of his father are barely touched on. It is still an unknown area."

"It's pretty clear that Ashton is not his real name. That gives us a nice slice of doubt to cast over him."

"Sure. And another area to follow up. This business is not becoming clearer but more complicated. Who the hell is Ashton's mother?"

"You'll find out. I have every faith in you."

"That helps a lot." But Jacko could not miss Ewing's optimistic tone. "What's made you so chirpy?"

"Your news, and," he turned to give Jacko a wide smile of satisfaction, "the fact that Liz has seen the last of him. She told me."

Jacko wished he could be as optimistic. What Liz decided to do would have no bearing on what Ashton wanted.

Jacko felt naked on the flight to Rome. He had been forced to leave the Browning pistol behind because of the London Airport security checks. Ewing had been completely unhelpful, pointing out that if he contacted the Embassy or one of the consulates there was danger of word getting back to London. And, anyway, Ewing did not want to get overseas officials involved in this sort of thing; and he carried no weight with them.

Harry Bateman had supplied a contact in Rome which meant that Jacko would have to overshoot his destination by a considerable distance and then motor back to north of Florence. All for a gun. But there was no way he could operate without one with Cirillo on the loose, let alone Ashton on the defensive.

In Rome the heat was still stifling. He caught a cab from the airport and gave an address which raised the brows of the cabbie for it was in one of the darker outskirts of Rome, a café where most people would fear to tread.

They pulled up in a narrow, cobbled street, with a small square in the middle, a fountain at its centre, the sound of which added an illusion of coolness. In fact the street was sunless and stifling and washing hung across it, unmoving in the airless canyon.

Scantily dressed residents hung out of windows to watch Jacko climb from the cab outside the café – seemingly without a name unless the peeling paint had taken the identity with it – with its tables and chairs blocking the pavement.

160

Jacko had trouble sorting out the money to pay off the cabbie; supplying currency was the one area where Ewing had been useful. The cab roared off down the street, swaying on the uneven surface with heads turning to watch it.

Jacko carried his one case into the steaming, dark interior of the café while all conversation stopped at the tables and all eyes followed his movements. He reached the counter and dropped the case between his feet.

"I want to see Cesare," Jacko said in English to the bearded man behind the bar. "Tell him Harry in London recommended me."

Thick dark brows were raised, and deep brown eyes like polished agate viewed Jacko in an impartial way. At one end of the bar the Gaggia quietly steamed away, adding to the heavy atmosphere. "Cesare?"

"Yes. He has something for me."

"You know him?" The bearded man started to wipe down a glass case stacked with rolls.

Jacko gazed round. It was too hot for customers in the interior, they all sat outside, but those who could get a view were craning to see what was happening. He wiped his brow, the sweat running off him. "Look," he said. "I'm sorry I don't speak Italian. But you seem to speak good English. Harry was supposed to have telephoned Cesare about me, from London."

Someone on the outside tables could obviously understand English and freely translated to the other customers.

"Harry did telephone. Last night. Are you Jackie?"

"Jacko. Is there somewhere where we can speak privately?"

"Of course." The bearded man suddenly spoke sharply and rapidly to those craning to see what was happening, and without exception they all found new interest in the street. He turned back to Jacko, lifted a flap in the counter, and said, "I am Cesare. Welcome to Italy. Any friend of Harry's is a friend of mine." The beard parted and very white teeth were revealed in a warm smile. "Come through."

They went through a kitchen where a buxom woman, cleaning up at the sink, turned to give Jacko a big smile.

161

There is something about Italian smiles, Jacko reflected; they are warm right through. He followed Cesare up some stairs and entered another world. One look round was enough to convince Jacko that Cesare was not short of a lira or two; the place was crammed with riches. He wondered if any of the customers had been up here.

Cesare asked Jacko to sit down and left the room to return a few seconds later with a gun. He placed a small table in front of Jacko and put the gun on it. "Three and a half million lire."

Jacko did not touch the gun. "That sounds a fortune."

"Not much over two hundred of your pounds sterling. Unmarked and very modern." Cesare shrugged. "Expensive, but very accurate and very safe."

Jacko picked it up to feel the balance. He decided to strip and check it thoroughly and as he did so, Cesare continued to talk.

"Beretta Modello 92. Used by the military and the police. Holds fifteen rounds. 9mm Parabellum. Wonderful, yes?" He stopped talking as he saw the speed with which Jacko was working. Cesare was suddenly fascinated, aware that he was in the presence of an expert. "I will say no more."

Jacko reassembled with the same speed and asked, "What's the trade-in price?" Seeing that he had not been completely understood he added, "I might not use this at all and I can't take it back to England. So I either throw it away or return it to you."

"Ah! Half price. Very generous offer."

"How do I get it back to you?"

"You bring it here. You want a drink? Or coffee, perhaps?"

Jacko shook his head. "I must push on. I won't even have time to see your beautiful city; that I would very much like to have done. Will you take traveller's cheques?"

"Have you your passport with you?"

Jacko grinned. Harry Bateman's influence had been flawed. He produced his passport and signed some traveller's cheques. "Can you throw in an extra clip?"

"Magazine? You make a hard bargain, Jacko."

As he stood up Jacko clapped Cesare on the shoulder. "You're pretty good at it yourself, Cesare. The gun is fine; I've used this model before."

They went downstairs, into the café and beyond the bar. On the pavement outside the tables were still full and curiosity rife.

The two men, now in complete accord, shook hands warmly and for a moment, as the expressions around him changed to one of unanimous friendliness, Jacko thought there was going to be a round of applause. As Cesare went back inside to ring for a cab for him, Jacko was bombarded by well-wishers he did not understand. It was a mood which could have gone either way depending on Cesare. But they all knew he now carried a gun.

Piero Cirillo relaxed on the Alitalia flight to Milan. Although he had been an Australian national for some years now, there was always that feeling of contentment about coming home. Given the choice he would have returned to Italy to live rather than Spain, but when he fled Australia he reasoned that Italy would be a logical place for the police to search if his identity ever came out. And it was easier to escape from Spain.

Cirillo had a police record in Italy which he had successfully concealed from the Australian authorities, and he was at present travelling on an Australian passport. As the plane dipped beyond the Alps and descended to Linate Airport his feelings were mixed. But one thing was certain; he would have no problem obtaining arms. His contacts in Italy were many and, if necessary, his Calabrian friends would come up to supply him.

Before leaving London Cirillo had booked a room at the Excelsior Hotel by telephoning a friend in Naples who was magically able to arrange it in spite of the high season.

Like Jacko, he carried one case and, as he unpacked it, his pleasure at being back in Italy was alloyed only by Ashton taking him off the Gorley job. Cirillo did not like failures, but he felt that Ashton had been covering up when he told him that Gorley no longer mattered. The attitude was too cavalier; killing was not a casual game where the rules could be changed halfway through. His feelings had been somewhat mollified, however, when Ashton agreed to pay him half the fee plus expenses. Even so, he had lost momentum over Gorley and he needed to restore it quickly.

As soon as he had unpacked he went out to hire a car for the next day. He could have flown down to Pisa which would have been much nearer where he wanted to go, but such a reservation would pinpoint him too much, and in a car he could go anywhere freely. When his arrangements were made he went out for dinner and then to look for a woman.

Jacko suffered the frustration of being driven into Rome in order to hire a car. So he wasted valuable time and the Rome snarl-ups added to his delays. By the time he set out most of the day had gone, and what remained of it seemed to disappear in reaching the Rome outskirts.

Driving on the right-hand side of the road did not worry him and, once on the autostrada, he tried to make up some time. When darkness fell so did the traffic but he knew that he could not drive right through the night without the risk of falling asleep. He kept going until the driving became hypnotic and then looked for a place to stay.

He found a service station about fifty miles south of Florence, used its facilities to wash and tidy up, but went back to the car to sleep; sleeping rough was nothing new; he could switch from luxury to extreme discomfort without thinking about it. He fell asleep on the back seat almost immediately.

Cirillo awoke refreshed in his luxury hotel bed, ready for the long drive south to Florence. He had a continental breakfast with black coffee and settled his account at reception after taking delivery of a heavy package. He drove off, hating the congestion of the Milan traffic. He did not relax until he was well clear of the industrial town, and even then, on the autostrada, was not entirely happy.

As the miles went by he unwound enough to think ahead, to getting matters back on the rails and shaking off some of the disappointments of London and Ireland. It was time to assert himself and he was on home ground.

Jacko woke up in cramped conditions, opened the car door and stretched. He ran round the parking lot six times before entering the service station to wash and shave, and have a hearty breakfast with an indifferent cup of tea. Refreshed, he returned to the small but reliable Fiat, and headed north towards Florence.

He was climbing now, the Appennino Tosco on his right forming the spine of Italy. The traffic picked up as he progressed and the rate of climb slowed him down, although the car was responding well, but how he yearned for his Ferrari.

He went deeper into the hills in order to by-pass Florence and from time to time he glanced at the road map on the seat beside him. He made two stops at small, hill-top towns, almost inevitably tourist attractions, with wide vistas of mountain scenery.

He would freshen up, have a cordial from the chill box and motor on. The air was fresher now but still very warm. When he calculated that he was within twenty miles of his destination he stopped once more and studied the map in detail, making pencil notes on a pad. Jacko filled up at a roadside pump, checked his oil and started out.

As he drove, part of his mind drifted comfortably but there was always a section of it that commanded full concentration on what he was doing. He resented coming to Italy, a country he loved, without really seeing it. Somehow, Tuscany was the one region he had not previously covered and it was unfolding before him but he could not afford to linger. It was a life or death game he was playing, and, as he drew nearer to his destination, he could feel the truth of it building up with each mile.

Cirillo had similar feelings. Concentrating on his driving and direction took some of the enjoyment of anticipation away from him, but for the first time in days he was feeling that luck was turning his way again.

When he turned off the autostrada and started to climb the hill roads he was less certain of himself but knew the mood would pass as soon as he was near the villa. He glanced at the big package on the passenger seat and decided it was time to check; that he had not done before was a sign of faith in his friends, or their acknowledged fear of him. It did not matter which.

He found a lay-by and unravelled the packaging to find a twin to the Beretta Jacko had, and the loose parts of a sporting rifle with tripod. Cirillo would have preferred a 7.65 pistol but had no quarrel with what had been supplied.

Maria Rinaldi had worried herself into an impossible situation. For days now, she had been tormented by the telephoned warning. No name had been given, nor advice on where the call had come from. She did not need to be told who had called for she had recognised the voice and, even if she had not, she would have known. Where he had phoned from she had no idea, except that she was sure it was from abroad.

Her husband Rocco had quickly noticed her concern and was quietly worrying about her. He had tackled her without success and watched her day-by-day deterioration with despair. He loved her and they enjoyed a rare kind of happiness.

From Rocco's point of view nothing had been the same since that late telephone call a few nights ago. She had returned to bed very disturbed and the mood had continued through breakfast the next morning. She had rallied when seeing him off but he recognised her brief change for what it was.

Over the next few days he implored her to tell him what was on her mind but she always made excuses. It was not until he insisted on taking her to the doctor that she offered him a garbled story about a brother being found dead in England. She would have been distressed, of course, but

166

it was not distress she was suffering. It was fear. What had happened? What had reared up from her past life?

Had there been another man Rocco would have been devastated but at no stage did he consider another man could be involved. Her feelings for him had not changed, she came to him for comfort. So he would have to take some positive action, and soon.

He hated the idea of going to the doctor and did not really think it would help. The answer lay in Maria herself. She was distraught beyond reason and if she continued like this it would drive her mad. And him too. He knew she was highly strung, but she was intelligent and he knew there was more to it than that.

Rocco knew his wife was reaching a critical point. She was disappearing inside a tormented mind and escaping from it less and less. Soon it would take her over completely and then it might be too late. As he kissed her goodbye that morning, holding her much longer than usual, he was determined that when he came back that evening he would take her to the doctor whether or not she liked it. It would be a start.

Maria, too, clung to him as if she understood what was in his mind but knowing it would not help. She needed to run away but could not leave him in the lurch. So she stayed and continued to destroy them both.

It was almost midday when she saw the car approach. It did not come up the drive but went past the wrought-iron gates to disappear behind the hedgerow. But she knew it was still there; it was so quiet, the air so still, that the sound of the engine reached her quite clearly. And then it cut out. The following silence was torture. Just a few seconds later she heard the crunch of footsteps on the rough-surfaced road. She could tell that it was a man's footsteps. And then the gate opened and she saw a man coming up the sharp incline towards the villa.

15

The man appeared to be unhurried but the incline was steep and the shingled drive could be slippery. And now, late morning, it was very hot.

She stood well back to watch through the lounge window. Maria Rinaldi was close to complete panic. All that stopped her from running from the villa was being rooted by fear.

If she screamed there was no one to hear. Their nearest neighbour was three hundred yards away. She could only watch the inexorable approach of the figure coming towards her with head down against the sun. This was the moment she had been dreading.

Breaking the spell of panic, Maria looked about her for a weapon. There was no such thing as a gun in the house. Although her husband was a jeweller he never brought jewellery home unless it was a present for her. And because of the isolation there was no burglar alarm.

She raced out the back and entered the garage from a rear door. All the gardening tools were kept here and she quickly selected a shovel and a hammer and went back in and locked the door behind her. Now she had broken the spell she quickly chased round the house locking everything she could. When she returned to the lounge window the man was no longer in sight.

Where was he? Nobody was trying the doors or windows. She remained still, holding on tightly to the shovel and the hammer, a slight figure, in a light summer sleeveless dress, filled with a terror.

Suddenly the door bell rang and she nearly dropped her crude weapons. Oh, my God. She could not breathe. She could not have moved her feet had she tried. Her breath came in great gulps and she simply stood there. Perhaps he would go away.

In his up-market jewellery shop on the Ponte Vecchio in Florence, Rocco Rinaldi was finding it extremely difficult to keep his mind on business. Midsummer was a busy time with tourists in their hoards, and business was good. But he was not concentrating, as the man and wife team he had as assistants were quick to notice.

The Ponte Vecchio was crowded with slowly moving crowds, and through its old arches, the Arno flowed implacably on as ancient buildings bulged over it. The scene was idyllic, but Rocco had no eyes for it; he had seen it so often and he was worried to distraction over Maria.

He reached the point when he knew he would have to return to the villa; his wife needed help and he must get back. During a quieter moment he told his assistants that he must leave and they were rather relieved for he was of little use as he was. He trusted them and they liked him so there were no problems and he handed them the spare set of keys and reminded them to set the alarms.

Rocco left for home with immense relief; he should have taken this step days ago. Maria needed more help than he could give her and he found comfort in the fact that what he was now doing was at least something positive. He could not get home fast enough.

The bell rang again, this time followed by a gentle tapping on the door. Maria did not know what to do. She still had the shovel and the hammer in her hands and then, in a rare moment of decision, dropped the hammer and gripped the shovel with both hands.

She went to the door, legs weak, mind totally confused. She was terrified of who might be the other side of the door. Again there was a long silence before the bell rang again. She knew there was no point in not answering for whoever was there would smash a window in order to get in and there was nothing she could do to stop that. At no time did she consider telephoning the police. Rocco would be furious, and anyway, they were too far away and would take too long.

She waited for the bell to stop ringing and then wrenched open the door and aimed the shovel at the vague figure before her. She was seeing everything in a mist and her one thought was to destroy whoever was there and to escape.

She was clumsy with the shovel and it was heavy but desperation helped her and she was lucky with the first blow. The man dropped to his knees and placed his arms over his head to guard against the blows which rained down from a woman who had the strength of the demented.

When he was on the ground, trying to roll away from her, Maria kept after him, trying to destroy him once and for all. When he did not move again, and her arms could no longer lift the bloodstained shovel, she stood over him, dishevelled and panting for breath. She gazed down and thought she had killed him.

When that thought penetrated further she started to think what Rocco and the police would say. Perhaps she could bury him. But her power had gone with her panic. She slowly began to realise what she had done.

As Maria threw the shovel down on the unmoving body a new kind of panic seized her. She had to get away; she should have done it the night of the call. She ran back into the house, collected her purse and some loose notes and fled into the garage. She jumped into the small Fiat, fumbled to get the key in the ignition, started up and the car rocketed out of the garage just missing the prone body, which she thought might have moved.

She did not wait to find out. With tears streaming down her face, hair hanging over her eyes, hands gripping the steering wheel as if it was the only thing in life she could cling to, Maria shot down the drive, burning the rubber on the shingle. As she reached the gates she jammed on the brakes, broke into a fearful skid that, by the grace of God, swung her round as she shot through, and on to the road facing east. She accelerated away in a cloud of dust.

*　　*　　*

Jacko had rolled just in time or the car would have passed straight over him. Barely conscious, blood streaming down his face from a gash in the head, arms bruised, bloodied and aching from the blows he had parried, he tried to rise and collapsed face down.

He spat out blood and tried again. It was the first blow which had caused the trouble. The side of the shovel had caught him on the head when he had not been prepared for it. If, through some last split-second reflex action, he had not marginally ridden the blow, it could easily have killed him. In his half-conscious state Jacko was aware that she had fled in the car and that he had to get after her before she killed herself on the road.

He got to his feet and staggered about unable to keep balance. In this condition he stumbled down the drive, barely capable of staying on his feet. He fell to his knees halfway to the gates and crawled before rising again to stagger on. He held on to the gates and worked his way along to his car.

When he was in the driver's seat he knew he was in no condition to drive, let alone start a road chase. The skid marks gave him her direction and he reversed into the drive and set off to find her. At least on these hill roads there were a limited number of turn-offs. His eyes misted as he drove and he had the greatest difficulty in keeping conscious. The attacks of dizziness passed over him in waves yet he managed to do all the right things, if much slower than he wanted. He just kept going without much hope; the woman was crazy; and all he wanted to do was to help her.

The Lamborghini was far too powerful and sometimes frightened him. Rocco Rinaldi had intended to trade it in many times but somehow never got round to it. On this occasion, though, he was glad to have it. He drove home as if inspired and the car held the hill roads as it had never done before. He arrived home about an hour after Jacko had left, parked on the drive outside the garage and immediately knew something was wrong.

The garage doors were wide open and the Fiat was missing. As he climbed out he saw that the front villa door was also open and a shovel was lying just outside. He called out for Maria as he hurried forward. As he passed the shovel he noticed the blood-stains and immediately felt sick.

"Maria. Maria." But there was no reply and he dashed into the villa still calling her name. He saw the hammer on the floor where Maria had dropped it and again his stomach turned. Holy Mother, what had happened?

He searched room by room and when he raced into their own bedroom a man stepped out from behind the door and pointed a gun at him.

"Where is she?" Cirillo demanded.

Rocco was shocked but was then strangely reassured by the question. At first he ignored the gun, his fear overcome by the strange absence of his wife. Then he flared up. "You fool. Would I be screaming her name if I knew?"

"Are you her husband?"

"Of course I'm her husband. And just who the hell are you?" Some of the steam was leaving Rocco and he was developing another kind of fear. The man had no place here and it seemed his interest was in Maria; why was he carrying a gun?

Cirillo did not trouble to answer. "Why are you so concerned for your wife?"

Rocco stared in amazement. "You can see for yourself why. She's missing. Why have you broken into my house with a gun?" He could feel his bravado evaporating.

"I did not break in; the door was wide open. I want to speak to your wife. Where would she go?"

"If I knew that would I be so distraught? For God's sake I'm worried sick about her."

"Okay, but why would she leave?"

Rocco thought it prudent to keep answering. "She's been acting strangely lately. I don't know why. I came home because I am worried about her. Can't you put that thing away?"

"Has she taken a car?"

"Yes." Rocco could have bitten his tongue out. Distress was addling his thoughts.

"What is the number of the car?"

Rocco had placed the accent as Calabrian. It had been a little difficult because there was something else mixed in with it. But he was no foreigner, his Italian was far too natural. He was taking in more detail and apart from the gun did not like the man's eyes; he had seen stones like that in some of his cheaper jewellery. "I don't know. It was her car. I didn't bother with it."

"If you don't give me the number I'm going to blow your balls off."

The threat was issued quietly and that made it worse for Rocco. He hated those eyes more than the gun. But he loved his wife more than he feared this stranger who, he was sure, intended to kill her. He must protect her, get rid of this man, and go and find her. "I cannot remember. It is not something I would try to remember."

"We're wasting time and I'm losing patience. I can take this place apart until I find her licence or insurance. And where would she be likely to go?"

If only he knew. Rocco accepted that the man could eventually find the number but that could take time and could be a life-saver for Maria. "Then you'll have to find it. I simply cannot recall it."

Cirillo lowered his aim. "Whether you find her or not you're going to be of no further use to her. Is that your last word?"

Rocco, protective of Maria to the last, wanted to move his hands in a futile effort to protect himself. He was sweating freely and his lower lip trembled as he said, "Yes."

Cirillo held Rocco's gaze as he took up the slack on the trigger. "It's your funeral," he said easily and shot Rocco through the heart.

As Rocco collapsed, Cirillo waited for him to settle, turned him over on his back, and emptied the remainder of his magazine into the corpse. Firing so many rounds as he did was an act of total frustration for Cirillo. He was sick of so many things going against him, and now he had released his tension on someone who was not even on his list.

When Cirillo finished firing he whipped out the empty magazine and quickly inserted a new clip. He spat at the dead body. Cirillo was rattled, and the more dangerous because of it. It took him the best part of an hour to find the registration number of the Fiat and once he had that he wasted no more time.

He returned to his car which he had parked round a bend and out of sight of the villa gates. As he started up he remembered the bloodied shovel outside the house. Obviously there had been some sort of fight, but between whom, and who had won?

Jacko could not concentrate through the clouds of dizziness. He had run into more traffic the further he had gone from the villa. Heavy trucks and tourist coaches did not leave much room on narrow hill roads which twisted and turned all the way.

In his more conscious moments he believed it was all a waste of time; Maria Rinaldi could be anywhere. The only thing he was sure of was that she had not come back for if she had he believed she would have to take the same road. He would have seen the small blue Fiat whatever his condition.

Jacko pulled in. He had given up trying to catch up with her. His condition was too bad for that, and, as it was, he had already made occasional halts in an effort to hang on. The head wound had not yet congealed and blood was trickling into his eye.

He drove on again with few options in direction. He considered it best to stick to the main road but was not yet sure where it would lead. He knew he was heading west and, therefore, would eventually reach the coast. As the traffic continued to thicken he supposed he must be near some sort of habitation and ten minutes later entered a fair-sized hill-top town.

There was a wide square where coaches parked and along one side, a row of shops, in particular an emporium

174

where a queue of tourists snaked into the street waiting for soft drinks and ice cream.

He parked as far away as possible from the others, took out a handkerchief, placed it on the windscreen and operated the water pump. When the handkerchief was soaked he sat in the car to wipe the blood from his face, making use of the central mirror. By this time it seemed that the head wound had congealed but he ruffled his hair to cover any sign. He climbed out and went searching for the Fiat.

The areas of parking were limited and there were few spaces available. Along the main town street which was also the through road, there was a constant flow of slow-moving traffic. Where the coaches backed on to the railings, at the end of the parking square, was a long area for tourists to look out across the hills and valleys and to take snapshots of the general beauty.

Jacko walked shakily along, legs weak, head aching, forever hoping for sight of the Fiat of which there were plenty but not the little blue one which Maria Rinaldi had driven away. Finally, and in despair, with the added burden of the increasing heat, he decided to get refreshment in the emporium. He climbed the steps, hanging on to the side rail, and entered the dark interior.

There was a crowd round a massive open freezer where people were helping themselves to ice creams, and, by it, a chill box dispenser for soft drinks. He helped himself to an ice-cold coke and wandered over to the pay kiosk to settle. There were plenty of tables and chairs and even hot meals available. Most of the tables were still empty but in the far corner, sitting alone, staring at two empty bottles in front of her, was Maria Rinaldi.

16

Jacko was not absolutely certain. After the blinding sunlight it was gloomy inside. And he had barely seen Maria at the door of her villa before the shovel cracked his head open. Just the same, he became increasingly sure it was her. She was staring down at the plastic table top completely unaware of what was going on around her. She was pale, dishevelled, with the appearance of a hopeless derelict.

Jacko slid round the drinks dispenser so that she would not see him. It was difficult to know how to handle it. If he approached and she started screaming the place down the police would come and he was armed and any accusation she might make could stand up.

He sidled round the dispenser again. Her position had not changed; she seemed to be in a trance. If Cirillo was looking for her too, and he was bound to be at some time, Jacko realised he would have to take a chance; she might sit there all day in that state.

He walked slowly towards her, skirting the tables, waiting for the screams, and thinking he was in no good condition himself to tackle too much. Two tables away she still had not seen him, and the tourist crowd were well behind him. It was a very large room, probably used for local dancing.

Jacko clung to a chair back as he suddenly felt faint; he would have to get his head looked at when he could. As the dizziness passed he continued on until he stood looking down at her. He took fingertip support from the chair furthest from her and pulled it out as quietly as possible. She must have heard, though, yet she gave no sign. He gradually eased himself on to the chair, sitting sideways in case he had to make a run for it.

He placed his coke on the table, the condensation running down his fingers. "Hello," he said in English in the friendliest voice he could summon. "Can I get you a coke?"

She gave no sign that she had heard and probably had not. Maria had retreated inside herself.

"Do you speak English?" He knew that she did but he had to try some sort of breakthrough.

Suddenly she looked up and gazed straight into his eyes. It was disconcerting, for her expression was cold and lifeless. Her lids opened like shutters and for some seconds were unblinking. Then the lids closed, her head inclined towards the table once more and her silence was worse than before.

With enormous relief he realised she had not recognised him; unless she had not actually seen him when she had gazed in that strange way. But it was possible that she did not know; she had opened the villa door in a mad frenzy and gone straight for him.

As he continued to stare at her he knew it would not be easy. "Keep this place for me." He left his coke, tilted his chair against the table and went back to the dispenser.

She was still there when he returned to push a bottle over to her. "Drink this. Put your hands round it; it will cool them. Can you understand me?"

Her lids flickered and she almost looked up again, but this time he was sure she had heard him.

"Drink it while it's still cold," he said.

Her hand came out slowly towards the bottle and when her fingers closed round it he was relieved. And then she pushed the bottle towards him and said, "I don't need your drink."

It was some kind of breakthrough but her tone had been lifeless, as if all hope had gone. But she had spoken.

"I'm sorry. I didn't mean to offend you. You look so distressed I thought it might help."

Maria did not respond to that. A shiver passed through her and she clasped her arms around her slim body as if cold, but it was baking hot inside the room.

177

There was a long silence which he wanted to break but, as it continued, was increasingly afraid of saying the wrong thing. Maria was delicate and so was the situation. He pushed the bottle across the table again: "Here try it, just a sip."

Without raising her head she asked listlessly, "Have you come to kill me?"

Jacko stiffened. He maintained his posture, not moving an inch towards her. "I wouldn't hurt a hair of your head. It upsets me to see you like this."

"Why? Why should you care if you haven't come to kill me?"

He had to be careful of what he said. "Because I came to protect you against those who would harm you. I'm here to help you, Maria."

She stiffened and her arms tightened round her and her nails dug into her flesh. He thought she was about to scream as her head came back, but he saw tears creeping out from the closed lids. She covered her face with her long-fingered hands and began to weep, her shoulders heaving gently.

Jacko's back was to the room and he hoped he shielded her from the customers but there was nothing he could do but let her cry. To attempt to console her might prove disastrous. He was uncomfortable because he felt helpless when his instincts were to go to her. She must have known Ashton was after her, and had been living a nightmare.

When she started to wipe her face with her hands he passed across a paper napkin for her to dry her face.

"I'm so sorry," she said in a tremulous voice. "I'm such a coward."

"Rubbish. Would you like me to get you some tissues?"

She shook her head, lips trembling. She wiped her eyes again, now red and watery, but she had come back to life. "Why should I believe you?"

"Because I'm the guy whose skull you cracked with a shovel and I should be very angry. But I understand why you did it. So don't give it a thought."

178

She gazed at him through a mist of tears and for a dreadful moment he thought she was going to retreat inside herself again. She tried to dry her eyes again by using the heels of her hands. "You? Yes, I can see that now."

Jacko managed a grin. He lowered his head and tenderly parted his hair to show her the spot. "Wham!" he said. "You certainly pack a wallop for a small one." He could see that she was still not sure of him; basically she was afraid of everyone, but he was making ground.

"My God, I could have killed you."

"With a skull like mine? No chance. Just a scratch. But who were you really expecting?"

She shook her head, still confused. "I don't know. But why would you want to save me? How could you know I was in danger?"

There was no point now in beating about the bush; if he did she would get suspicious again. "We've been checking on a bloke called Dickie Ashton. Your brother, I believe."

The rivulets were drying on her face and she was listening intently. Mention of Ashton had sharpened her senses. "My brother?"

"Isn't he?"

"Who are you working for? Why are you involved in this?"

Jacko was relieved. They were down to discussing the matter; it was the breakthrough he had not really expected. "I can't tell you that except to say I should be regarded as being on the side of the angels. As unlikely as it may seem, I'm one of the good guys. I really am here to protect you. Will you settle for that?"

She was not quite convinced. "But there has to be a reason? What is he up to?"

"You know what he's up to. You believe he sent someone to kill you. And I think you are right. My job is to find out why. I've got to delve into his background."

"You'll have a job."

It was the nearest she had got to a humorous remark.

"That's why I called. I came to warn you and to see if you can fill in some of the background. You seem dubious about your brother."

"Are you a policeman?"

"No. Policemen who enquire after your brother have a habit of dying. Who tipped you off by the way?"

"It was an anonymous phone call. But it was his father, I recognised his voice instantly. And then I knew it was serious."

"His father is now dead, probably killed by Dickie himself." He did not want to scare her again but she needed to be shocked into telling the truth about Ashton.

She displayed no sorrow. "He was just as bad as Dickie; worse in the old days. He must have mellowed in order to have warned me but he was a monster, like his son."

"You keep making little remarks from which I gather Dickie might not be your brother." Jacko recalled Michael Ashton had done the same.

Without realising it, Maria reached out for the coke. It had lost its chill by now but she removed a straw from one of the empty bottles and drank thoughtfully. After a while she said, "I suppose I've always known it would have to be told sometime. But you are right; Dickie is not my brother nor Michael's; look what they did to him."

"You know about Michael?"

"Oh, yes. Dickie's father told me when he telephoned. It was meant to scare me and it did. I've been scared ever since."

Jacko watched her suction up the coke, her hands shaking. He wasn't sure whether or not she trusted him yet for there was a resignation about her now as if nothing more mattered. But she was beginning to speak the truth as though glad to be rid of it. "Why was it such a secret for so long?"

"About Dickie? There was an arrangement with Dickie's father and my mother. My mother was down on her luck and struggling to bring up us kids after my father died." She paused for a long time, her expression guarded.

"I always thought," she went on, "that Dickie's father had something to do with my father's death. My mother and he were carrying on long before Dad died."

"Was his name Ashton?"

"Oh, yes. At least that's the name he married under. But he could have used any name. It was ages ago and at that time we called him Uncle John. He carted Dickie around with him like an appendage, as if he meant something special to him, and I think he did. John doted on Dickie. Perhaps he saw something of himself in the boy, and he wasn't wrong, was he?"

"But he did marry your mother?"

"Oh, yes. They married in Paris. Mother had resented Dad's failure at that time and she needed money. John was dripping with it. Part of the arrangement, as I remember, was that we kids used the name of Ashton and not Dad's name. We changed it by deed poll. I must admit it made life simpler. I think the inducement for all this was that John settled a large amount on my mother and set up a trust for Michael and me. We were never short from then on and have not been ever since. We were sworn to secrecy about the name change and told that we must accept Dickie as one of us and that he had always been our brother. My mother hinted that, in fact, he was our real brother through an affair with John that Dad did not know about."

"So you found it an easy deception?"

"Oh, yes. We were young. Both Dickie and his father could be charming and our new father provided us with what we wanted. He was very generous and has been all along. But there was another side to him. He knew how to instil fear into us behind mother's back. He terrified Michael and me; he made us believe that if we ever told anybody about Dickie we would come to some terrible harm. And we believed him. As the years went by we forgot it had ever happened. It was quite easy to do and he bought our loyalty up to now."

"Yet it's obvious you thought that one day the balloon would go up? You've been living in fear of it happening."

"I'm a very nervous person, mister ... what's your name?"

"Jacko. All my friends call me that."

"Well, Jacko, you can see the state I'm in. Yes, both Michael and I thought that one day it would come out and it would reveal something very unpleasant. It's difficult to explain but both John and Dickie had a way of warning without saying a word. Beneath the charm were thick layers of evil. It communicated and was never so impressive as when we were young; that's when it really sticks. It's always there, Jacko, that unhealthy feeling that something is not right and why are we still being paid so generously after all these years? We've even been advised on investments, so are quite well off. Like him or not it is a strong incentive for keeping quiet about something that seems unimportant. It becomes quite easy to do."

"Until something goes wrong?"

"Yes. I suppose the threat of something going wrong has always been in the subconscious. With me, anyway. I don't think Michael was too concerned. He had his own life and as long as the cheques came through he was happy."

Jacko fiddled with his coke bottle. "He left notes to indicate that he, too, had some sort of premonition that one day matters might come to a head. Is your mother still alive?"

"She lives it up in New York. There is no way that she would destroy the goose who lays the golden egg. Whatever Dickie is up to that warrants this, he is quite safe from my mother. She won't let him down as long as the money comes through."

"You must have missed your father."

Her expression softened. "I loved him. He could always remove my fears and he always knew them. I've been afraid of something or other all my life; even of happiness. But I was right, wasn't I? It's been destroyed."

Jacko took a chance to reach across to squeeze her hand which was still round the bottle. "Interrupted, maybe. It will come back. Have you your mother's address?"

"Why?"

"In spite of what you say I think she should be warned."

"She's in no danger."

"Don't you believe it. You wouldn't have it on you? It wasn't given in Michael's notes."

"I know it by heart. I've no pen or paper with me."

Jacko produced both and made a note of the New York address Maria gave him. "Thanks for that. I think I'd better get you back to collect some things. What time does your husband return?"

Maria glanced at a wall clock. "Six. But he's been worried about me so he might return earlier. Why do I need to collect my things?"

Jacko looked surprised. "Because you can't stay in the villa and wait for Dickie's man to pitch up. You've got to leave. Does your husband know anything about this?"

"No." Maria raised her hands in protest. "Before you say it I know I should have talked to him but I wanted to protect him from it."

"I'll take you back. You're in no state to drive." He gave her a little admonishing glance. "It was a wonder you managed to get here. Where's your car?"

"Round the side."

"If you can arrange to have it collected I'll drive you back in mine." He smiled. "I'll drive carefully; I'll have to after that wallop you gave me."

"I'm so dreadfully sorry. I was terrified."

He helped her up. "It was a good job I wasn't a copper." The blinding sunlight hit them as they emerged from the gloom and they walked over to Jacko's car.

"You must get your head seen to. It looks terrible. There's a clinic on the Florence road, or I can call our doctor when we get back."

"Don't worry about it. Let's get you home. I'll stay with you until you and your husband have sorted out where you intend to stay. Keep away for about a month and I'll try to keep in touch to let you know when it's safe to go back." He switched on and just before moving off, added, "Thanks for what you've told me. It's been most helpful." He pulled out behind a coach and managed to pass it before the road narrowed.

"There's a lot missing. I don't know a thing about their earlier life."

"You've made a bridge, Maria. It's somewhere to start." For a reason he could not explain he suddenly felt queasy, his stomach knotting.

Cirillo followed the skid marks as Jacko had done and because he had not seen the small light blue Fiat on his way to the villa from the other direction. He drove steadily and without much hope but continued on because it was the only way he could react.

Cirillo was burning up inside. It was not so much that he was making mistakes as that the luck was going against him. He had not wanted to shoot Rocco but was left with no alternative unless he wanted to risk being described to the police. Not even that was sufficient to gall him; he had *shot* the man which would set up a murder enquiry, when he should have arranged some sort of accident, ideally with the Lamborghini. But there had not been the time. Accidents were not so easily arranged and he had to get after the woman. But it niggled him that he had been unprofessional even though there were extenuating circumstances. It was not the way it was supposed to go and it left him wide open.

Now with the registration number locked in his memory he was fully alert to all small, light blue Fiats as he drove along in the direction both Maria and Jacko had taken.

Jacko concentrated on his driving, head still muzzy but clearer than it was. They had lapsed into silence while considering what had happened and what should happen next. And they were travelling at moderate speed.

Maria gasped when Jacko suddenly slammed on the brakes and the car broke into a rear-wheel skid which he quickly corrected.

"What's the matter?" Maria called out. "Are you ill?" She was shaken and scared again.

184

"I suddenly went dizzy," he lied. "Must have been the blow. It's okay now." But it was far from all right. He had just seen Cirillo pass them in the opposite direction which meant he had already been to the villa. So why was he not waiting there for Maria to return?

17

Dickie Ashton sat in his London office and read a brief report from the detective agency he had employed; he ignored his constantly buzzing intercom.

He was well aware that obliterating his past was taking up too much time. He could justify his activities; he was an immensely busy man who thrived on work, but he could not evade certain duties for ever. There were issues he must deal with unless he wanted to raise questions from his colleagues. He was not answerable to anyone but nor could he obviously neglect issues which affected them. The last thing he wanted at this stage was comment on his ability or integrity.

Cirillo was supposed to have dealt with his other problems but after a quick start had been bogged down for too long. Nothing seemed to be simple any more. It was too late to find someone else, and frankly, in spite of his chagrin, Ashton did not think there was anyone else capable. Bad luck had crept into the affair at an unfortunate time. He had to wait for the tide to turn. There were only three more people to dispose of and he hoped that one of those had already been dealt with in Italy. And then, of course, would come Cirillo himself and Ashton fully accepted that only he could do that. Then he would be clear to get on with his life.

As he read the report once more he suddenly realised that his last premise was not quite true. The man running parallel to Cirillo must be traced and destroyed; God knows what he might have picked up by now.

Ashton slipped the report containing the Canadian address into a pocket. The more he thought about it the more convinced he became that perhaps this, too, was one he must attend to himself. It was a matter of honour, but he did not see the sick irony of that conclusion. He would arrange his affairs so that he could soon leave for Canada.

He rang Liz Mitchell and her answering machine clicked in. When later in the day she did not ring back in reply to his message, he rang again. This time she answered.

"What about dinner tonight, Liz? Anywhere you choose."

"I'm seeing Thomas. But, anyway, I told you I would not be seeing you again."

"Oh, that. People say these things." He chuckled. "We've known each other too long, Liz. You can't cut off a friendship just like that; particularly without cause."

"I'm not cutting off a friendship, Dickie. I simply won't be dating you again. I'm devoting my time to Thomas in future, that's all."

"I'm pleased about you two. I really am. So you're seeing him tonight."

"Yes."

"Another time then, Liz."

As soon as she had hung up Ashton dialled Ewing's ex-directory number which he was not supposed to know. He was lucky with his first call. He did not explain how he had come by the number but said straightaway, "Thomas? I think it might be a good idea if we met."

Ewing answered cautiously, "It might."

"What about dinner tonight?"

"I'm tied up tonight. Another day perhaps."

"Like you, my schedule is very tight. Tonight is the only day this week. Is your present appointment so important?"

"Presumably you have a sound reason for this meeting?"

"Of course. I'm bound to have after you set the hounds after me." He laughed heartily. "I want to explain a few things."

"I'll see what I can do. I'll get someone to ring you back with a message."

"Thanks, old boy. See you tonight."

Ashton obtained a perverse satisfaction from breaking up Liz's date. He knew that Ewing would not tell Liz who he was meeting. That should fix the haughty bitch for a while. And then he must set about fixing Ewing himself.

Jacko could not understand why Cirillo had not seen him; they had passed quite close to one another. Detail came back with after-thought. Cirillo had looked really grim, eyes on the road. He had not so much as glanced at Jacko or his passenger.

Revelation came slowly; Cirillo was searching for a particular car; it could only be Maria's, nothing else made sense. So how had he found out what car she had? He could see how and hoped he was wrong.

"Are you all right?" Maria was worried about him. "You look as if you've seen a ghost."

That was far too near the mark. "I was wondering if we need to go to your villa at all. It might be safer to avoid it." He could feel her gaze on him.

"All my things are at the villa. I shall need them. Besides Rocco will wonder where I am."

It was not going to be easy and if he pressed it too hard she would be suspicious and scared again. Sight of Cirillo had unsettled him; it could only be bad news for Maria. "Couldn't you collect your things later or have them sent over by a friend?"

"Over to where? I've yet to fix something up and I must talk to Rocco about that. No, it's better to go to the villa first."

Jacko was far from happy but there was nothing he could do. He kept driving but for once his mind was elsewhere.

Cirillo reached the emporium and had the same reaction as Jacko. It was a natural place to stop and the only sizeable place around. He parked his car, made sure it was locked and searched the streets. He did not enter the emporium. The photograph Ashton had given him was years old and of poor quality and he was not sure he could recognise anyone from it. Oddly enough there had been no photographs in the villa. But the car was a different matter.

He found the small blue Fiat round the side of the emporium after half an hour of searching. So she was here somewhere. He strolled thoughtfully to his car, got in, and drove back towards the villa.

After five minutes of reflection he started to drive at speed, his mind made up. Some time or other Maria Rinaldi would have to go back to the villa. Cirillo began to think his luck might change.

As they approached the villa Jacko searched desperately for an excuse not to go there. And then he resigned himself to it; ultimately it would make no difference whatever might have happened. He could only protect Maria so far, after that she was on her own and he had the terrible feeling that the moment was not far off.

He drove through the gates and up the drive quickly seeing the shovel still lying there. The door was still wide open and a Lamborghini was parked to one side of it.

Maria gave a cry of delight on seeing the Lamborghini. "Rocco's home. He's home."

So why had he not come out to greet them, Jacko reflected; he must have heard them approach on the shingle. As he pulled up behind the Lamborghini he grabbed Maria's arm as she was about to climb out. He was convinced Cirillo had been here. "You stay there while I check things out. Just in case."

"But he's here, Jacko. That's his car."

"I guessed that. Let me go see if he's all right."

He was still holding her by the arm and now she grabbed his hand as the joy dropped from her. "Why shouldn't he be all right?" It was barely a whisper.

"I just want to be sure. Stay in the car until I come back."

"No! No." She struggled with him digging her nails into his hand.

He did not let go but she was working herself into a frenzy and started to call out Rocco's name. "Calm down, for God's sake. Take it easy."

At last she struggled free. Let her go, he thought. It has to happen one way or the other, sooner or later.

She jumped from the car and ran into the villa calling Rocco's name much as Rocco had done with hers when he had first arrived home. Jacko followed slowly, not wanting to intrude if everything was all right and not wanting to be on the scene too quickly if it were not.

Maria ran around downstairs calling out, her desperation mounting as she received no reply. And then she ran up the stairs as Jacko waited in the large hall. He heard her run across the landing, presumably to their main bedroom, and then heard a strange sound as if she had choked, and a soft thud difficult to define. Then there was no sound at all. Jacko drew his Browning and went slowly up the stairs.

Maria, he saw, had fainted from the shock of seeing the man she loved so desperately, and whom she had tried to protect from her problems, riddled with bullets, and had fallen across his body.

Before doing anything Jacko checked every room. He knew Cirillo could not yet be back but he might have set a trap. He took binoculars from the car and scanned the surrounding hill tops; there were plenty of positions with ample cover for any gunman.

When he returned to the bedroom Maria was still lying there. He eased her away from Rocco's body then carried her to a bed in another room.

It was difficult to know what to do next. If he called the police he would have to leave; his would be a difficult story to accept, but, in any event, he could not risk that kind of exposure.

He soaked a towel in the bathroom and dabbed Maria's face. She was deathly white and breathing very shallowly. Hooking a hand behind her head he lifted it slightly and squeezed the towel until water trickled over her face.

He eased her head back on the pillow and folded the towel before placing it across her forehead. He stood up and looked down at the slim, so vulnerable figure and wondered what was left for her and whether she had the courage to cope.

As Jacko watched over Maria, a deep loathing for Ashton grew, one he would have to control if he was to be objective.

So far this affair had been a job to help out Ewing. What sort of person Ashton was had not really mattered to him, he was not concerned with politics or banking. But it had all gone beyond that. He would fix Ashton if it was the last thing he did; and as the resolve entered his mind he was aware that that was what it might well turn out to be. Ashton and his hired killer did not mind who they killed.

Cirillo turned off the road that led to the villa and climbed to higher ground. He was nervous now; the road he was on was narrow and little better than a cart track. Lacking Jacko's almost uncanny sense of direction, he was not at all sure he was heading the right way.

Now on the track he had no alternative but to keep going. Fortunately nothing came the other way. At one point he stopped to look back but the main road was lost to sight and he was above the noise of traffic. There was shrub either side of him, quite green up here, and he saw a nearby stream gurgling down the hill side between outcrops of boulders.

The more he climbed the more concerned he became about turning round in order to get back. By now there was a curve in the track about every twenty yards and he suffered the sensation of being totally lost. He kept going because it was the only way he knew of doing a job whatever the peripheral fears.

He reached an area which flattened out and there was a small religious monument at one end of the very rugged plateau. He crossed himself from habit without understanding the gross hypocrisy of what he was doing.

He climbed out of the car and took stock. It was fresh up here but the sun was still strong. He walked round the perimeter and could see nothing except sections of the track he had climbed. The town was out of sight and so was everything else except the superb Tuscany vista.

He climbed down a slope holding on to bushes and roots as he went and then crawled crabwise along the side of the slope at the bottom of which appeared to be a perpendicular drop of about two hundred feet to a high valley floor. He picked out some widely spread dwellings a long way below him.

The Lamborghini was the first thing he recognised. Even so high above it, its shape was unmistakable; it was a pity to let such a fine car go to waste. He was sure he could even see the shovel, but the car behind the Lamborghini could not be missed; it was not the small blue Fiat, though. Nor was it a police car; the police would have had someone outside the villa. Whoever had arrived in it must have found the body. Yet there was no sign of activity.

Cirillo watched for a while, puzzled that nothing seemed to be happening. Then he made up his mind and returned to the car. The first thing he did was to turn it round so that it was facing the track he had come up; there might not be another opportunity to find an area to turn.

He opened the trunk and took out the rifle and tripod. He loaded, checked his ammunition and took the equipment to the spot which overlooked the villa. From a firing point of view the place was far from ideal; the angle downward was too acute for good shooting. It did not worry him; he was now doing what he did best.

There were pros and cons in using a tripod mounting; it would vastly steady the aim but he could not adjust it until he had a target in his sights and that might not give him the time he needed. He made adjustments to the feet and pushed them well into the dry earth to obtain maximum stability, then he mounted the rifle. It was well hidden behind shrubs with only the gun muzzle protruding.

He first sighted on the Lamborghini, the telescopic lens bringing it into sharp focus. And by shifting aim slightly, he picked out the shovel; it had not been moved as far as he could see. Having obtained his focus he moved it to the still open front door of the villa. He tightened the clamp just sufficiently to hold the rifle in place, but not too tight to take a quick change of alignment.

192

His position was over the gun because of the slope but he could contend with that. As he sat back on his heels he was increasingly puzzled by the second car and the lack of life. There must be someone inside the villa. And if it was not the woman she must surely return. His one worry was light. Once dusk came he would have to postpone any action and he did not fancy returning down the track in half-light. All he could do now was to wait.

When Maria opened her eyes they gazed blankly at the ceiling and she did not see Jacko standing beside her. It was doubtful if she saw anything in recognisable form. The shock of finding her husband dead, in the state she was in, must have pushed her close to the edge of insanity.

Jacko took one of her hands but it was ice cold and he did not think she was aware of what he was doing. Basically, she had no will to return to the real world. Life as she knew it no longer existed and she wanted no other. But he could not leave her like that.

"Maria. Maria." Jacko looked for a response. All he could detect was the slightest tremor of the lower lip. He returned to the bathroom and came back with a glass of water which he threw in her face. Even that had a minimal effect but she did blink once or twice.

He pulled her upright. She needed a doctor but there was no safe way to get her one. The immediate need was to get her out of the villa to some safe place, but until he could get her to talk he had no idea where to take her. All he was sure of was that the man who had called himself John Smith would return.

He carried her to the bath, put her in it, now feeling a slight resistance to him. He plugged the outlet and ran the cold water around her. Almost immediately she began to gasp. And then she started to struggle as he held her down. And as she struggled she yelled and then screamed, a piercing sound of sheer terror.

"It's okay. It's me, Jacko. I'm only trying to help. Now get out and change your clothes."

She was not quite ready for that and tried to return to the safety of her coma so that she had no need to face the tragedy which lay in the next room.

Jacko slapped her face twice quickly. He was deliberately brutal. "Get out of there quick, get dressed, or you'll be joining him." Time was running out.

"I want to join him," she screamed. "Don't you understand? There's no life for me without him. He *was* my life. Leave me alone."

"That's how you feel now. You want Ashton to continue like this or do you want to stop him?"

"Just what do you think I can do? I can't even face myself."

It was a big step forward but he had to continue the hard line. "I can't stay with you any longer. I have to go. I don't want to leave you alone to face Ashton's man but I have to get away for my own safety. I'll call the police and you sort it out with them. I hope they come before Ashton's man returns."

Maria struggled from the bath as fast as she could, slipping and sliding and hanging on to him. Her wet clothes clung to her, moulding her thighs, her hair hung in streamers, dripping water everywhere.

Jacko helped her out and held her until her shivering eased off. "Dry off and get dressed," he whispered urgently into her ear. "As fast as you can. And then you can tell me where to take you. You can get someone to call the police from there. Bear up, Maria. This is the one time to be strong."

As she went into one of the spare bedrooms he could hear her weeping pitifully, but she was moving and dressing and, as far as he could judge, doing it as if her life depended on it. And it did.

Cirillo was still mystified by the total lack of activity at the villa. If the police had called at all the place would still be crawling with them. He used the telescopic lens as binoculars and scanned the windows but the light reflection was against him and he could see nothing. He tightened the clamp a little again after re-focusing on the doorway.

At least he felt safe up here. It was wild and beautiful and lonely. Nobody had used the track and he had left his car well clear of it. By luck he had chosen the right spot, but a change of luck was well overdue.

He kept his gaze on the villa door, occasionally tracing back to the villa gates to check any new arrivals. The gates themselves were just out of sight but he could clearly see most of the drive.

Something caught his eye. A deepening of shadow inside the villa doorway. He was in a firing position inside a second. He loosened the tripod screw so that he could quickly traverse and watched a faint movement just inside a door. Then a man and a woman appeared. The man was supporting the woman who seemed to be ill. And then revelation came and his adrenalin rose like flame. It was rare for Cirillo to get excited but he was now. The man he hated most in the world was right in his sights. It was the bastard who was always turning up at the wrong time; the bastard who had interfered all along. It was a sweet feeling to aim straight for the heart. As they hesitated on the doorstep, he tightened the screw, perfected the aim and took first pressure on the trigger.

They swayed just outside the doorway and the low sun caught them in its full glare. Cirillo could have made the shot without a telescopic lens but the thought was subliminal, taking no time in his mind.

The woman staggered, pulling the man with her, which made him hesitate fractionally but the sight adjustment was minute. He was filled with the satisfaction of imminent revenge, and about to take up the second pressure when the professional in him clicked in like a computer programme.

The man was not his priority target. If he shot the man the woman might run or hide behind one of the cars or even run back into the villa and call the police. And he would have to try to catch her with a quick shot. Ashton would want him to get the woman first. Hatred of the man was influencing his judgement.

Cirillo then sighted on the woman. He waited for the man to steady her, took careful aim, and fired. As he saw her collapse he switched his aim to the man.

Holding Maria close, Jacko felt the impact of the bullet striking her and, as she collapsed, immediately pulled her towards the villa. He sprang back as the sound of the shot belatedly reached him, flattened himself inside the doorway as another shot whistled over his head as he was falling. Once prone inside the door he pulled Maria in by her arms. By the time she was under the cover of the hall he knew she was dead and he could see the spreading stain on her dress.

He was angry, and frustrated because he was pinned down. The sound of the shot and its reverberation round the hills, informed him it was a rifle fired from a distance. Ashton's man must have found high ground.

Jacko held the lifeless body of Maria and felt like weeping as she had done. And then came the growing hatred; a great happiness had been destroyed between Maria and Rocco who had lived and loved until Ashton had seen them as a threat to his craving ambition.

He held her for some time without really realising it. The temptation to go out and shoot back came late and futilely. It was impossible to judge direction when sound carried around the hills as it had. He had a rough idea where it had come from but it was well out of range of his Beretta.

The assassin might come down to finish the job but he did not think so; it was too risky and the light would have deteriorated by the time he arrived. It was more likely that he would wait for Jacko to leave the villa. Jacko could feel he was out there somewhere; he was becoming attuned to him.

The villa now felt as dead as its owners. Its friendly atmosphere had cut out with the death of Maria and it had become a morgue. He carried her upstairs and laid her down beside Rocco so that they were touching each other. He was sure they would both have wanted that. His action would confuse the police when they inevitably came, but it would make no difference; he knew who the killer was but could not ring the police because he could not speak Italian and he wanted no enquiries over someone reporting two murders in English. It would be too easy to be connected with the deaths as the obvious suspect. There was nothing more he could do except choose his time to leave.

The killer was probably out there waiting for him to do just that. So he waited for late dusk when any kind of shot would be speculative. Professionals did not act on uncertainties.

When the time came he made for the car in a running crouch, climbed in, and switched on the engine. Rolling down the drive without beams was difficult. Darkness was wrapping round the hills and a sprinkling of faint distant lights was springing up like the first feeble stars.

Jacko turned left at the gates, in the opposite direction to the small town with the emporium. He knew where he wanted to go but found the going tough as the darkness deepened. He did not switch on his beams until he saw bouncing headlights cresting a rise on the incline above him and knew that for safety's sake he would have to respond. He was well aware that the man who had shot Maria and her husband would have made note of his car when looking through telescopic sights. He was also aware of the temptation there must have been to shoot him first; the danger was still somewhere around these hills.

Jacko took the first recognisable turning south and shortly after that joined a much wider road to pick up a good deal more traffic with it. For once he was glad of the extra company. He sat back and settled himself for the long drive down to Rome, not so much to return the Beretta, he could cut his losses on that, but because he instinctively judged it to be the best thing to do.

Cirillo, on the other hand, drew other conclusions. When he missed the fast-moving Jacko with his second shot he knew there would be no chance of a third. He was holding a murder weapon in his hands and he had another in a shoulder holster.

He hung around hopefully but not really expecting anyone to appear. He anticipated Jacko's reluctance to ring the police; the Englishman was bound to be armed and would not want the police to discover that, nor to find him with the two bodies. But he had missed his opportunity.

His consolation was that he had got the woman. He was convinced she was dead and it had to rank as one of the finest shots he had ever made.

At the first hint of dusk he began to worry. It would be difficult for him to cope after dark in unfamiliar territory. It was time to suspend action. His regret at not getting the man still almost outweighed his success with the woman. He was left with the feeling that the job was only half done.

He dismantled the rifle and tripod and very carefully wiped them clean; he had always had difficulty in firing with gloves on. When finished, he picked up the rifle with a handkerchief wrapped round his hand, and flung it far out over the edge to land in thick bush some two hundred feet below. He then did the same with the tripod but going to another spot and flinging it in another direction. He drove down the winding, descending track not needing lights but nervous of the encroaching dusk. He was glad when he hit the lower road and could now put on full beams. He had to work out a route back to Milan.

18

Julie Ashton moved into her New Jersey apartment a few days after the telephone call warning her that Dickie Ashton had killed her son Michael. She had never doubted the validity of the claim by her caller.

As with his call to Maria, Gorley had not announced who he was for he knew she would know and had reason never to forget his voice. He had given her no more information than he had to Maria.

Dickie had been late reaching the stage of megalomania and this was all that surprised her. Even as an early teenager he had shown himself to have big ideas, dreams then, but ones that he had worked upon. There must have been a period of reasonable stability when he was merely astutely crooked instead of being mad and crooked.

None of this had worried Julie while she had the protection of John, although there were times when she craved also protection *from* him. But, by and large, he had looked after her, mainly because it was in his own interests. She knew he had good reasons for using the camouflage of her own family. But in his heyday, John could be really exciting and it had not disturbed her when her husband had suddenly had a fatal accident.

Julie had closed her mind to the event. She had her suspicions but never voiced them. It was one of the points about John she had loved; if he wanted something he went straight out and took it, and at the time their affair was torrid.

Her decent-living first husband had made a hash of his posting to France and their life had gradually deteriorated until living was difficult. If he had not died she would have left him for John anyway. But it came as a surprise that

John actually wanted to marry her; on condition, and with the right financial back-up.

It was then that she knew he had something to hide. But she was never inquisitive and as long as there was plenty of cash she was happy. Anyway, she did not want to suffer an accident like her first husband had. She did not even ask John whether or not he had been married before, nor did he raise it himself. For all she knew young Dickie had been born the wrong side of the blanket, but she could discern something of the reason why John took the boy around with him. As Dickie had grown older there were times when his similarity to his father was uncanny.

Since the telephone call Julie had become increasingly edgy. Now the move to New Jersey was complete she had more time to reflect. That John had taken the trouble to phone at all implied that the danger was very real and that he still cared for her in his way. And it meant he had kept tabs on her.

She had been careful to settle all her outstanding bills before moving and did not leave a forwarding address. She also closed down her bank accounts and opened new ones. Julie had lost none of her flair for protecting herself. She cancelled all credit accounts and would open up new ones as soon as she could. Every precaution she took against being traced was based on her knowledge of Dickie's father to whom she was still married so far as she knew; they had come to no agreement over divorce.

She worked on the premise that if John could trace her then so could Dickie. Both had the money to use the best enquiry agents and if Dickie wanted to find her he would apply the same effort, graft and corruption as his father had in the old days. In spite of her earlier indifference Julie was beginning to get scared. For once in her pleasure-seeking life she had no man to protect her at a time of crisis. And she did not trust other women to the same extent. Women formed her friendships, but John in his heyday had been a bastion. Only a fool would have taken him on.

After all these years she realised she was missing John for all his many faults. She had no idea he was dead, killed by his own son, which was as well, for had she known she would not have been just filled with nervous anxiety. She would have been terrified.

"I got plenty of information but failed to save the woman."

Jacko threw down the empty air ticket covers in disgust. He related the events in Italy keeping to the barest of facts. He was tired, in need of a bath, disillusioned and upset about Maria. But the first thing he did on landing at Heathrow Airport was to ring Ewing, finally tracking him down at his office.

Ewing was waiting on the steps of the house when Jacko arrived in a cab. They had gone into Jacko's lounge and Jacko flopped down on to the nearest chair, unshaven and weary.

Ewing himself was looking tired as if he had been up all night. He was still furious at the way Ashton had broken up his date with Liz. Ashton's apologies had poured out, of course, and his excuses were cast-iron, but Ewing well knew what he had done and had later explained to Liz, to be accused by her of double standards; it was all right for Ewing to forbid her to see Ashton but a different set of rules applied to him and at her expense.

They had sorted out the problem, both knowing that Ashton had deliberately set out to cause that very situation, but it showed what Ashton was willing to stoop to, which they should both have already known.

Ewing explained none of this to Jacko. He felt desperately sorry for the ex-SAS man as he sat across from him. Neither of them suggested drinks and there was an air of despondency between them which was totally foreign in Jacko's company; his irrepressible optimism was missing and Ewing was not the man to replace it. But he tried;

"Your job is to get information on Ashton's background, not act as saviour to his targets. And you are doing that very well. It's beginning to knit together."

Jacko was slouched in the chair, arms dangling between his legs. "Saviour? That's bloody rich. I haven't saved one of them since I came into it. Frank Stewart's gone, Michael

Ashton, Gorley, and now Maria. They've all gone and all I have is a handful of information. Has it been worth it?"

Ewing leaned forward and tried to resurrect them both. "They were already targets which you had to find out. And you did, Jacko. You did. You've obtained important information, perhaps, even, sufficient to place a big official question mark over Ashton. And your job has never been bodyguard to any of his victims."

"You weren't with Maria when she was shot. Nor when she found her husband lying on the floor with his chest full of bullets. I should have known the bastard was out there waiting. We passed him. Shit." Jacko covered his face in dismay.

Ewing realised just how little he knew about field operations and his respect for Jacko, already high, grew. "Perhaps you've done enough. You've got much further than anyone else has managed. If you want to opt out I won't press you to continue."

Jacko took his hands away from a face now haggard. Slowly he said, "There are times when I think you don't understand a bloody thing. You political sods should get out into the real world. Have you been listening to me?"

Ewing was startled by the attack. "I was trying to help you."

"Balls to that. I don't want sympathy. I want you to understand what the hell has been going on, and you don't. You measure it by information received. Real people have been knocked off. What would you be thinking if one of them was Liz?"

"That was unfair." Ewing straightened. "Just what the hell do you expect me to say? Okay. I've never been in the firing line but that's not my fault. Would you feel better if I played chicken on the M1?"

Jacko held up his hands. "Okay. But don't ever ask me again if I would rather opt out. The name of the game has changed for me. I was holding Maria when she died. And I intend to get the bastard who did it. Both him and Ashton."

Ewing sat back relieved. "You were right, I misjudged you. Well I have some news for you which might throw a little more light or might confuse the issue further. Joseph Archibald Adams, born in Coventry in 1917, emigrated to Canada in 1946. He apparently had a wife and five children. It's taken a little time for the Canadian authorities to trace this. Your hunch was right to check Adams in Canada."

"That takes us forward?"

Ewing was disappointed with Jacko's reaction; he was in an awkward mood. "Couldn't John Gorley have been Adams?" he asked Jacko.

"Adams, Ashton, Gorley, and his London rooms were in the name of West, all the same bloke?"

"Why not? He could have been changing his name most of his life."

"Okay, let's accept it. Now what? He's dead and the certainties went with him. Dickie Ashton won't oblige by filling in the gaps."

"But you can surely see what Dickie Ashton has to hide. His father was obviously a wrong'un. Using all those names, he had to be hiding a great deal."

"Is Dickie responsible for the sins of his father? The human rights mob would love that. Persecution. Dickie would know how to use that to advantage. Haven't we got anything stronger?"

"The Canadians are working on it. Ashton or Adams or whatever his name is did not set out to make things easy for authority to trace him. On the contrary it would appear as if his purpose in life was to pull the wool over everyone's eyes."

"Okay, we think we've got a name. Let's hope the Canadians dig up a bit more to work on."

Jacko had dinner with Georgie Roberts that night. After Ewing left he had bathed and changed and rang Georgie hopefully, surprised how willing she was to drop everything to see him. She would cook a meal for him at her place.

203

When she opened the door she gave him a big hug which he returned, but he was afraid to let himself go. He was not sure what held him back. Georgie felt it, though, just that little resistance to real affection which neither of them quite understood.

But Jacko felt more comfortable and more relaxed in her company than anyone else's. He was at ease with her, and he knew that he loved her really deeply, and it was perhaps this that frightened him a little; not his feelings but his failings. Georgie deserved much better; it would not be fair to her to tie her down to someone like him.

At dinner, over which she had clearly taken considerable trouble, he voiced his doubts. "Georgie, I know I've said it before but you could get any man you want. Look at you; you're a dish."

"That's not true, Jacko. I want you and I'm not getting too far. Why are you afraid of me?"

He was glad that he was chewing so he could delay the reply. "I'm not afraid of you, Georgie, but of what I might make of you. I've been the wrong side of the law for quite a while; that's how I landed this job; I was offered immunity but only for the past. I'd only have to put one foot wrong again and they'd have me. They've been waiting some time."

"So why not call it a day and settle down? You don't have to go back to old ways. If you married me you'd be tied to the law." She had not meant to be funny but they both laughed.

"Is that really what you want?" He could not believe she was serious.

"Jacko, of course I bloody want it. I'm putting my heart on the line for you. You should be saying this, not me. For a tough guy you really are a wet at times."

"I'm not tough, Georgie. I just happen to have certain talents. You really think it would work? I'm not very domesticated."

"Nor am I. We could live on junk food and raise our cholesterol levels; that would be living dangerously wouldn't it?"

He grinned. "You're a marvel, Georgie. You certainly know how to hook a man. If that's what you really want we could give it a go. But give yourself some more time to think about it first. I don't want you to make a big mistake."

Georgie pushed back her chair and came round to him. "Okay, I've thought about it." She sat on his lap as he changed position, and put her soft arms round his neck. "Let's practise," she said. "You obviously need some." She placed her lips close to his ear and whispered, "And then I'll tell you about the contact I've made in Canada."

Watching his donkeys always had a calming effect on Dickie Ashton. He had a genuine concern for them. There had come a point in his life when he suddenly found himself preferring animals to humans. He had not stopped to think why but, had he done, he might well have decided he trusted them more. He did not have to worry about them revealing anything about him. He could talk freely in front of them. And they were generally more predictable than humans, certainly those humans he knew. And, unlike so many humans, they were satisfied with their lot.

It was one of the reasons he had arranged to meet Cirillo at the donkey sanctuary. Because of the complexities that had arisen, he had found it necessary to meet up with the Australian much more often than was healthy. But it could not be done over a telephone and, finally, he had conceded to the odd meeting provided they could not be observed.

So he had been forced to give his stable maids and housekeeper the morning off in order to meet Cirillo safely. They stood with their back to the rails to face the old country house. It was again time out from the City for Ashton, and that aspect was increasingly worrying.

"Are you sure it was the same man?" Ashton asked.

"I had him in my sights. It was him."

"You should have killed him while you had the chance."

"I came close to it. But if I had I might have missed out on the woman."

Ashton nodded his agreement. "You were quite right. At this stage it was more important to remove her. And he didn't reappear?"

"Not while I waited. Once it was dark the chance had gone. But I don't like the way he keeps pitching up. We're running parallel. I thought you were going to deal with it."

Ashton was irritated. "I can't get a trace on him. My contacts can find nothing out. He's being kept very close to the cuff. There is a way but it will not be easy." In order to get back at Cirillo he added, "Our arrangement was for these people to have accidents. You've been popping them off like dinner plates at a fair. You've left a trail of murder enquiries. That was not the agreement." He turned to face the pasture and watch a mischievous donkey called William nudging some of the others.

Cirillo spat. "That was the idea. It doesn't always work out the way you want. The guy down at Chelton was accepted as a suicide. Frank Stewart could have been knocked off by any of his cronies; the police thought it was gang war. And the enquiries in Italy won't get anywhere because it will appear like a motiveless killing. And the other guy's prints will be all round the villa so I wouldn't complain too much if I were you. What about this guy in Ireland?"

"I have it on good authority that he drowned. We've been lucky over him."

Cirillo was not satisfied with the reply. There were times when he did not trust Ashton at all, but he had to admit that he paid well, and promptly. Matters seemed to have settled down between them but he was not going to bank on it.

"When are you flying to New York?" Ashton asked.

"Tomorrow. I had to use another passport and needed a visa. That job shouldn't take long. I'm surprised you don't use one of the Mob on the spot. It would save you money."

"I thought about it." Ashton turned to smile at Cirillo. "I prefer to keep it in the family. Better controlled that way." He had indeed considered it; it would have been very easy to contact someone in New York, but he wanted to be under no obligation to the Mob. With Cirillo he knew where he stood and how to deal with it later when the final job was done. Unexpectedly he said, "Be gentle with her. Make it quick. I wouldn't want her to suffer." He was gazing out across the fields as he spoke.

Cirillo stared in surprise. Apart from anger it was the only touch of emotion he had seen Ashton display. "Sure. I'll do what I can." He would have been even more surprised had he realised that Ashton was really talking to himself through Cirillo, as though he could not face the request directly, and that the target he was referring to was not Cirillo's but his own.

Cirillo found something disturbing in Ashton's quiet reflective gaze. He would agree that he was relying on a long-term hit-man's instinct for trouble, but it was there and for a moment felt it directed against himself. It was then he decided that, when the last contract was complete, and the last payment made to him, he would do one last job for free.

19

Jacko sat on an aisle seat in the 747. He had jumped from helicopters at dangerous heights, parachuted with ludicrously long free-falls, apart from the many dangers he had faced on land, but he did not like flying. In all the other situations he had been master of his own destiny but at 31,000 feet above the Atlantic, on a British Airways Jumbo, he had to sit away from the windows and endure the expertise of others. He did not like it.

He was still haunted by Maria's pale face and tried not to dwell on it. He finally settled for a movie and lost himself in it until he fell asleep and dreamed of the wonderful time he had had with Georgie.

When he landed at Kennedy Airport he took a cab from there to the Americana Hotel on Seventh Avenue. He checked in, having reserved a room from one of the London agencies, and before he unpacked his bag checked on the telephone number of Julie Ashton in Brooklyn. He made the call and there was no reply. He tried another one in Greenwich Village, taken from a notebook he had brought with him, and had no better luck. It was not a good start.

He unpacked, showered, changed and tried both numbers again without response. There was no point in calling at either address on spec, so he curbed his impatience and went down to the spacious lobby. It was worse than London, with tourists, or business men attending conferences, milling around. He went outside and started to walk slowly north up Seventh Avenue towards Central Park. Unfortunately there was no air-conditioning on the Manhattan streets.

He turned right at Carnegie Hall and along to Sixth Avenue, went north a block and turned into 58th Street to stop at the corner of Fifth Avenue. Across to his right was Tiffany's, and two blocks up from there, the high rise of the General Motors Building. It was all so familiar, it was as though he had never left the place.

He turned up Fifth Avenue to 59th Street to see a crowd gathered outside Central Park where the horse-drawn carriages queued to take the tourists for a ride. One of the horses had collapsed in the intense heat and frantic efforts were being made to unharness it. By the time Jacko reached the crowd the horse was on its feet again, shaky but safe.

The incident took his mind off what he must do but he was impatient to press on, and frustrated by the lack of contact. He walked a little in the Park and, fleetingly, was homesick for the London parks. He suddenly decided to get back and be on hand by the telephone in his room.

He rang the Brooklyn number again without success and tried the Greenwich Village number once more. A man's voice said, "Unless you're a beautiful woman, make it quick; I'm on my way out."

"You were on your way out years ago, mate. Don't give me that bull."

There was a long silence, then the voice exploded, "Willie Jackson. Jacko! You Limey bastard, where've you been?"

"I'm here at the Americana. Can I see you urgently?"

"Sure, you can. I'm on my way over. Great to hear from you, you son of a bitch." And then, in an affected British accent of the kind Jacko would never use, "Bloody marvellous, old boy."

Jacko was still grinning when he put down the phone. Glenn Patton, once of the US Green Berets. The SAS and the Green Berets had trained together in Wales, West Germany, and California, at spaced intervals under various NATO schemes. It had been hard going; it was always harder when the nationalities were mixed as if each had to prove themselves the better. But it was a way to respect and to everlasting friendships.

Patton arrived a short time later and the two men

embraced like long lost brothers. Patton was taller than Jacko, and rangier, loose-limbed with no outward evidence of stamina. He was balding, thin hair brushed straight back, brown eyes bright and humorous, face lined and brown. He looked older than he was but always had done, and would probably look no different in ten years' time. He was still deceptively fit.

When they had brought themselves up-to-date with each other's affairs Patton was in favour of going down to the bar and celebrating; it had been a few years since they had seen each other.

Jacko shook his head, ordered a bottle of Bells and snacks from room service and explained, "I don't want what I have to say overheard. Let me work first and then maybe we can celebrate."

"Well, why don't you come down to the Village and stay with me there? You'll be free."

"Are you married?"

"Not at the moment. I've tried it twice but I'm no good at it. My fault; I guess I'm just an awkward bastard."

"Join the club, mate, but I've so far managed to steer clear although that might change." They were sitting in opposite chairs with the bed sticking out like a peninsular between them. "I don't know my movements yet; I'll be coming and going at odd times. Let me take a rain check. But I want a big favour."

"Name it."

"I want a pistol. Not a Saturday night special but something reliable. A Browning will do fine."

Before Patton could answer there was a knock on the door and the drink and refreshments were brought in. Once they had charged glasses, and had toasted each other, Patton became serious. "That's quite a demand."

"Well, I couldn't bring the bloody thing across with me, and I don't want to tout round for one. It's for a good cause, Glenn. I wouldn't call on your friendship if it wasn't."

"I know that. But these days I'm kinda working for Uncle Sam; I wouldn't want to push his nose out of joint."

"I'm doing the same thing for our lot. We've got a bad bastard who's hired a hit-man to tidy up his past. I'm doing it because chummy has friends all over the place including the police."

Patton smiled reflectively. "A situation not unknown to us over here. I take it you want an unmarked piece?"

"Right."

"For protection only? A straight answer, Jacko."

"I'm not gunning for anybody. I'm here to protect someone. But I'd feel naked if I ran into chummy's hired help."

Patton drained his drink and looked accusingly at the empty glass. "Okay, as long as you're on the side of the angels you'll have it before the night is out. I seem to recall you always liked a spare clip. Let's go down to the bar."

As much as he liked his old friend, Jacko did not want to go down to the bar. He wanted to ring the Brooklyn number again and if there was no response this time get over there. But Glenn Patton was sticking his neck out for him and there was nothing he could do.

They went to a Broadway bar but Patton was true to his word, drunk or sober. He finally took Jacko to a small restaurant in Greenwich Village, excused himself while they were seated at one of the candle-lit tables, and returned from the area of the kitchens. "I've got to leave you now, Jacko. You stay here for a while, drinks on the house." Patton gave a twisted grin. "I'd lose my job if I hung around to see what happens next. For an old friend, okay?" He turned and left.

Within minutes a fat man with an apron round his waist appeared with a shoe box and placed it on the striped table cloth in front of Jacko. "Sale or return. When you've finished bring it back."

By the time Jacko got back to the hotel it was after 1am, too late to try the Brooklyn number, but he did anyway. There was still no reply. He decided to call there early in the morning.

Before he turned in he checked Patton's supplies. The shoe box was held together with Sellotape. He tore off the

211

lid, removed the packing and saw that Patton had been true
to his word. A Browning automatic pistol, by the look of it
well used, lay at the bottom of the box with a waistband
lightweight holster, and in separate cotton wool packing
were two loaded clips. Jacko started to take the cotton
threads out of the magazines before falling asleep on top
of the bed, still dressed.

Jacko woke at his usual time to find the gun still in its box,
lid off and the magazines lying separately beside him, a
small bunch of cotton fluff at one side. He was slipping;
he should have put them away.

His head still muzzy, he put away the gun and access-
ories. He took a cold shower. Even with the heat of the
day already building up the water was ice cold. He dried
off feeling fresh, shaved, and put on cotton trousers and
shirt with a light jacket to hide the gun. He slipped a
magazine into each pocket of his jacket and went down
for breakfast.

Back in his room he rang the Brooklyn number once
more; there was still no reply. He locked his room, handed
in the key at the desk, and went looking for a cab. With
twelve thousand yellow cabs around it was reasonably easy
to get one and Jacko gave the Brooklyn address.

"You British?"

He had barely sat down when the cabbie got the dialogue
going. "English."

"Same thing. You want me to show you a place or
two in Brooklyn? Like the Fragrance Garden for the
Blind? Terrific at this time of year; the whole Botanic
Garden is."

"No, thanks, mate, just get me to that address."

They headed down-town and talked on across the
Brooklyn Bridge and a busy East River, eventually to
enter the ethnic patchwork borough of Brooklyn. The cab
driver dried up and stopped outside a well-proportioned
apartment block in a respectable area; Julie Ashton did
herself well.

"Will you wait for me?" Jacko handed over some bills.

"I'll give you ten minutes, okay?"

Jacko found the janitor and asked which floor was Julie Ashton on.

"Everybody's looking for her. She moved out a couple of days ago."

"Any forwarding address?"

"Nope. Just split in a hurry."

"You said everybody is looking for her; many?" Jacko passed across a twenty-dollar bill.

"A few. One or two women friends. A mean-looking guy came by yesterday. I have to tell them all the same; I don't know where she is. She didn't skip; she's all paid up. Sorry."

"The mean-looking guy," Jacko described Cirillo, "would that be him?"

"Could be." The janitor rubbed his narrow chin. "Yeah, I guess it could. Gave me a few dollars like you but I couldn't help any."

Jacko went back to the cab. So Ashton's man was here. He supposed he should not be surprised. But once again he had got there first. Where the hell had Julie Ashton gone?

Ewing opened the jiffy bag. It was well stapled, marked urgent and personal, and it had been delivered to his home before he left for the office, by private messenger. He took it into his small study and prised off the staples. The sheaf of papers inside was quite thick.

He laid them on his desk and there was a single sheet of paper on top with the bold typewritten message; THE ASSETS OF LIZ MITCHELL AS AT 2 JULY. He immediately felt sick. He sat staring at the bundle without touching it.

He knew who had sent it but how many people had been bribed to obtain the information? After the initial shock his first reaction was to send the bundle straight back to Ashton without looking at the contents. But Ashton would deny all knowledge and send them back again, unless Ewing sent it anonymously as Ashton had done. But it was not his style.

In spite of his resistance Ewing was curious, as Ashton had known he would be. And if he did send them back there was no way he could prove that he had not examined them; Ashton would not believe such a claim and would remain secretly satisfied.

Ewing knew the purpose was twofold. It clearly showed that Ashton had inroads into the most private of information. And it was intended to make Ewing realise that he was quite incapable of financially supporting a woman such as Liz. Was he?

That was the great temptation. How would he ever know if he did not take a look at what was lying on his desk in front of him? Ashton would not have manipulated the figures; he would not need to, and if he had, then the slightest suspicion and his ploy fell flat.

For some time Ewing sat at his desk without so much as laying a finger on the package. There was an elastic band round the middle to keep the papers together and he saw his hands come out in front of him to remove it. He picked up the papers and stared at them wondering whether he should tell Liz; if he did she might do something silly and try to tackle Ashton who would hope for such a performance.

He was still undecided on how to deal with the matter when he found himself going through the pages one by one. He took his time, but did not attempt to make a running addition as he went, nor did he dwell long on any one sheet. Even as he examined them he realised that this very act could make things very awkward between him and Liz. She would have wanted him to return them to Ashton.

At the end of his examination he grouped the papers together once more and put the band back on and slipped the bundle into the envelope which he re-stapled. He produced a label on which he printed Ashton's name and address and stuck it over his own address. He was still undecided on whether or not to tell Liz. But he was sickeningly aware that she was far wealthier than he had ever imagined.

Ewing sat there knowing he should be at the office and

having no will to go. Finally he had to leave but did so in a thoroughly miserable state, and still undecided. He had locked the package in his desk drawer with the vague feeling that he was doing the wrong thing.

Only one thing was certain; Ashton was right. If the figures he had provided were only half right, Thomas Ewing would be totally unable to keep Liz on his income and match her present life-style. He reflected that he had probably realised it all along but, now it had been brutally thrust home, it was far, far worse than he had thought.

Later that same day Liz listened to a call from Dickie Ashton on her answering machine. "Liz, I'm not trying to make a date, or to pester you. Something's cropped up on your investment side I think you should know about. I'm ringing as a banker."

When she reluctantly called him back he made no attempt to chat but said, "I think you should know that somebody has made a back door attempt to check on your holdings. Can you think of anyone who might benefit from that information?"

At first Liz disregarded it, then went cold; it was crazy. "Why would anyone want to do that?"

"That was my question to you. I can only assume some-one wants to know how much you're worth."

When she remained silent Ashton went on, "If it will help I can check with friends elsewhere to find out if the enquiries are general or just through us." When she still did not reply, he continued; "Let's not forget how we first met; it was business, not pleasure at that time. I still hold those interests to heart, Liz, no matter what you think of me personally. Do you want me to make some enquiries?"

"Have you no idea who is probing?"

"Oh, no. These things are handled by a friend of a friend who knows a friend; you know the sort of thing. Thought you should know."

"Don't do anything. But give nothing away either."

"If that's what you want. I'll check to see if anyone here has acted unduly; difficult but I'll try. I can't imagine anyone wanting that sort of information, can you?"

After she had hung up Liz had a reaction. She thought it through and wondered if Ashton was deliberately misleading her. But what could he gain by it? He had already broken a date between Ewing and herself, presumably from spite; would he do the same in this way? She felt that Ashton would keep his business and personal affairs apart; he was far from being a fool. If he was simply trying to stir it up between Ewing and herself he was doing it in a rather childish way. Just the same, she would not want Ewing to have an inkling of her true wealth, he was a proud man and it could make things difficult between them.

Liz was uneasy. She did not really believe that Ewing would go behind her back to check on her wealth, although he would know that she would never tell him. But it sowed a seed of doubt and it was difficult to keep her mind off it. Should she tackle Ewing? She did not know. Nor did she know that in this instance Ashton's business interests ran parallel with his personal affairs; there was far more to it than stirring it up, but she could not see the depths of his evil.

Jacko was unable to contact Glenn Patton until later that day. They met at the RCA Building in the Rockefeller Center because Patton had to go that way. The sun was still high enough to cast squat shadows of the enormous building and they watched the fountains giving an illusion of coolness.

Jacko came straight to the point. "Are you in a position to help me trace a woman? I think she's English but has been living here some time. This is her Brooklyn address."

Patton glanced at the piece of paper. "I guess she's not there now?"

"Moved out in a hurry, from what I can gather. Left no bills and no forwarding address. The gun-toting bloke I told you about enquired about her before me. I don't like it. I would like to save the lady if I can."

"Sounds as if she knew he was coming." Patton tucked the address away.

"So did some others. In England, and Italy; it didn't help them, Glenn. They're dead."

Patton gazed at Jacko through dark glasses, his face expressionless. "Are you in a mini-war or what? Am I doing the right thing in helping you, Jacko?"

"I wouldn't come to you if it wasn't straight up. I wouldn't want to land you in the shit. Unfortunately I've no credentials to show you. I don't want my name to crop up. If I was operating openly, the chances are I'd be pushing up the daisies by now. As it is our hit-man and me are not unknown to each other. It's a matter of who has the luck."

Patton's smile was faint below the glasses. "I've been in the same position. But the fact is, Jacko, you seem to be conducting a war on our patch. We're a peace-loving lot. We don't want guns banging off in New York."

"Okay, I'll use a knife." Jacko knew his friend was winding him up; there were more murders on the streets of New York in a week than in the whole of Britain in a year.

"Is there something about you I should check on?"

"That's up to you. It won't come out good."

"I've got to cover my own tracks, Jacko. Is there someone who I can call on who will give you backing?"

Jacko understood his friend's dilemma. "Try the British Home Secretary."

"Are you having me on?"

"If you're in doubt, try him."

Patton mulled it over. "So this is urgent?"

"A matter of who gets to her first." Jacko was relieved.

"I know a guy in the Company who might help. Be as quick as I can."

By this time Jacko was satisfied that Patton was in the Company himself, or the FBI. But he was still stretching a favour. Green Berets and SAS friendships went deep, often founded on mutual dangers.

As they parted, Patton said, "Let me know if you want back-up, but you may have to open up a little first."

Cirillo went back to the Julie Ashton address when it was

dark. He went into the converted building and rang the bell of the janitor's small apartment.

"Oh, it's you again." The janitor started to close the door when Cirillo pushed his way in and closed the door behind him. They stood in a cramped hall, cum-office, which had a small desk with papers strewn over it.

"This shouldn't take long," Cirillo said. "I just want to know where Mrs Ashton moved to."

"I told you earlier, mister. Nobody knows. As sure as hell she did not tell me." He sometimes found the strange accent difficult to follow.

"That's what you told me, sport. I want you to do a little better."

The narrow-faced janitor was nervous but not yet taking Cirillo too seriously. "If I don't know, I don't know. You want me to lie?"

"Just think a little harder. You can do it."

"Mister, if you don't get out of here I'm going to ring for the police. And you're disturbing my wife in the next room."

"Your wife died last year. There's a young married couple after your job, so make it easy on yourself. And if you try for the phone you'll have joined your wife before you even touch it. Now stop wasting my time."

Cirillo had produced no weapon, but like most killers was able to impart fear into a person with a look. There is an inner darkness about a professional assassin's eyes, a soullessness that holds no hope.

The janitor began to fidget, his bony fingers intertwining. "I still can't help you, mister. Look, you can have the money back you gave me this morning." The next moment he went hurtling across the desk, cracking his head on a wall with billboards hanging from it, and finally crashed on the floor to one side of the desk. When he looked up, nose and mouth bleeding, it seemed to him that Cirillo had not moved, yet he had not seen the blow coming.

"Let's start again," said Cirillo, not unpleasantly. "You just needed a little prompting, that's all." He made no effort to help the janitor who seemed to prefer being on the floor rather than be knocked down again.

"It won't help. I can't tell you what I don't know."

Cirillo sat on the edge of the desk. "I'm going to help you along. I want from you a list of her friends; callers. You must have got to know some by name, perhaps even well. Maybe they even tipped you from time to time. I don't need casual callers, just the regulars. And if you stretch yourself, you might even know some of the addresses, or, at least, roughly where they came from."

Cirillo smiled down at the janitor who was not reassured. "You'll find it easier to write if you sit at the desk. Let me give you a hand."

The janitor wanted no more physical contact with Cirillo. He pushed himself back and scrambled up, picked up one or two of the papers he had dislodged and sat tentatively at his desk. "There weren't all that many," he groaned; "not regulars."

"That's good," said Cirillo. "I don't want to go traipsing all over New York."

The janitor produced pen and paper and started to write slowly. And as he wrote he thought that he must warn these ladies as soon as this strangely speaking man left. And maybe the police, too.

There were five names, and according to the janitor, four were married and one widowed. A firm address had been supplied for one, and tentative addresses for the others.

Cirillo stood behind to look over the janitor's shoulder as he wrote the names down. They did not come quickly, the janitor pausing from time to time as he dug into his memory. His writing was shaky but Cirillo seemed to have no problem in reading it.

"That's all I can remember," the janitor said finally. "I don't know whether they know where she went or not." He stubbed his finger at one of the names; "That one definitely does not know. She called the day after Mrs Ashton left."

Cirillo leaned over and took the sheet of paper and

scrutinised it. He folded it and put it in his pocket. "You see, I told you you could help."

The janitor looked up; "It doesn't mean they know where she is."

"One of them is bound to know. I'm obliged to you. Thanks, sport. Give my regards to your wife." Cirillo shot the janitor through the back of the head, the silencer muting the sound.

20

Jacko was tempted to follow the same line as Cirillo, but he was unwilling to apply the same brutal pressure in order to get a result. He was not averse to force against the right person but he was satisfied the janitor had told him the truth. It was this thought, and the fact that he had handed over the follow-up to Glenn Patton, that persuaded him not to go back to see the janitor.

For once, in this bloody enquiry, he had been spared the risk of arriving to find one more corpse. Which was as well, for fifteen minutes after Cirillo had left, the janitor had a visitor who often called for a late night session of cards with his friend, and, having roused a neighbour, had subsequently called the police. At the time Jacko was impatiently reflecting on what he should do, the police were milling around the apartment block and ambulance men were carrying the corpse out strapped to a stretcher, and a full homicide enquiry was already in progress.

To make sure he missed no calls Jacko stayed in his hotel room and watched television, and generally built up his frustration. Time and again he fought off the craving to ring Patton, or even to call round to his place in Greenwich Village.

He did not know that Cirillo, a name he had yet to learn, had gone back to the apartment, but he would have taken bets on it. He was sick of the advantage always being with his enemy.

When the telephone did ring later that night he almost jumped out of his chair. He turned off the television sound as he grabbed the receiver. "Glenn?"

"One name. Get a pen."

"I'm ready."

"Mrs Marcia Dunn. Lives outside Grasmere on Staten Island." Patton gave a more detailed address and continued, "Sorry I'm so late but the janitor at the apartments where Julie Ashton lived has been shot through the back of the head. Probably a ·22 but we're not sure yet."

"That has a familiar ring. He must have got what he wanted."

"I am doing this as a favour, Jacko. I couldn't get anyone to drop everything without knowing much more than I do. The janitor was the obvious guy to approach but we arrived too late and had to tackle the neighbours who were all up by that time, roused by flashers and sirens all round the block."

"I understand. Don't think I'm not grateful. It's just that this bastard is always in first and leaves a trail of slaughter."

"Oh, we could see it was a pro job. I might have to subpoena you to give us his name."

"I don't know his bloody name. I can give you a physical description which would fit half your Latins. London seems to think he knocked off an Assistant Commissioner of Police in Canberra. He also knocked off an Assistant Commissioner in London, Joseph Samson. But nobody can prove a thing. I met him on neutral ground when we both had to walk away from it. But I couldn't prove he was the killer. I just know it."

"You could go through some mug shots for us. I can arrange it at a convenient time."

"There's no such thing as a convenient time with this bloke. I've got to get to this Marcia Dunn at the crack of dawn before he reaches her."

"She doesn't know it but she's already under protection. Don't sweat on that. If she's the one you want don't fret."

"You've got a lot of pull, Glenn. You FBI?"

"Did I ever deny it? I'd rather you looked at the mug-shots sooner than later."

"Sometime tomorrow, Glenn. Our Marcia may not be the one. Anyway, I doubt very much that you'll have anything on him. I don't think he's operated over here before. It's just a hunch but I think he started in Italy, moved to Australia when the heat was on some years ago, and then fled from there. But I'm pretty sure he was a European operator until now."

"We still might have him on file. It can only cost you time."

"That's the one thing I haven't got unless you rob me of the rest of the night. I want to stay sharp."

"Don't give me that crap. I've known you go for days without proper sleep, and so have I. Don't try to keep him to yourself, Jacko. Don't make it a personal vendetta; that could be fatal."

"Don't worry. If I can hand him to you I will. If you get him first that's okay by me." It was not convincing and Jacko knew it.

And so did Patton. "You haven't changed, have you? Still the same awkward so-and-so. Look, I can't keep a detail at Grasmere for long unless you come up with something solid for us. Everything I'm doing is on the old-boy network. But it can't last, Jacko. I'm answerable and I've got to give some explanation."

"Let me find Julie Ashton before matey does and then I'll give you the full story as I know it. There are still a lot of answers hanging and people like Julie Ashton have some of them."

"Just don't be too long. If you're going to Marcia Dunn's place you're better off hiring a car. Take the Verrazano Bridge to Staten, and Grasmere is almost due west of Fort Wadsworth. Meanwhile we're doing a make on her but I don't expect to come up with anything. Here's a number where you can leave a message for me."

Jacko made a note and hung up. There were only a few hours to dawn. He slipped off his top clothes and lay on the bed to doze away what was left of the night.

*   *   *

As he crossed the Narrows on the Verrazano Bridge, the water was slate grey beneath him. The Narrows stretched up to Upper New York Bay where it split into two, the Hudson River on the left and East River wriggling through between downtown Manhattan and Brooklyn; the island of Manhattan was caught between the two, chopped off at the top by the Harlem River. It was early morning, the sun still low, casting the long shadows of skyscrapers across the Hudson. It was a beautiful time of day for what was going to be another scorcher.

Jacko took to the New York traffic as if he had been born there. He felt at home here, he always had, and it was second only to his native London. Yet this day he felt something of a foreigner, as if he was violating the friendliness thrown out to him. He was on a job, and it was a bloody one, and it should not be like this at all.

When he drove on to Staten Island he homed towards Grasmere, stopping well short of it. The almost isolated white-walled villa was what he would call a chalet bungalow, one dormer window set into the roof. It was not a large place, but respectable, and it sat quietly in the surrounding open-plan lawns, with the post box raised like a periscope at the edge of the drive.

He spotted two men who could have something to do with Glenn Patton. The area was too exposed for an ideal stake-out and both men had been reduced to sitting in cars at strategic points in the wide open street. Both had marked him though, even before he pulled up outside the villa.

Jacko gave one of them a nod as he climbed out of his car but there was no response. He was quite sure Patton would have warned them of his arrival and given them a description. He went down the short drive and rang the bell.

Marcia Dunn was in a royal blue dressing-gown when she answered the door. She was plumping out, her grey hair tinted with a blue wash, and she was delicately made up. A pleasant looking woman with a nice smile. Jacko placed her at around fifty-five years old.

"Good morning, madam. My name is Willie Jackson. I'm trying to locate a Mrs Julie Ashton who, I believe, is a friend of yours."

Her expression immediately changed, the nice smile locked in, her eyes now startled. She was rooted for a second or two but was then about to close the door. Jacko knew he would have to move fast.

"I'm here to help her. You see that man across the street? In the cream Ford?" He realised she would have to step out to see the car and there was little likelihood she would do that. To make matters worse one of Patton's men had left his car and was walking towards them. "Well, he belongs to the FBI and is keeping an eye on you. Don't worry."

Jacko could see he had handled it badly and had merely managed to confuse and instil fear into her. Why would the FBI want to keep an eye on her; the question was written on her face. The lanky FBI man was now sauntering down the drive towards the house brandishing his warrant card and offering a reassuring smile.

"Officer Hahn, ma'am." And turning to Jacko, "You Willie Jackson?"

Jacko produced his string of credit cards.

Hahn examined them and handed them back. He looked Jacko over. "The chief gave a fair description." He turned back to Marcia Dunn who was now hanging back in the doorway, scared and not knowing what to do. "It's okay, ma'am. This is one of our British colleagues from Scotland Yard, London. You help him as best you can. We'll be here if you want us."

As he turned away Hahn shot Jacko a look which said, 'I got you out of that mess you made,' and went back to his car.

"You'd better come in."

Jacko followed the plump figure down a short hallway and into a comfortable, bright, chintzy lounge.

"I hope I wasn't rude," said Marcia. "Would you like some coffee?"

Jacko could see there was little chance of a quick exit. "That would be very nice." He sat down near the windows so he could see out into the street; Hahn was smoking a cigarette in his car.

Marcia came back with a loaded tray and it was obvious that she had already had a percolator on the hob. Jacko asked for black and one sugar and Marcia sat in what was obviously her favourite chair opposite the television set which was showing a pre-war film with the sound turned off.

"So you've come all the way from London to find out where Julie is?"

"That's right. I'm trying to stop her getting into trouble." Jacko was resigned to it being a bad morning; his words were not coming out as intended.

"Has she done something terrible?" Marcia's expression was hopeful.

"Why do you say that?" Jacko did not want the coffee but made an effort to drink it.

"Well you said . . . " Marcia stopped herself. "I'm sorry. Julie's a good friend of mine. I think she came from London at first. But she's lived all over the place." She put down her cup, little finger extended, and added, "I'm afraid you've had a long journey for nothing, Mr Jackson. I don't know where she is. She moved suddenly and didn't tell me where she went." There was more than a hint of resentment in her tone.

"Perhaps she didn't have time. Maybe she'll contact you." But Jacko was thinking that if Marcia was any kind of gossip then that was unlikely. Julie was frightened which suggested she had received a similar phone call to Maria Rinaldi. To cut off all her friends was a desperate measure.

"If she didn't have time then she's certainly had it since. No, she won't call; not now. I've done nothing but be friendly to that woman."

Jacko felt out of his depth. Perhaps it was too early or he was tired, but he could see himself getting nowhere. "What about her other friends?"

"She hasn't been in touch with them either."

Jacko had a brief vision of the exchange of telephone calls between Julie's friends, all denying knowledge of her whereabouts. He had to hope that one of them was lying. "Is it possible to give me the names and addresses of all her friends?"

"Why? Don't you believe me?"

Would he say anything right this day? "Good Lord, yes, of course I do. I don't expect to get anywhere but there is a faint possibility that one of them may have forgotten some important detail. And there's another thing, Mrs Dunn; has it occurred to you that Julie has told you nothing in order to protect you? That she thinks so much of you that she would not take the risk of endangering you? Why do you think there are FBI men out there keeping an eye on you?" That was better.

"You're scaring me. Why should I be in danger?"

Jacko took the plunge. "Someone, for reasons I don't know, wants to harm her. And, like me, might approach you. Unlike me they might not believe you don't know where she is. Can you do a list for me? It could be very helpful; to both of us."

When Jacko left the villa he walked down the street, crossed over and approached Hahn who was still in his car with all the windows down.

"She's scared," said Jacko.

Hahn raised a brow. "I didn't scare her. What did you say?"

"Tell me what you don't like about me and get it over with." Jacko was bending down, one arm along the top of the car.

"I was taken off a case to help you. I'd been working at it for weeks."

"Well, ain't that too goddam bad. I didn't detail you. I'd never heard of you. And if I do again it'll be too soon, mate. If you have a beef then tackle Glenn Patton."

"Is that how it is? You two are buddies?"

"We played soldiers together. With real ammunition." Jacko pointed to the villa. "She's scared and has good reason. There's a pro after one of her friends and unless he's already found her he'll pitch up here some time. Just over medium build, solid but sinewy. Lean Latin looks, brown as a berry, speaks English with an Australian accent laced with Italian. He's left a trail behind him. He did the janitor over at Brooklyn last night."

Hahn quickly forgot his grudges. "We'll keep an eye open, and will pass the description on to our relief. He can hardly be missed out here."

"Don't you believe it. He's already shot two top coppers. He's cleaning up as he goes; doesn't believe in witnesses. Is there anyone on at the back of the house?"

"Yeah. In the next block."

Jacko nodded. "Can you patch me through to Glenn Patton?"

Hahn raised headquarters and said, "You'd better sit in the car."

Jacko climbed in, the interior stifling even so early in the day, and took the speaker from Hahn when Patton was on the line. "Glenn, she's given me a list of friends of Julie Ashton. They are scattered over Manhattan, Queens and Brooklyn. They are all on the line. Is there anything you can do to protect them?"

"How many?"

Jacko glanced at the list. "There are seven names but I reckon no more than five are really involved. The other two are really long shots and rarely visited. It's unlikely the janitor would have known who they were."

"That still leaves five. I can't spare the men, Jacko. I stretched a favour for Marcia Dunn; I just wanted to be sure that you got to her first."

It was no more than Jacko expected. "If you have lunch with me I'll give you the whole story. You might change your mind."

"I doubt it, but I'll see you at the Americana at, say, 12.30."

It was the best he could hope for. Jacko acknowledged and handed back the speaker. "It looks as if you might be getting back to your own case quite soon," he said to Hahn.

"It needs a lot of agents to cover five dames," Hahn said regretfully.

"I know. I'm grateful for the help so far." Jacko climbed out and leaned down to the open window. "Thanks," he said. "You may not be on this job for much longer; but it's only fair to warn you that the pro would think nothing of putting a slug in the back of your head as he did to the janitor and others. Your designation won't save you. Keep your eyes skinned."

Hahn grinned warmly. "Now I know you played soldiers. Only a soldier would use a crappy word like designation."

Jacko grinned back. "You, too?"

"I guess so. You're not such a bad guy, Jacko. Thanks for the tip; I'll keep sharp."

Jacko was walking back to his car when Marcia Dunn came rushing out, dressing-gown flapping, arms waving. She stood in the middle of the street not knowing whether to go to Jacko or Hahn in the car. By this time neighbours were also interested and she was picking up an audience, most of them hidden.

Hahn climbed from the car and ran towards her as Jacko did the same. The two men each took an arm and led her back into the house. "He called, he called," she kept repeating in a highly agitated voice.

They got her seated in the lounge, calmed her down and waited until she was reasonably coherent. She was panting, still in a state of shock. "I know it was him," she said at last. "He had this strange, twangy accent."

"Like this?" Jacko gave a fair imitation of Cirillo.

"That's it, that's it. Weird."

"What exactly did he say?" asked Hahn calmly.

"Well, the phone rang, and I answered and this man with the strange accent asked me if I was Marcia Dunn and I said I was before I could think straight. Then he asked if he could speak to my husband as there was a deal he wanted to discuss. If my husband had left could I pass on his number."

Marcia looked up at Jacko and Hahn who were still standing, and appeared ashamed. "I told him I had no

229

husband, that he had died eight years ago." She gazed from one to the other, quite tearful. "I shouldn't have said that, should I?"

Jacko and Hahn exchanged glances and Hahn said, "Don't worry, ma'am. You told the truth. What happened next?"

"He apologised profusely, said he had made a terrible mistake and would talk to his office about it, and rang off."

It was some minutes before the men thought it safe to leave Marcia Dunn alone. Her life had changed that morning and she was in a state of shock.

Outside, Hahn said, "You get after the bastard. I'll have a word with the boss. We can't walk away from her. You go get him, Jacko."

Laura Beatty was a tall, well-preserved elegant woman. She had retained her looks, endured the odd tuck to her features and looked ten years younger than her fifty-six years. She was a very attractive brunette with a charming smile and ready wit. She was, and always had been, an asset to her husband Lew who made a fortune out of real estate.

She was due to go to her usual morning coffee session in mid-Manhattan when the telephone rang. She was actually on her way to the door and it was touch and go whether or not she answered the phone. She stopped in mid-stride, held a pose most models less than half her age would have envied, then with a shrug of annoyance, crossed the hall to the study to pick up the nearest phone. "Laura Beatty."

"Oh, Mrs Beatty, it is really your husband I would like to talk to. Would it be too much trouble for you to fetch him?"

She recognised the Australian accent and even the Italian faintly mixed in. "And who are you?" She stopped just short of being imperious.

"Sir Peter Barrett."

"You did say Sir Peter Barrett?"

"I did," replied Cirillo. "My accent puzzles you? Perhaps I should explain that I'm Australian of Italian extraction. Could I have your husband's number? I simply want to arrange an appointment with him."

Cirillo jotted the number down. "What time is he usually back? Maybe I could take the two of you to dinner while I'm over here."

"That sounds delightful, Sir Peter. He is rarely home before 6.30. I do look forward to meeting you."

Cirillo put the phone down. He had rented a small downtown apartment, with its own bathroom and telephone. He had no direct contacts in New York but many oblique ones and they had been useful in providing what he needed; there was a price, of course, but well worth the service.

He sat on the single bed and examined the list of names. Laura Beatty, Rachel Gleckler, Jean Douglas, Lynn Minciotti, and Marcia Dunn. He had now telephoned them all using the same ploy about their husbands. He recognised he was unlikely to get anywhere by asking the whereabouts of Julie Ashton on the telephone; they might all have been warned.

His success was mixed. He had known Marcia Dunn was widowed but wanted to establish that she still lived there. Her reaction had surprised him; she had almost panicked as if expecting his call and at the end he was sure she had been. Was that cockney bastard over here too, now?

Rachel Gleckler's husband was recently retired which made it more difficult to isolate her. But the remaining two had husbands who were still in business.

Because of Marcia Dunn's reaction Cirillo decided to go to Staten Island first to see if he was right about her. If needed, it still left him time to get to the haughty Laura Beatty before her husband came home.

He drove to Battery Park to catch the Staten Island Ferry, in order to avoid Brooklyn. He was mobile little more than half an hour after Jacko left Marcia Dunn's house. But it was some time later before he reached Grasmere.

231

In his usual way he stopped far short of his destination to study a road map and to satisfy himself on the exact location of the dwelling. When he drove past, the place was busier than when Jacko was there but, like him, he had no difficulty in locating Hahn in his car, and further back, another cop. He drove slowly round the block to find the third man. He drove straight back to the ferry terminal.

The short journey across the bay, passing Liberty Island, the statue magnificent in the full blast of the sun, gave him time to think. Marcia Dunn had been warned and was being protected. That was far from being insurmountable, particularly at night, but were the others being protected in the same way? The others he had called had responded perfectly normally. There was only one way to find out.

They had lunch at the Americana. Jacko was fidgety. Patton unfolded his napkin with a smile. "It's getting to you, Jacko. That's not like the Jacko of old."

"The Jacko of old would have operated on his own terms. I'm trying not to embarrass you, Glenn. And I'm still trying to save lives. For all I know, chummy has already taken some more, and they're already lost among your statistics." He picked up the menu and created a barrier between them.

After they had ordered lobster and side salad, Jacko told his story about Dickie Ashton, leaving out only the names of Thomas Ewing and Liz Mitchell.

Patton listened to most of it while eating and made no interruptions nor showed any sign of interest. But at the end of it, while Jacko tried to catch up on his meal, he said, "The guy must be a psycho."

"Which one?"

Patton made a dismissive gesture. "The hit-man is taken as read. How can you be a professional killer without being psycho? Mind you I've known one or two like Ashton over here, but this guy doesn't seem to know when to give up while he's still safe."

Jacko finished chewing. "If he kills enough without detection he'll win. He can't have far to go. Julie Ashton might be the last. Can you help me with these ladies?"

"I can't protect them. It will simply take too many men and I'll never convince upstairs of the urgency of a foreign favour."

"It's taking place on your patch, mate. Have you put out an all-stations on chummy?"

"Sure. Are you going to call on all these women?" Patton thoughtfully reached for his wine.

"I can't telephone them. If Julie Ashton has tipped any of them off they'll think I'm the hit-man. It can't be done over the phone. If I pitch up personally without any form of authority, and with my accent, they'll close the door in my face and scream for the police."

"You want me to send my men, don't you?"

"That's damned nice of you to suggest that, Glenn. You're a real mate."

Patton smiled. "It's okay, Jacko. You didn't trap me into it. It was an alternative and not so time-consuming as stake-outs. I'll get the nearest agents to tackle the five remaining ladies and try to find out where Julie Ashton has gone." He paused, and then added awkwardly, "But I'll still have to take the detail off Marcia Dunn's place. I'm sorry, but we're up to the eyeballs coping with our own wars."

In London, Dickie Ashton telephoned Cirillo from a call box near his penthouse. It was an arrangement they had set up once Cirillo had settled in and had passed on his number to Ashton. Ashton rang between 6 and 6.30pm, 1 and 1.30 New York time. If Cirillo did not answer Ashton would try again at midnight. Ashton wanted the job completed before he made his flight to Toronto for the penultimate execution.

The arrangement irritated Cirillo. It meant he had to be back in his apartment for every lunch time, and the rooms were hot and stuffy, the air-conditioning unit on the window sill old and erratic. It was also difficult if he was in the middle of action, although the later call was designed to cover this.

When he returned from Staten Island, however, he was keen for the call to come through and when it did he answered at once.

In a roundabout way, to allow for crossed lines or tapping, he explained what had happened and that he had yet to contact Aunt Mollie to tell her the good news about her inheritance. And then he said, "Her cockney cousin is over looking for his share. The bastard is here."

There was a silence while Ashton took in the implications. He was disturbed by this news yet knew he should not be. It was an increasing problem he hoped would go away instead of steadily intensifying. "I'll deal with it," he said at last.

"You've said that before. And he still keeps coming at me. He's getting in my way." Cirillo made no attempt to camouflage his meaning.

"I said I'll deal with it. That's the best I can give." And then, in a moment of frustration and spite, added, "If you're so bloody good why can't you take care of it yourself?"

"I can. That's no problem. All I need to know is where the bloody hell is he? Can you find out where he's staying so I can explain the terms of the will?"

"I might call you back tonight. Whatever happens don't call me." There was an unlisted number he could have given Cirillo but he was taking no chances. It had been a long trail, much longer than he expected, but, bit by bit, they were getting there, and after Julie Ashton the rest should be easy, even Cirillo himself.

Ewing and Liz Mitchell went to the Baccarat. They were quiet, caught up in the web being spun around them, their usual brightness suspended. It should have been a happy occasion. When they were seated by the window, Ewing opened a document case he had brought with him, extracted the files Ashton had sent him and laid them on the table in front of Liz.

"Those are details of your holdings, investments of all kinds, and your UK bank balances. They were sent to me by Dickie Ashton to show me that I can't possibly afford you." Ewing's voice was strained.

"He sent them to you?"

Ewing looked across the table at the beautiful image of the woman he loved, and felt that this was the end. "I can't prove it. I phoned him and accused him of it, but he denies all knowledge. Naturally."

Liz's expression softened. She held out her hand to him and he took it without conviction. "He rang me to say that someone had been trying to find out my financial affairs by the back door. He was warning me as one of my bankers, he said." She smiled bitterly. "He was clearly trying to implicate you."

"Thank God we've had the sense to be honest with each other. I hope you believe me, Liz. Not only did I not enquire after them but it took me some time before I looked at them."

"It would be too much to expect you not to. Forget it, darling. It's done. That creep is really the lowest reptile on earth."

"But he's done what he set out to do. He's made his point. I can't afford you." Ewing indicated the documents. "I couldn't keep up with that. I wouldn't normally be eating here because I can't afford to."

"Then I'll pa . . . " Liz stopped in mid-word. Oh, God. She stared at his changing face. "It doesn't bloody well matter." But she could see that it did to him, and in that moment she hated Ashton more than she had hated anything in her life before. She was shaken by the depths of her own passion, the violence in her rising until her hands trembled on the table. "Are you going to let him win?" she asked shakily.

"He has won, Liz. Whatever you say, whatever we do, the bastard has won."

"Then we'll live together instead of getting married. Who cares?"

"We do. We're caring types. Liz, I can't pretend things

235

are the same. You've played down your wealth, and it might have worked had I never known the true story. There are many men it would not have worried at all. But I had to fight my way up and that much money scares the living daylights out of me. I have to live with myself and self-respect is something I value."

She was close to tears and heads were turning towards them. "I'll give it to charity." Her voice was quivering.

"Don't be silly. I wouldn't let you. This isn't a disparity of respective incomes we are talking about, I could live with that, but of complete life-styles."

Liz stemmed her tears, and then rose gracefully from the table and walked away.

Hostile glances were cast at Ewing. He was feeling as if his life had ended.

21

Jacko accompanied Hahn to see Jean Douglas in a Victorian-style sector of Brooklyn. He went merely for something to do and because, in spite of their initial brush, the two men had struck up a rapport.

The lanky Hahn had been taken off the detail to protect Marcia Dunn. Now that Marcia knew she was being protected Patton had put a man inside the house with her, which released the other two men. It was a compromise deal which meant that wherever Marcia went her protector went with her, a situation she began to enjoy and which started tongues wagging.

Hahn spoke to Jean Douglas, again middle-aged to elderly as Julie Ashton's friends were almost certain to be, and he handled it well. Once identification was made they were invited in to a cosy, if frilly apartment, to discover that Jean Douglas knew no more about the location of Julie Ashton than Marcia did.

Jacko resisted the temptation to put a few questions of his own; he had only to speak in his near-cockney accent to get her more confused than she was and that would mean explanations. So Hahn handled it all. It began to look as if Julie Ashton had told nobody where she had gone; and that confirmed the depth of her fear.

Because of the time and the distance, Hahn rammed his flasher on the roof of the car and set off his siren so they could travel north to Queens at speed. But from Lynn Minciotti, in her comfortable chalet, they learned no more than from the others. Other agents were tackling Laura Beatty, Rachel Gleckler, and Carol Kolston, but both Jacko and Hahn had the uneasy feeling of failure. Julie had gone to earth.

They returned to Manhattan to pick up the other reports. The only woman not yet contacted was Laura Beatty, quite simply because she was constantly out. If the FBI could not find Julie Ashton who could? But the FBI could not pull a woman's ears off; Ashton's man could although he, too, seemed to have disappeared after the phone call to Marcia.

Jacko was depressed. He needed a drink but even though Hahn was willing to join him, the FBI man had run out of time, so Jacko was left on his own. He had a late dinner on Broadway and went back to his hotel. There were no messages and when he tried to raise Patton at his home there was no reply. It was as though everybody was telling him that they had done their best and there was nothing more they could do. It was up to him and he did not know where to start. If only he knew where the Australian was staying; that could solve everything.

It took Cirillo all day to check out the addresses the janitor had given him. The traffic had been a pig and he had lost himself a couple of times, and had made enemies in trying to extricate himself. To avoid attracting attention required much better driving than his. But having been warned by the stake-out at Marcia Dunn's, he now wore a dark, well trimmed beard and he had added to his eyebrows.

By 5pm he had discovered nothing about Julie Ashton but he was satisfied that there was no surveillance on the other women. His life depended on knowing that.

He just had time to try Laura Beatty's apartment again in mid-Manhattan. Her husband was due in at six but he had already called twice and she had been out both times. He had not allowed for the traffic; by the time he reached her apartment block it would be too rushed a job. He did not want the complication of her husband arriving home while he was with her.

By the time he reached his own lodgings he was depressed and frustrated and dirty with the sweat of effort. Tomorrow he would start on all five ladies. He did not know that Jacko had an extra name in Carol Kolston.

But the answer had to lie with one of them. He opened the windows to hear a nearby radio blaring, and lay on his bed.

He was puzzled by Marcia Dunn having protection and not the others. It pointed to her being the one with the information. Why else would she be guarded? He had telephoned all the names on the list so what made her different? He would go over again in the morning and then to Laura Beatty's who would be telling her husband about a call from Sir Peter Barrett that evening. It did not matter. What did was that he received news about the man who was running parallel with him. Everything would change if he could send him to his grave.

Daley had trouble parking when he saw the cab pull in and Ewing and Liz climb out. It was obvious that they were going to the Baccarat which helped, and when he finally found a slot for his car he returned to the restaurant. He crossed the street and took up position.

Daley produced a two-way radio and reported the location of the two he had followed on the instructions of Sonny Rollins. Then he closed down and waited.

When Ashton received the relayed message he drove to the West End in one of his lesser known cars, and parked as near to the Baccarat as he could get.

Daley saw Ashton walk briskly up to the restaurant and slow down as he neared it. He did not know Ashton nor, as yet, that he was obliquely involved in his surveillance. He merely watched to fill in time.

Daley saw Liz Mitchell leave alone. As she went past, he saw Ashton drift into a doorway and turn his back to her. It was clear that he knew the woman and did not want her to see him. When she had disappeared Ashton showed himself again and went on to wait outside the Baccarat entrance.

It was a little while before the man who had arrived with the girl, tall, rather good-looking and dignified, came out, looking as miserable as the woman had done. Ashton approached him, and, for a moment, Daley thought there

239

was going to be a fight between two City types. The tall man pushed hard and Ashton reeled back as if he would fall through a sheet glass window. The tall man made no effort to save him and strode on angrily.

Ashton, clearly shaken, recovered and ran forward to catch up with the other man. Daley slowly followed not sure when his job was done. He held back as he saw the men arguing forcefully beside a car. After a while it seemed to simmer down and, almost unbelievably, they both climbed into the car.

Daley's own car was parked some distance away. He produced his radio and asked for instructions to be told he had already exceeded his brief and was to go home.

In the car the bad feeling continued and Ashton realised that it would take some time for Ewing to calm down sufficiently to talk sense to him, and that Ewing was very unlikely to agree to return to Ashton's apartment. The only way he had managed to get Ewing to travel with him was to insist that he could restore the damage done to Ewing and Liz.

Ashton bore the tirade that it had all been caused by himself; Ewing was bound to strike out. And it was true although he would never admit it. But when Ewing eventually began to run out of steam Ashton waited for the right moment. Ewing might temporarily be drained by his anger, but that anger would still be there.

They were on the South Circular before Ewing said, "Where the hell are we?"

"What does it matter? I can drop you wherever you want."

"I've said all I want to say. Take me back, I was mad ever to get in with you."

"No you weren't. You want Liz back. I can fix it."

"You've already fixed it, you bastard."

"Let's not go over all that again. You've called me all the shits you can come up with, so let it rest for a while. None of that can get her back for you. But I can."

"Just as easily as you separated us, no doubt." Ewing felt exhausted and depressed. There was little more he could say to express his deep revulsion of the man driving beside him. He had entered the car really to express his feelings over what Ashton had done to break up his happiness but in the end he knew that none of what he said made the slightest difference to this man who was beyond caring what he did to anyone.

"I can get her back for you, that's all I'm willing to say."

"By confessing to her? It will make no difference now. You've put up a barrier between us."

"If there is a barrier, I can remove it."

In spite of his detestation of Ashton, Ewing was interested simply because he was in love with Liz. Nothing could change that. "What are you going to do? Swindle her out of her money?"

Ashton pulled into a lay-by. They were on the fringe of open countryside, and a line of plane trees overhung them like a green canopy. "Why would I want to do that? No, I intend to see that you get some to make up the difference."

In the clamminess of the car and the outside humidity, Ewing became cold. At first he could not speak, and then he said, "Whom do I have to kill for you?"

"Oh, come on Thomas, what do you think I am?"

The question was ludicrous. Ewing began to laugh light-headedly.

"All I want is a little information."

Ewing turned to gaze at Ashton, unable to take him seriously. "What sort of information?"

"The name and whereabouts of the man you employed to nose into my affairs."

"You're off your head. I've employed no such person. That would be a job for the police, if they could stay alive to do it."

"If that's what you think, wouldn't it be easier for me to take you out of the scene?"

"Oh, I've no doubt you've thought that one through. But I'm not an Assistant Commissioner of Police, killed in the line of duty. And you would have to take Liz as well. And I've had much more time to take precautions against such a threat than poor Samson did. You can't go on killing forever."

"So you have got someone persecuting me."

"Is that what I said? Dear me. No denial from you? That's tantamount to a confession, Ashton."

"I wouldn't waste time on denying anything as insane as that. Do you want her back or don't you?"

"Of course I want her back, but I cannot give you information I know nothing about."

"Someone has set up an investigation into my affairs. God knows why. Someone obviously is spreading a smear campaign. I can only think the reason is political; perhaps I'm doing too well in that direction for some. I want to put an end to it once and for all. If that means paying out a good deal of money, then it's worth it to me just to rid myself of the nuisance."

Ewing tried to concentrate. Ashton was talking as if the whole murderous business was no big deal, just like brushing off an irritating fly. But he knew that he would not be discussing the matter with Ashton at this moment if it fitted so casually in Ashton's mind. Ashton was worried sick. "Well, I hope whoever is investigating you, succeeds. It's time the stone was turned over."

"You don't understand. All I want to do is to get on with my life and make some useful contribution to the affairs of this country. Is that a lot to ask?"

They sat in the car, the light gradually fading now with a pink hue covering the western sky. Ewing was having difficulty in grasping that they were having this conversation at all. It was totally unreal. "What about the killings?"

"What killings are you talking about? Are we on the same subject?"

"I am. Samson; your brother Michael, your sister Maria, and God knows how many more. Those killings."

"Perhaps I can't do business with you; you're mad. I know Samson only by name, my brother Michael committed suicide because his live-in-lover had a fatal accident, and the last I heard from my sister was that she was alive and well in Italy. Just what are you suggesting?"

Ewing realised he would get nowhere. He reflected that Ashton was so far gone in his campaign of self-justification that he might even believe what he was saying. "Even if there was someone after you, do you expect whoever knows of him to betray him? Do you really think that could happen? And if it could, what would you do? Have him killed? You imagine that someone would be willing to be an accessory to murder so that you can tidy up?"

"There you go again, talking of killing. All I would do is make him an offer he could not refuse. As I intended to do to you."

"Take me back, Ashton. Can't you grasp that I don't want your hand-outs?"

Ashton switched on. "Okay. It's your funeral." He turned to study Ewing in the dusk. "I wouldn't have brushed if off as a hand-out, though. The figure I had in mind was three million, split around various off-shore banks. That would set you up with Liz, wouldn't you say? Just for a name and address."

Cirillo was up at first light having slept badly. He had received a phone call from Ashton just before going to bed which had cheered him, and left him with a labour of love, but he was anxious to complete the job and was restless. His instructions were, as they had always been, a matter of priorities. It was like a re-run of Italy; get rid of the woman first. Ashton must have his reasons but Cirillo was not sure they were right, yet admitted to himself that once the woman was out of the way he would not have to rush over the last task.

He went back to Staten Island to check on the house outside Grasmere. The stake-out had been removed. He drove round again, unable to believe his luck. He parked a block away and walked to the house. It was still early morning but was already hot.

He stood in the shallow porch, took one last look round, there was no house directly opposite, and turned to ring the bell. The door opened after a short wait and Cirillo was surprised to be faced by a man who was still wiping shaving foam from his face. That would have been quite normal but for the Smith and Wesson tucked in his waistband.

The two men were both surprised and each recognised the purpose of the other about the same time. Cirillo had the advantage of experience and cold-bloodedness. He drew his silenced gun and shot the FBI man who flung his towel in Cirillo's face just a little too late; he was still trying to draw his gun as he crumpled to a heap in the hall.

Cirillo knew what would happen next if he did not hurry. He stepped over the body, closed the door as far as the outstretched legs allowed and dashed inside. Marcia Dunn was in the kitchen.

As Cirillo entered, she was frying eggs with her back to him. "Who was that?" she asked without turning. "One of your colleagues?" Even when Cirillo did not answer she was not suspicious and went on, "How do you want these? Easy and over?"

Cirillo was almost on her by then and at the last moment she felt the terror that was behind her. She turned, saw Cirillo and the gun, and with surprising presence of mind hurled the frying pan and its sizzling contents at his face.

Cirillo ducked, felt the hot fat go down his back as the pan spun over his head, saw Marcia about to burst her lungs in a scream which might wake the neighbourhood, and lunged at her, catching her round her open mouth. She reeled back against the cooker, burning her hand on a ring as she put it out to save herself. Cirillo closed into thump her on the jaw to stop the scream of pain. Satisfied she would be out for a while he returned to the hall.

He pulled the FBI man clear of the front door and closed it. He then dragged the body into the living-room. The man was not quite dead; he had been caught in the lung and blood frothed from his mouth. Cirillo ended it with an almost nonchalant shot through the heart.

He went round the house, found the police radio and the shoulder holster and guessed he had not much time. His back was still burning and he tore off his jacket; the back was covered with fat, and streaked with half-cooked eggs. He found the FBI man's jacket in a bedroom; it was too large but serviceable; it would do.

He hurried back to the kitchen, filled a bowl with cold water and poured it over Marcia's head. She barely stirred. Her mouth was open showing the badly cut lip where he had struck her, and there was a vague smell of burning flesh.

Cirillo was desperate now. He had planned none of this and the cop had come as a complete surprise. He poured more water over Marcia and she started to come to. As soon as she did she felt the awful pain from her burnt hand and started to cry out.

Cirillo slapped her face, not too hard this time, but enough to bring her to her senses. He had to be quick and he must get a result. He forced her up and she stood shakily before him, her soaked dressing-gown drooping from her shoulders, her hair dripping water and running down her face.

Cirillo grabbed her by the hair and said, "Come with me. And if you so much as whimper I'll plug you. Understand?"

Marcia held her injured hand by the wrist to ease the crucifying pain. In two days her humdrum life had become a nightmare.

Cirillo forced her into the living-room and made her face the dead FBI man lying flat on his back on her best carpet. "Look at him," he snarled. "That's what will happen to you if you feed me with bullshit. Now, where is Julie Ashton?"

Marcia cringed. She had not particularly liked the woman; why was this happening to her over someone she did not know all that well, and what had the silly bitch done for this to happen? Marcia produced a strange sort of dignity. She was crying but held herself well in spite of the gun waving in front of her face. "I don't know," she replied. "I simply don't know."

Cirillo shook her by the hair. "Then what the hell is a cop doing protecting you? You've one more chance and if you don't deliver you join him."

"I'm going to join him anyway," she said with incredible calmness. "I think they were protecting me because they expected a visit from you, not because I know where Julie is, because I don't." And then with anger, "You stupid man, do you think I wouldn't tell you if I knew?"

"Give it one last try. Think, for crissake."

Marcia's mind was numbing over. She barely heard him. She simply stood there shaking her head and quietly crying.

"Okay. I'm going to ask you one more thing then I'll leave you alone." He dragged her over to a small sideboard along one wall. He picked up a framed photograph from several spread along the top. "Name these."

He held the photograph in front of her; there were about fifteen women beside a Greyhound coach. Most of them were laughing or smiling, the group close together for the photographer.

"All of them?" Marcia wiped her eyes.

"As many as you can." Cirillo's profession demanded a good memory for faces, and he would remember most of the names she would give him. But he really wanted only those on the list the janitor had given him.

Marcia struggled through them, barely able to see but the enlarged snap had been taken on one of their outings and she knew most in the group very well.

Cirillo made particular note of the faces he needed to recall, went over them again mentally and when satisfied he would remember put the frame down, turned Marcia round and said, "I'm sorry to do this to you lady. You're a gutsy sheila." He shot her through the back of the head and she dropped on top of the FBI man.

As soon as she fell Cirillo picked up the frame again, wiped the edges and the glass then smashed it on the sideboard to remove the print which he rolled up and pocketed.

Outside, Cirillo carried his ruined jacket over his arm for it contained too much forensic evidence to leave there, and he still wore the other man's jacket. He strode away towards his car as a woman came out of a nearby doorway.

"I hope you are looking after Marcia real well," she called out. "You must be the new relief."

She was digging for information; Cirillo managed a nod and a grin and strode on, not wanting his accent to be heard and remembered. But she had seen him which made the killing of Marcia Dunn superfluous. What did it matter? What did was getting off this damned island before the dead cop and Marcia were found. It was one of the few times he felt close to disaster. He would have to move fast and decided to cross by the Verrazano Bridge and to lose himself in Brooklyn. From there he would have to get to Laura Beatty's place in Manhattan. It was a long way round but it was too dangerous to take the ferry and find there was a reception committee the other end.

22

"Hasn't Sir Peter called you yet?" asked Laura Beatty.

David Beatty lowered the *New York Times* property section, and smiled over the top of the paper to show a head of thick grey hair and an expression of amusement. "He certainly didn't ring in the middle of the night, honey, or you'd have known about it."

Laura Beatty fussed around the breakfast table. "You know what I mean. There might have been a call on your answering machine while we were out last night, you know, the one you always tell me I mess up if I touch it."

Beatty folded the paper and raised his coffee. "Well, don't you?" he asked good-naturedly. "I don't know how you manage to do it to something so simple, but you do. No, Laura, there were no messages. The guy's a phoney."

"Why do you say that? he was charming with that accent of his."

"What was he knighted for?"

"How should I know?"

Beatty rose. "I must be off." He went round the table to kiss his wife fondly. "He sounds like a con artist. Beware."

"You always say that about people you don't understand."

"This one hasn't a face, Laura. We know nothing about him and I find it strange that he would ring you during the day expecting me to be in."

"He didn't. He wanted your office number in order to contact you."

Beatty went into his study to collect his document case. When he reappeared he gave his wife a long hug and said quite seriously, "My office number is listed, honey. If he rings again make sure you get his number. I find it odd that he made no effort to contact me. Perhaps he's a burglar trying to find out if anyone was in."

Laura Beatty looked disappointed. "I hope not. He sounded so nice. Have a nice day."

Cirillo pulled off his false beard as he drove. He was in a quandary. He was certain that a search was on for him based on a description given by his main enemy. But now he had been seen by Marcia's neighbour with a beard and that limited his choice; the police would soon have conflicting descriptions but at this stage he did not think it would help him. He had to come up with something else.

He loathed using disguises, and usually operating in low key, in-and-out jobs, generally had no need of them. Now he had finished plucking at the beard he decided he would have to use the blue contact lenses. He hated wearing them because they hurt; he should have practised more often in them. But with lenses, glasses and a medium-sized moustache he might provide sufficient cover to see him through.

His driving did not improve with the strain but once he was off the bridge and losing himself in the streets of downtown Brooklyn he felt a sense of relief. He must now get to Laura Beatty as soon as he could.

Jacko felt trapped. He was awaiting more positive information from the FBI and nothing was forthcoming. There was no point in him taking to the streets vainly searching for Julie Ashton. He still felt that one of the women on the list Marcia Dunn had given him held the answer but the FBI had come up with nothing. They were satisfied that none of the women knew. And because he was hanging around for some sort of breakthrough he was confined largely to his hotel where he could be readily contacted. When the break did come it was not in the manner he expected, and the news was shattering.

In London Liz Mitchell called on Thomas Ewing at his London home that same day, but five hours ahead of New

York time. It was evening, the heat still unrelenting, and she had dressed to impress.

Ewing opened the door, saw her standing there smiling up at him and wanted to hold her where she stood. Instead he said, "Hello, Liz, it's always a sheer delight to see you."

"I've come to apologise," she said. "May I come in?"

Ewing hastily stepped aside saying, "Of course."

They went into the lounge and Ewing got them both Camparis with soda and ice, and they sat tentatively opposite each other.

Liz raised her glass and said sweetly, "So I don't rate a kiss any more?"

"You know that is ridiculous. I'm just trying to make it easier for us."

"And have you?" Liz waved a hand, annoyed at herself. "I didn't mean that. I'm sorry I walked out on you last night. It was unforgivable."

"No. No, it wasn't. I don't think either of us felt any different. I left shortly after you; I didn't eat." Ewing gazed at her with yearning. "It would be so easy for me to forget all about it, Liz. I have never loved anyone as much in my life as I love you. That can't change. It's just that I know that somewhere along the line it will get to me and that would be when the trouble starts. I can't help it; it's the way I am."

"Has it occurred to you that that is one of the traits I admire about you. It all seems so crazy. I simply cannot see why we should not live together like everyone else these days."

"But we are not everyone else." Suddenly he laughed and looked away from her. "Who knows, I might inherit a legacy."

She sat forward; there was something about his tone. "You think you're coming into money?"

He was sorry he had said it and shied away. "Anyone can dream. And anything can happen."

It was not like him to be evasive. Liz was puzzled. Then she pushed it from her mind and said, "Is there nothing at all we can do about Dickie Ashton?"

Ewing shook his head. "Not legally. I don't hold out too much hope that we ever will."

"You mean he can go through life destroying people without leaving any kind of clue?"

"He's clever, he has power, masses of money, and he uses other people to do his dirty work. There are other Dickie Ashtons in the world, Liz. But they don't all want to become public figures."

"So you've come up with nothing?"

He smiled. "You sound like an American cop."

"I'm serious, Tom."

"I know you are. We have nothing that will stand up in a court of law, and even if we had I wouldn't gamble on the result. He has the means to intimidate and corrupt." He paused, then added quietly, "They say everyone has his price. A great deal of money is a powerful incentive to turn a blind eye, or conveniently to forget something important."

"It seems incredible to me that there is simply nothing. I've given you odd items myself."

"You've given opinions and observations. What he has done to us is not indictable. Nor could it ever be proved that he was behind it." Ewing sipped his drink and then added, "The only material thing we have is a gun."

Ewing rose and crossed to a bureau. He opened the central drawer and produced the plastic bag with the North Korean 7·65 mm automatic in it.

"Is it safe?" Liz exclaimed. "Is it loaded?"

Ewing had not thought about it. When Jacko had handed it to him to keep for possible evidence he had taken it for granted that the gun was safe. But then Jacko was used to handling firearms. He peered through the plastic. "The safety catch seems to be on. I think a little red dot appears if it is not. I have no idea whether or not it's loaded. It never occurred to me. I'd better put it away again." He put it back in the drawer and as he sat down Liz asked;

"Why can't it be used in evidence now?"

"The gun was obtained by an agent who was working on the case. We believe Ashton killed his father with it. But until the father's body turns up there is nothing one can do. The gun is just an item which might be useful in proving that the father was there the night he was killed."

"You *know* he was killed?"

"No, Liz. We are convinced; not the same thing. And a certain witness would be reluctant to give evidence."

Liz gazed at Ewing with new interest. "You've been going deeper into this than you've told me. Just what have you been up to, Thomas?"

"I've already told you far too much. Anyway, I don't think we will get anywhere."

"That's your depression speaking."

"Perhaps. I must admit to feeling low. You know why."

Hesitantly she said, "Tom, may I stay the night? For old times' sake if you like. If we can't marry we don't have to live like monks."

"There's nothing I'd like better. I'm only ever happy when with you. But think about it, Liz. It will just make things worse."

Liz recrossed her long legs. "Not for me it won't. Please, Tommy. Let's at least have one night to remember above all others. Please, darling."

Cirillo had left his hired car in Brooklyn when he became trapped in the traffic there. He had travelled back to Manhattan by subway which saved him considerable time. He now waited across the street from the block where Laura Beatty lived. He expected the worst, and by now the two bodies on Staten must have been found. It ruled out calling on Laura in person which he would prefer to do. But at least he now knew what she looked like.

Laura Beatty was obviously a woman who went out a lot. Each time he called the previous day she had not been in. Now he considered he was flying blind; he did not know whether she was in or out and he would have to hope for the best. If he waited long enough she would probably appear one way or the other.

Mid-Manhattan was a very high priced area and it was also busy. This helped him in changing his position from time to time but not in picking out possible stake-outs. As yet he had seen nothing to make him suspicious but the balloon would go up some time and he was now depending on luck. After receiving Ashton's call the night before he was highly satisfied; now, in the time it took him to ring the door bell at Marcia Dunn's, it had all changed.

And then it changed again; Laura Beatty left the building little more than half an hour after he arrived. He did not need to check with the photograph in his pocket; she was a striking attraction for any age group. She wore designer clothes and walked as if she owned Manhattan. Cirillo kept cool, made sure she was not being followed, and then slipped in some few yards behind her. He had reached the corner of the block when two police cars with sirens blaring over the noise of the unending traffic, tore round the corner and skidded to a halt outside the apartments building.

Cirillo kept walking. It had been a near thing but that was how things sometimes went; he saw it as a good omen. Meanwhile Laura Beatty was searching for a cab and he closed up on her.

He was standing right beside her before she turned to notice him. He smiled at her and it sent a chill through her. "Don't twitch a muscle," he said, still smiling, "or I'll blast your face away just where you stand. I've nothing to lose, Laura. Now be a good girl and we can share a cab together. I just want to ask you a few questions and then you can go."

Glenn Patton arrived in a flurry at the Americana where Jacko, having received his phone call, was waiting for him at reception. Patton took Jacko straight outside, not speaking until they were in his car.

"It's a different ball game now, Jacko. The bastard has shot one of my officers and has killed Marcia Dunn. I've arranged for all women on that list to have twenty-four hour protection. You got your wish."

"I didn't want it this way. Is your bloke dead?"

"Yeah, he's dead. This guy is leaving no witnesses but he slipped up on one. We've dug out a neighbour who saw him and greeted him. She said he only smiled back. He fits the height and weight but was wearing a beard. The point is, is he still wearing a beard? Descriptions have gone out with and without and we've got the boys with her over at Staten trying to come up with a composite.

"We can be pretty sure," he went on, "he got nothing out of Marcia because she knew nothing. A picture was taken from the top of the sideboard. There must have been a reason so we must assume it contained some of the others. He now knows what some of them look like. We must take it that they were all in it."

"So what now?"

"We've men posted all over the goddam place. I don't like waiting, so let's visit the nearest one, Laura Beatty, just a couple of blocks from here."

When they arrived the two cars were still parked outside obstructing the traffic which was arching round them. Two men were inside the wide vestibule and were talking to the uniformed porter. One of the men, seeing Patton, detached himself and took his chief aside, glancing questioningly at Jacko.

"It's all right, Hank," said Patton, "he's on our side; take no notice of his funny accent."

"She's not in," said Hank. "Some of the boys are still upstairs but there's no sign of a break-in. Nothing's been disturbed that we can see."

"I won't be happy until we can get hold of her. Get out a call for her."

"We've already done that. She fancies herself, there are several pictures of her around the place."

"Can I see one?" asked Jacko.

Hank glanced at Patton for approval. "Sure. Tenth floor. Number twelve. You British?"

"English," replied Jacko and hurried to the elevator bank, Patton with him.

"I don't like it," said Patton as they went up.

"Neither do I," replied Jacko. "He's crafty enough to have waited outside after the Staten job."

They went over the large apartment coming up with little other than that the Beatty's were not short of money.

"Has anyone contacted the husband? She could be with him."

There were two men in the apartment, still collecting what information they could and some of it was now produced. "He's in real estate. We heard you were on your way so we thought we'd wait before we contact him. We didn't want to put the fear of God into him. Waddyer think, sir?"

"He must have a receptionist; call her. Make out you're someone from Saks' or something. Play it by ear."

Three minutes later they had established that Laura Beatty had not put in an appearance at the office, but that usually about this time, she had coffee with friends at Tiffany's. A few minutes later they established that so far she had not arrived and her friends were puzzled. Apparently Laura was a punctual woman.

"He's got her." Patton turned to Jacko who agreed.

There was a depressing silence in the room for some minutes before Patton said, "Everybody's out looking for her, we can only wait for a result."

Cirillo sat next to Laura in the cab so that she could feel the gun against her side. He showed it to her briefly so that she would be in no doubt. She was so terrified that he had had to help her into the cab, her legs almost giving way under her.

The cab driver lifted his brows as Cirillo winked; he had seen it all before, but a lush at this time of day was a little unusual. Cirillo asked for Penn Station and the cab set off.

Cirillo pushed Laura into a corner away from the driver's range of view through his mirror. When they were settled she said in a shaking voice, "You're the man who called yesterday."

"Bang on, Laura." He grinned, "Sir Peter."

255

"What do you want. Money?"

"No, no. I've got plenty of that. I simply want to know where Julie Ashton moved to. Tell me that and you can go back. No big deal."

Laura tried to stop shivering. She had led a protected life, nothing remotely like this had ever happened to her; it was the kind of thing she heard about rather than read, for that kind of trash would be in the yellow press. But now it was actually happening and she could not cope. Too well bred to cry she simply tried to hold herself together in one piece. She shook her head slowly. Cirillo could anticipate what was coming and concealed his rising anger.

"I don't know," she replied. "She has been extraordinary secretive about it and dealt direct with my husband." Laura simply was not geared to the situation. She was terrified and wanted it all to end but it took some moments before she realised she had implicated her husband. "Oh, my God." She almost passed out.

"And he won't tell any one of her friends because he's been sworn to secrecy. I like someone who can keep a trust."

Laura was unable to say anything. She wanted to scream but knew that would be the end. She shuddered with revulsion as Cirillo put his arm round her. He held her firmly and whispered in her ear, "Don't spoil it now, darling. I'm putting on a show for the cab driver." He coughed loudly and she moved her head away from his face as he shot her dead. She jerked in his arms and sighed and he remained holding her upright; killing her was the only way he could see to stop her warning her husband.

A short while later the cab pulled in and the driver called out, "Penn Station", because he knew Cirillo was not a New Yorker. Cirillo slipped more than enough money in the slot to keep the driver happy, made sure Laura was propped up, climbed out and said, "She's decided to fly. Take her to La Guardia. She's sleeping it off but she'll be round by then; if she's not just give her a shake. This should take care of it." He handed over a generous bundle of notes; the driver glanced back in the cab and then pulled out with a laconic smile; there was one born every minute.

Cirillo had Beatty's office telephone number; he rang from a pay phone at the station and asked for the exact location of the real estate offices. He called another cab and headed for Eighth Avenue at 48th Street. The cab driver had to drop him at the corner of Eighth because the one-way system flowed east there. He walked down past the Belvedere against the flow of traffic.

The building was not as smart as he expected, nor the entrance as impressive, but when he rode up to the seventh floor his opinion changed. Signs of affluence began to show in thick corridor carpeting and subtle but adequate lighting. He reached two huge double glass doors with the name Beatty and Swanson forming a gold half circle across them. He went through the Swanson half of the door into a large reception hall with potted palms and framed photographs of property from Florida to the South of France. On the pastel shaded wall behind the panelled counter were more modest photographs of local estates.

A rangey blonde gave him a sweet smile and he spoke in an accent that fascinated her; "I'd like to see Mr Beatty. Tell him it's Sir Peter Barrett."

Beatty came out in person to escort Cirillo to his office. As they walked down a short corridor Beatty said, "My wife told me you called. As you didn't make contact I told her you must be a con man." He smiled widely. "My apologies. Please go in."

Cirillo sat in a soft leather armchair, waited for Beatty to seat himself behind the large modern desk, drew out his gun, pointed it at Beatty whose jaw dropped as his colour drained, and said, "You should have the spirit of your convictions. You are right. How people love a title."

Beatty was rigid, eyes staring. Then he summoned a little courage and said, "This is a gag, right? That thing's not loaded."

Cirillo aimed quickly at another armchair, fired, and a bullet tore straight through the back of the chair taking with it a trail of stuffing, and finally embedded itself in the wall. "Tell your receptionist you are taking no calls till further notice."

Beatty shakily rang through, wondering what on earth was happening to him.

"Right, sport, all I now need is the address of Julie Ashton."

Beatty almost relaxed. "There's no need for the gun to get that. All you had to do was to ask. But it's not in here. It's in the files outside." He started to rise but Cirillo soon had him seated again.

"Don't give me that crap. This is an address you've kept to yourself; you'll know it from memory. If you've forgotten the detail, just punch a few keys on that machine there and get the answer." Cirillo indicated the computer on one side of the desk.

Beatty sat still for a moment. He had kept the address to himself because Julie Ashton had convinced him that it was essential that, for a while at least, she should not be found even by her friends. And Beatty had kept his word. He now prudently considered that the gun pointing at him relieved him of that obligation. He began to tap the keys.

"Beatty's place, quick." Patton shouted the instruction as he put down the telephone. They had waited at the Beatty's apartment with the forlorn hope that Laura might return. Various reports were coming in from agents and police raking the town for sight of her or the killer.

They all rushed to the elevator and it was not until they were in the car and racing towards West 48th Street that Patton explained. "A cab driver picked up a guy who had what might be an Australian accent, together with a smart dame who he said was a lush; she could hardly stand. They went to Penn Station where the guy got out with an instruction to take the woman to La Guardia."

Patton was ejecting the words above the scream of the siren as he skilfully coped with the heavy traffic. "Somewhere along the line the driver turned to see if the woman was all right, couldn't see her and thought she might have fallen off the seat. He pulled in. She had fallen all right and had a bullet hole over her heart. The description fits Laura Beatty and the pick-up point was just on the corner of the block."

They reached Beatty and Swanson to find chaos was already there with the police. Beatty was still sitting in his chair, with head back and a bullet hole in his forehead.

The story emerged that a man called Sir Peter Barrett had called and had been with Beatty for a while. When he left he told the receptionist that Beatty did not want to be disturbed for a while, and apparently Beatty had already told her on the intercom that no calls were to be put through to him until he said so.

Eventually one of the partners had wanted to speak urgently to Beatty. He could not be raised on the intercom and then the door was found to be locked. They had called out and inevitably, after no result, had forced the door to find him as he now was.

Jacko had insight of Cirillo getting his last target. But where was she? While Patton's men questioned the staff, he and Jacko went round the desk to stand behind the dead Beatty. The computer screen was still flickering. On it was a list of names and addresses and among them was Julie Ashton with an address in New Jersey.

Patton sent a screed of orders out over the radio and then made a couple of telephone calls from the office. When he looked round, Jacko was already on his way out and Patton chased after him, catching him by the elevator.

"You can't do it alone, Jacko." Patton looked at his old friend and saw an expression he had not seen on him before. He had seen Jacko in action, had trained and patrolled with him, and had always been impressed. He had seen his prowess with small arms, and the nerve of the man. And he had heard things about him; as he studied Jacko now he began to think that some of them might be true. There was no point in saying any more but he decided to keep as close to Jacko as he could. Anyway, with the luck they had been having, they were probably already too late.

They raced downtown to take the Holland tunnel to New Jersey. There were three cars in the small convoy and even with highly trained drivers and blaring sirens it was difficult to negotiate the heavy peak traffic. When they reached New Jersey it was no better; here was the highest population density of any state in the country. It was the worst possible time of day to make headway, coupled with the heaviest time of year for tourism.

They were heading for a point between Atlantic City and Cape May fingering out into Delaware Bay. As they sped along, slicing through the traffic in sometimes hazardous manoeuvres, the news came through the police radio that they were too late. Local police had found Julie Ashton dead from a single bullet wound; there had been no time for arranged accidents, and, anyway, at this stage the trail of corpses would have made one more quite meaningless.

Jacko, sitting in the rear of the car beside Patton, who had left the driving to one of his best men, felt the deep depression of failure. That was it; so far as he knew the job was complete and Ashton was off the hook. It was the bitterest of pills to swallow.

They had passed the broadwalks and trams and gambling casinos of Atlantic City and were on the way towards Cape May. They had to continue simply to assess the problem and where to take it from there. The Atlantic was a deep royal blue to their left, a stretch of green lawns one side of the street lined with an apparently endless row of cars parked nose to tail.

Jacko went cold. "Let me out here."

He spoke so assertively that the driver pulled in without reference to Patton.

"You've seen him?" Patton demanded.

"No. It's a gut feeling. The line of cars, they spark something."

"A sense of déjà vu?"

"Look, just let me get out. Okay."

"I'll come with you." The two men climbed out and Patton instructed the two following cars to continue on and told his own driver to wait. He turned back to Jacko. "There's something on your mind?"

"I can't explain it." Jacko was scanning along the sidewalk where the cars were parked. "He has to come back, unless he's got a boat somewhere. He's done everything too much in a hurry for that. He's here. I can feel the bastard; smell the stench of him."

The whole sidewalk was loosely packed with people, most of them visitors. Jacko realised the ridiculousness of his position. But something had built up between Cirillo and him from the moment they had met at Highbury in London; that had involved another line of cars.

Jacko suddenly gripped Patton's arm and stopped. His expression was so intense that Patton asked for no explanation. It was like seeing an animal with a scent; nothing else mattered but the prey; nothing else existed.

"That's him." Jacko spoke so quietly, so coolly, that Patton wondered whether he really meant it. Then he saw a man walking along in front of them, heading in the direction of Atlantic City. Apart from general shape he did not match the descriptions that had gone out. His hair was quite different, long and untidy. It was almost impossible to see his face as his back was turned to them, but there was sufficient visible to see there was no beard.

Patton glanced at Jacko and saw that his friend was in no doubt. Jacko had the scent. There was clearly something about the stance, the movement, or even some kind of emanation that Jacko had picked up, right or wrong.

"You want me to pull him in?"

"We must make sure first."

But Patton was convinced that Jacko was already sure. The last thing he wanted was a shoot-out in a crowded area. "Don't do anything dumb."

Jacko did not reply. When the sidewalk opened out to encompass a wide area of lawns to one side Jacko closed up and said, "Well, if it isn't Mr Smith. Still polishing cars?"

The reaction was electric and sent people screaming for cover. Cirillo turned and produced his gun in one movement. Jacko pushed Patton away and hurled himself over

261

the bonnet of the nearest car to roll off it and raise himself behind it in one continuous action. He had felt the shot go close and as he reappeared behind the next car fired back at a running Cirillo and caught him behind the knee.

Cirillo collapsed but rolled and raised his gun just as Jacko shot him through the hand. Jacko came round the car and closed his ears to the shouts of Patton and the screams of scattering onlookers; he neither saw nor heard them. Cirillo climbed up on his good leg and tried to raise his gun but his sinews were shot through. As he reached for the gun with his left hand Jacko sent a shot straight through it.

Now for the first time Jacko saw what he had wanted to see; Cirillo was afraid, facing a situation so many of his victims had faced. Even so, as he propped himself against a car he raised his injured gun hand which still awkwardly gripped his pistol, and Jacko shot him through his other kneecap. Cirillo collapsed with no legs to support him.

Jacko advanced quite openly on him as Patton and his driver dived at him to grip him by the arms. But nothing could stop Jacko now; he threw them off, his cold fury giving him whatever strength was needed, his mind was numbed yet at the same time filled with thoughts of the terrified Maria Rinaldi who had died in his arms.

Prone, and bleeding from knees and hands, Cirillo tried again, knowing it would be his last chance. As his gun left the ground Jacko put another bullet through his hand and at last the gun dropped.

"You're not going to shoot anyone else with those hands, you bastard. And your legs aren't going to carry you to any more assassinations." Jacko kicked Cirillo's gun away as Patton and his man made a more determined effort to grab him. But some of the steam was now leaving Jacko as he viewed the pitiful heap at his feet.

"You mad bastard," said Patton as he took Jacko's gun from him. "To try that sort of fancy shooting in a public place like this. Christ, you could have been out of practice."

Jacko felt the pressure draining away. "I am out of practice," he feebly replied. "I just turned it on for him.

262

Check his gun with forensic and it will match with Julie Ashton, the Beattys and Marcia Dunn. And that's only this side of the pond."

"Did you imagine we wouldn't?"

Patton's driver was looking at Jacko in awe. As he released his arm he said to Patton, "I've never seen shooting like that before."

"I have," said Patton dryly. "From the same guy. Get those crowds back. Let's start clearing the mess."

As Jacko gazed down at Cirillo, whose wig had slipped and eyes watered below the contact lenses giving him a completely bizarre appearance, his mind reverted to Dickie Ashton. Ashton had won; Cirillo was a pro, the police would get nothing from him. The real instrument of murder was still alive and well and free.

23

Dickie Ashton disembarked at Toronto and arranged a car hire in the name of McNeill which was borne out by his passport supplied by a contact of Sonny Rollins. He was in a mixed mood. Before leaving London he had received news of Julie Ashton's death and of Cirillo's capture.

Cirillo worried him somewhat although, like Jacko, he considered Cirillo too professional to talk; but at the first suggestion that he might he would put out a contract on him and had already instigated enquiries to that effect.

He covered the seventy-odd miles to Guelph with no difficulty and located the small house in the quiet street and parked right outside. His information was that Rose Drew would be alone in the house until her daughter returned in the late evening; he would be gone long before then.

He rang the bell and felt strange as he gazed down at the small, elderly lady who opened the door to him. There was a visible bitterness about her and he supposed he should not be surprised. He raised his hat, which he wore in spite of the heat, and said, "Mrs Drew? My name is Owen McNeill. I've come from London with some rather good news. You've inherited some money. May I come in?"

She stared at him vacantly, then her expression fleetingly changed; she stood aside as if resigned to anything that might happen in her humdrum life. She took a good look at him as he went past; his only concession to disguise was a false moustache and spectacles, which matched the passport photograph.

When they were in the small lack-lustre sitting-room Ashton felt ill-at-ease at a time he should feel some kind of elation. He decided to get it over with as fast as possible but before he could move Rose Drew said;

"You're Richard, aren't you?" She gazed at him without resentment and in her mousy way, as if she had just mentioned the weather.

Ashton was shocked. "What on earth made you say that?"

"Because I've had nothing else to think about since your father walked out and left me with five kids to bring up and no money. Oh, I always knew you would come back. One day. You or your rotten father. Even after all these years, I can see it is you. You look like he did, not so tall but the eyes are the same, and the lies trip out in the same way. Have you come to kill me? Am I an embarrassment at long last? Well you'd better get a move on, your half-sister will be home soon."

"Half-sister?" He was so stunned by what she had said, that it had made him both curious and careless.

"I thought that would surprise you. Didn't your father tell you that you're not my son? Didn't he have the guts? You're a bit on the side; he was your father but your mother was a rotten little whore."

Ashton struck her back-handed before he could stop himself. It wasn't supposed to be like this; he did not want to leave a mark on her.

Rose Drew collapsed on to a chair, holding a hand to her face but still conscious. There was a slight smile of satisfaction on her face. "Just like your father," she said. "I was certain who you were from the moment you spoke. Now you've confirmed it. Every bit as rotten as he was. Did he tell you he lived by crime and extortion and blackmail, and yes, murder too? While we were still together. He didn't even tell me he was leaving. He only took you with him because he knew I would kick you out the moment he left and you could prove to be a complication to him later on. God, how I've waited for this day; I knew it would come some time."

Ashton tried to control himself. She was goading him into making mistakes.

She gazed up at him, a prematurely old lady, aged by a grim struggle to survive and a hatred she still nurtured.

"I changed my name to my mother's soon after he left. I couldn't bear to be called by his. How many times did he change your name? He did it the moment he left me so nobody could trace him." She stared up defiantly, knowing she would soon die but taking her revenge first. "Did you know we are still married? We never divorced. Whatever marriage he had along the road was bigamous. Did he tell you that? He was rotten to the core and so are you. Get it over with you little bastard. I hope you rot in hell."

There was no further point in pretending; he had expected nothing like this. Instant recognition; my God, how right he had been to come. "Are the others still alive?"

Rose looked guarded. "They were too young to know anything. They are no danger to you. I've protected them from the whole rotten business. They wouldn't know you from Adam."

Ashton nodded as if agreeing. She had made it infinitely more difficult for him to do what he had come to do. He had been taken completely out of his stride, yet he could not delay. Rose Drew was smiling at him, almost challenging him, as if she had waited all these years for just this moment of fatal confirmation of what she believed. Her life had turned full circle.

"They'll get you for it," she said. "That will make it worth it."

Ashton came as near to a decent act as he had ever come. He made no effort to contradict her. He could have told her that officially he had never left England and that he had an alibi over there in the unlikely event of him ever wanting one. He decided to let her take her dreams of revenge with her.

Rose Drew was found dead late that night; her daughter had been to a concert in Toronto. Rose was in bed, the clothes pulled over her, face down in the pillows. She had apparently suffocated. Nobody saw anything sinister in the death; she was an old lady. It was two days later that a neighbour mentioned the visitor on the day of her death, but he had openly left his car outside and had not been there for very long. It had all been so open, in fact, that it was not worth mentioning to the doctor, and the police were the last people anyone would want to tell.

EPILOGUE

It was a quiet dinner, hardly a celebration, but the four felt they should meet to compare notes and to try to cheer themselves up. It was Jacko who had forced Ewing to include Liz. In his typical way he would not tolerate the reasons Ewing put forward for trying to keep away from her. Georgie Roberts was the fourth.

They had selected a small, highly recommended restaurant in the West End where the food was known to be good. And it was. But overshadowing the wit and laughter was a deep sense of failure. They all knew that Dickie Ashton was riding high and was already bouncing around more publicly. None of them knew about Rose Drew nor were they ever to learn. Like everybody else they were unaware that Ashton had left the country for two days, while he was known to be down on his donkey farm.

Halfway through the meal Ewing said to Jacko, "Ashton offered me three million to give him your name and address."

Jacko looked up. "Dollars or pounds?"

"Oh, pounds, old boy."

"Did you accept?" Jacko continued eating.

"How could I refuse? He reasoned with that much money I could keep Liz in the way to which she is accustomed."

"I didn't realise I was worth that much," said Jacko, apparently unimpressed.

"I told him your name was Joseph Gaunt and that you were staying at the Waldorf Astoria."

Jacko grinned. "What about the money?"

"Some of it has already come in. It's all from off-shore sources."

"So you and Liz will be all right now. Well, that made it worthwhile."

Liz said awkwardly, "He's told me none of this."

"How could I? It would be poetic justice if I kept the money, but if I did that I would certainly have to share it round. But I can't keep it; it will all go to charity; every penny."

"You're too high-minded," said Jacko.

"If I had not been you might conceivably be dead."

It was a sobering thought and there was silence for a while until Georgie said pointedly, "Perhaps Jacko can learn something from your principles." She put a hand on Jacko's arm. "Is he safe now?"

Ewing inclined his head realising her fears. "Ashton was afraid that Jacko might squeeze something from the man he had hired to kill had they met in different circumstances. The luck went against us. Ashton must know by now that Jacko, and he still doesn't know who he is, can prove nothing against him. And Ashton has completed what he set out to do; he's cleaned up, there is nothing else to find. The FBI have identified the killer as Piero Cirillo wanted in Italy for murder and other crimes. Cirillo seems to be holding his tongue. Nothing's perfect."

When they broke up they put on a show for each other but none of them was fooled. Liz went back to Ewing's place, which pleased Jacko for he could not see Ewing's money hang-up. And Jacko took Georgie back to his house. Perhaps they all needed each other and the resulting solace.

The following weekend Dickie Ashton was found dead at his donkey farm. He had been shot inexpertly five times but one shot had proved fatal. It was unusual that he had no staff present at the farm that weekend which suggested to those who knew him that he was probably entertaining a lady whose name he did not wish to be known.

Ashton had not, as yet, created such a public figure for himself that his murder should take up too much news space. Many noticed it nevertheless. Ewing was advised of it through the PM's office before he read about it, and it left him with a strange feeling of unease.

He went back to his apartment in a sombre mood. He could not pretend he was not vastly relieved that Ashton had left the scene after so many murders. It was justice. But who had done it? Jacko would have needed only one shot. He opened the central drawer of his bureau and went very cold; the 7.65 mm automatic was missing. He sat on the arm of a chair, numbed and not knowing what to do. Finally he called the only man he knew who seemed able to sort out his problems and whom he implicitly trusted.

Jacko, hearing the near panic in Ewing's voice came round at once. He was shocked to see that Ewing appeared to have aged in a few days; his tie was loose and his hair unkempt where he had continually run his hands through it. Jacko poured him a stiff whisky and one for himself. "Here," he said, "this is better than your usual tipple. What the bloody hell has happened?"

Ewing told Jacko about the missing gun, and then added, "I showed it to Liz a few nights ago. She has stayed here twice since then. She was the only one who knew it was there. She was supposed to be with her mother for the weekend; I've been afraid to check."

Jacko drank half his whisky in a gulp. Liz? Why not? Ashton had tried, and still might have succeeded, in breaking up her affair with Ewing. And then he saw the irony of it; it was the gun with which Ashton had killed his own father. The old man had found an instrument to use from the grave. "Have you spoken to her since?"

"Oh, yes. I telephoned. She seemed perfectly normal, quite bright in fact. Naturally, I did not raise my fears, although it was difficult not to."

Jacko saw the justice of it too, but in a way that Ewing could not. Ewing was bound by law; Liz was bound by a woman's logic which at times can be devastatingly accurate. He drained his drink, told Ewing to do the same then poured two more. He was thinking of the trail of blood and murder he had followed from England to Italy and across to New York. The death of Maria Rinaldi would always stay in his mind, and so would his loathing of Ashton and Cirillo.

He looked across at Ewing and raised his glass. "Cheers, old mate. Stop worrying. Are you sure you put it in the drawer?"

"I showed it to her. I shouldn't have done but I did."

"Did you check that it was loaded or not?"

"God, no. The damned thing scared me. I left it as it was, in the plastic bag you put it in."

Jacko smiled. "Maybe Liz did take it, afraid that you should have a gun in the house. But you can rely on one thing absolutely; nobody shot anyone with that gun. I would never hand over a lethal weapon like that without removing the ammunition, *and* the firing pin which I still have somewhere. Shame on you, Thomas.

"Whoever shot Ashton should get a medal, but as sure as hell it wasn't Liz. I won't let her know what you thought, and you'd better make it up to her in some way so that she will never know your doubts."

KENNETH ROYCE

EXCHANGE OF DOVES

'You understand that our policy is not to deal with terror-
ists. An exchange could not be sanctioned.'

The Home Secretary was adamant – until he was told
the identity of the hostage. Suddenly the exchange of
doves became a possibility: an innocent girl for a man
under illegal interrogation by British Intelligence.

Sam Towler, ex-SAS, unhappily seconded to MI5, is
ordered to carry out the exchange that no one will ever
acknowledge. An exchange that goes horribly wrong
and leaves him on the run with an injured woman and
every evidence that he has become a priority target for
his own side.

HODDER AND STOUGHTON PAPERBACKS